International Praise for Miss Read

"Miss Read reminds us of what is really important. And if we can't live in her world, it's certainly a comforting place to visit." —*USA Today*

"An affectionate, humorous, and gently charming chronicle . . . sometimes funny, sometimes touching, always appealing."
—*New York Times*

"[Miss Read] has achieved a sort of universality."
—*Chicago Sunday Tribune*

"Miss Read has three great gifts—an unerring intuition about human frailty, a healthy irony, and, surprisingly, an almost beery sense of humor. As a result, her villages, the rush of the sun and snow through venerable elms, and the children themselves all miraculously manage to blend into a charming and lasting whole." —*The New Yorker*

"Humor guides her pen but charity steadies it . . . Delightful."
—*Times Literary Supplement*

"We need more books like this . . . quiet, homey stories about down-to-earth people." —*Anniston Star*

"Miss Read has created an orderly universe in which people are kind and conscientious and cherish virtues and manners now considered antiquated elsewhere . . . An occasional visit . . . offers a restful change from the frenetic pace of the contemporary world."
—*Publishers Weekly*

"What you will find in the novels of Miss Read is an aura of warm happiness." —*Columbus Dispatch*

"Miss Read has created a world of innocent integrity in almost perfect prose consisting of wit, humor, and wisdom in equal measure."
—*Cleveland Plain Dealer*

"Someone has said she writes for ordinary people extraordinarily; when I read her I keep thinking of the acute perception and wit of Jane Austen. [Miss Read] is unique, and oh, so ~~~~~~~ read." —*Times*

"Miss Read [possesses] a tranquil eye ~ windy times."

NO LONGER PROPERTY OF
SEATTLE PUBLIC LIBRARY

D0950430

CH

Books by Miss Read

AFFAIRS AT THRUSH GREEN

Miss Read

Illustrated by John S. Goodall

HOUGHTON MIFFLIN COMPANY

Boston   New York

To Jenny
with love

First Houghton Mifflin paperback edition 2002
Copyright © 1983 by Miss Read
All rights reserved

For information about permission to reproduce
selections from this book, write to Permissions,
Houghton Mifflin Company, 215 Park Avenue South,
New York, New York 10003.

Visit our Web site: www.houghtonmifflinbooks.com.

Library of Congress Cataloging-in-Publication Data
Read, Miss.
Affairs at Thrush Green.
ISBN 0-395-36554-6
ISBN 0-618-23857-3 (pbk.)
ISBN 978-0-6182-3857-6
I. Title.
PR6069.A42A7   1984
823'.914   84-6702

Printed in the United States of America
DOH 10 9 8 7 6 5

Contents

1 A Snowy Morning

CHARLES HENSTOCK awoke with a start. He must have overslept, it was so light in the bedroom. He turned his head and squinted sideways at the bedside clock. To his relief, the hands stood at twenty past seven.

Still bemused, he gazed above him, relishing the warmth of his bed and the elegant swags of plasterwork which decorated the vicarage ceiling. Those skilful workers some two hundred years ago certainly knew how to delight the eye, thought the present incumbent of the parish of Lulling.

Not that Lulling was the only parish in his care. A mile to the north lay his old parish of Thrush Green, and north and west of that delectable spot were those of Nidden and Lulling Woods. It was a large area to care for, with four splendid churches, and Charles Henstock constantly prayed that he might fulfil his responsibilities with diligence.

His wife Dimity lay curled beside him, still deep in sleep. They had started their married life together at Thrush Green, in the bleak Victorian rectory which had been burnt to the ground some two years earlier. The general opinion was that the fire was a blessing in disguise. The hideous building had stood out like a sore thumb among the beautiful stone-built Cotswold houses round the green.

But Charles still mourned his old home. He had known great happiness there, and even now could scarcely bear to look at the empty site where once his home had stood.

A pinkish glow was beginning to spread over the ceiling.

The sun must be rising, but still that strange luminosity which had roused him hung about the room. More alert now, the good rector struggled upright, taking care not to disturb his sleeping partner.

The ancient cedar tree was now in sight, its outspread arms holding thick bands of snow. The telephone wire sagged beneath the weight it was bearing, and the window sill was heavily encrusted.

Very carefully the rector slipped out of bed and went to the window to survey the cold February scene. Since his early childhood he had delighted in snow. Now, looking at his transformed garden, his heart beat faster with the old familiar excitement.

The snow covered everything – the paths, the flowerbeds, the tiny snowdrops which had so recently braved the bitter winds and tossed their little bells under the hedges. It lay in gentle billows against the summerhouse door and the tall yew hedge.

Beyond the garden, St John's church roof glistened under its snowy canopy against a rose-pink cloud and, high above, the golden weathercock on the steeple caught the first rays of the winter sun.

The beauty of it all enraptured Charles. He caught his breath in wonderment, oblivious of the chilly bedroom and his congealing feet. What enchantment! What purity! An overnight miracle!

'Charles,' said Dimity, 'what has happened?'

'It's been snowing,' said her husband, smiling upon her. 'It's quite deep.'

'Oh dear,' said Dimity, getting out of bed. 'What a blessing I brought the spade indoors last night! No doubt we'll have to dig ourselves out.'

Dimity had always been the practical partner.

Charles Henstock's appointment to the living of Lulling, and its combined parishes, had been welcomed by almost all who knew him.

He was much loved in the district for his modesty, his warm heart, and the willing care he gave to his parishioners.

The fire at Thrush Green rectory had shocked the community, and Dimity and Charles received much sympathy. It seemed particularly appropriate that he should now live in the beautiful Queen Anne house and enjoy such pleasant surroundings.

Nevertheless, there were a few people in Lulling who viewed their new pastor with some reserve.

Charles had followed his old friend Anthony Bull who had held the living of Lulling for almost twenty years, and had made his mark in the parish.

Anthony had been the very opposite of Charles Henstock. In appearance he was tall and handsome, with a fine mane of hair which he tossed back from a noble brow with the ready expertise of an actor. Charles was short, tubby and bald, and lacked any sort of dramatic technique in the pulpit.

There were quite a few of Anthony's followers who admitted unashamedly that they had attended St John's for the enjoyment of their vicar's eloquent sermons as much as for the High Church ritual for which the church was noted. Anthony Bull's magnificent vestments were the admiration of all, and particularly of the needlewomen in his flock. The fact that he was fortunate in having a wealthy wife who adored him, and was generous with her money, was one which did not go unnoticed in the parish. Never had Lulling Vicarage been so beautifully furnished, or its gardens kept so immaculately. Mrs Bull, it was common knowledge, was prepared to pay almost twice as much an hour for domestic help as was customary, and there were a number of infuriated housewives who were obliged to see their own charwomen vanish towards the vicarage, or else to pay wages which they could ill afford.

The vicarage was now more sparsely furnished with the

few pieces of furniture salvaged from the disastrous Thrush Green fire and some modest articles newly acquired. The Bulls' magnificent Persian rugs had given way to some well worn runners in the hall. The priceless Chinese vase which had held exotic blooms all the year round on the Jacobean hall chest, was now replaced by a sturdy earthenware pitcher holding garden flowers or the silvery moons of locally grown honesty, throughout the winter months.

Nevertheless, Dimity, with help on only two mornings, kept the lovely old house shining, and nothing could detract from the beautifully proportioned rooms with their great windows looking out upon one of the most superb settings in Lulling.

No one expected the Henstocks to attempt the same standard of living as their predecessor. They were less concerned than he with material trappings, and even if they had wanted to keep the house as expensively furnished, their modest income would not allow it.

But everyone agreed, even those who lamented Anthony Bull's departed glory in the church itself, that the welcome to be found now at Lulling Vicarage was warmer than ever. It was good, they told each other, to have such a fine pair living at Lulling.

Some quarter of a mile away in the High Street of Lulling the three Miss Lovelocks were surveying the snow from their front bedroom windows.

The old ladies were still in their night attire. The collars of their warm flannel nightgowns were buttoned modestly around thin scrawny necks. Miss Bertha and Miss Ada were wrapped in ancient camel-coloured Jaeger dressing gowns, and Miss Violet in a voluminous light plaid garment purchased some twenty years earlier on a visit to the Shetland

Isles. Bony feet were encased in sheepskin slippers, but even so the old ladies shivered as they surveyed the snowy High Street.

'So unexpected,' said Miss Bertha.

'Not a *word* about it on the weather forecast,' said Miss Ada severely.

'But it's very pretty,' said Miss Violet. 'Just see how lovely it looks caught in the railings!'

They gazed across at the railings outside the Methodist chapel. There certainly was something attractive about the white thick fur that blurred their usual starkness. In fact, the whole street was transformed in the early sunshine.

The roofs glistened like sugar icing. Doorsteps were hidden under gentle billows, and dark ribbons showed where traffic had trundled by in the road itself, highlighting the vivid whiteness of the rest. The pollarded lime trees along the pavement wore thick caps of snow, and the scarlet pillar box, outside The Fuchsia Bush café next door, was similarly topped.

A small black and white terrier rushed out from a house nearby, barking ecstatically and stirring up a flurry of snow dust in its excitement. Now and again it stopped, head up, pink tongue pulsing, legs quivering and stiff, before dashing off again in another frenzy of delight in this strange element.

'Well,' said Miss Bertha, 'this won't do. We must get dressed and see what's to be done.'

'I think *porridge* for breakfast would be a good idea,' said Miss Violet. 'We don't need much milk if I make it fairly runny.'

'And I really prefer a little salt on mine,' said Miss Bertha. 'So much *cheaper* than sugar.'

'And whoever is down first,' called Miss Ada to her

departing sisters, 'switch on the electric fire in the dining room. *One* bar, of course, but I think it's cold enough to indulge ourselves this morning.'

The Misses Lovelock were renowned for quite unnecessary parsimony.

A mile away to the north, the inhabitants of Thrush Green greeted the snow with much the same surprise. The young welcomed it with the same rapture as Charles Henstock's. The old looked upon it with some dismay.

Miss Watson and Miss Fogerty, headmistress and assistant at the village school, discussed this unexpected quirk in the weather as they tackled their boiled eggs.

'I hope Betty remembers to put down newspaper in the lobbies,' said Miss Watson. 'It saves such a lot of mess.'

'I'm sure she will,' responded little Miss Fogerty. 'I only hope the children don't try and make slides in the playground before we go across. So dangerous.'

Miss Watson sighed.

'It's mornings like this that makes me regret staying on here,' she confessed. 'To think we might have been happily settled in dear old Barton. There's probably no snow there at all!'

Miss Fogerty tried to rally her old friend.

'It was not to be, Dorothy dear. I'm sure of that. And after all, we've always been very snug in this school house.'

'Maybe, maybe,' agreed her headmistress, 'but I still wish we could have retired when we had planned to do so. It has been such a disappointment.'

Even Miss Fogerty, devout believer in divine intervention in human affairs, could not help agreeing.

The two old friends had hoped to retire together to a small house at Barton-on-Sea. Property, of the type they wanted, was expensive and scarce. A great many people, it seemed, wanted to live in such a pleasant area. They too wanted a small, easily managed house with only a little land to maintain.

The two ladies had spent several weeks during their holidays in looking for a future home. On more than one occasion they thought they had found it, only to come up against snags. Sometimes the surveys had disclosed faulty drains, crumbling foundations, unaccountable subsidence, dry rot, wet rot, or plain shoddy building. In other cases the owners had backed out at the last minute, unable to buy the property they had hoped to purchase, or suddenly deciding to take their own off the market.

In the meantime Agnes Fogerty's arthritis had become worse and the Thrush Green doctor, John Lovell, had recommended a course of treatment which would spread over some months. Added to this was pressure from the local education office, upon Dorothy Watson, to postpone her retirement.

What with one thing and another the two hard-pressed ladies agreed to stay on in their present circumstances, and great was the relief felt by all their old friends at Thrush Green.

On the whole they had been relieved to have this respite after the frustrations of house-hunting. They both enjoyed their teaching, and had the satisfaction of knowing that their efforts were appreciated. The genuine delight of the parents and friends of the school when they had told them of their decision to stay on, was of great comfort to them, and did much to mitigate the disappointment of failing to find a house.

But this morning, with the snow blanketing all, and with memories of past snowy winters at Thrush Green school, the two friends knew that they must put all those wistful might-have-beens behind them, and face the realities of snow-crazed children, wet floor-boards, clothes drying on the fire-guards and, worst of all, no possible hope of playtime being taken outdoors. The dog-eared comics, the well-worn jigsaw puzzles, the ludo and snakes and ladders boards must emerge from the cupboard which held the wet-playtime equipment, and all one could do was to pray for a rapid thaw.

Dorothy Watson folded her napkin briskly.

'May as well make a start, dear,' she said, rising from her chair. 'And if it's not too slushy at playtime, I propose that we let the children make a snowman.'

'But only those with wellingtons,' Miss Fogerty reminded her.

And with this proviso the two friends prepared to face the day.

Next door, in one of the finest houses on Thrush Green, Harold Shoosmith and his wife Isobel, were also at breakfast.

Theirs was a more leisurely affair than that of the two schoolteachers, for Harold had been a retired man for several years, and relished the fact that he could dally over his breakfast coffee.

Isobel had first met him on one of her visits to Thrush Green. She had been at college with little Agnes Fogerty and they had kept up their friendship over the years. It was a great joy to both to find themselves neighbours in middle age.

The shouts of children took Harold to the window, still cradling his coffee cup.

'My word,' he exclaimed, 'they've made the most splendid slide the whole width of the playground!'

'Agnes and Dorothy won't approve,' commented his wife.

'They wouldn't be such spoil sports as to ruin it, surely,' said Harold. 'I wouldn't mind a go on it myself. They're keeping the pot boiling marvellously!'

Isobel joined him at the window which overlooked the playground. Sure enough, the sight was exhilarating. Some dozen or more children, scarves flying, hair on end, were chasing each other in a long line down the twenty-foot slide. Their breath steamed in the frosty air, their faces glowed like winter suns, and the din was appalling.

Rows of smaller, or more timid, children lined the route adding their cheers to the general racket. There was no doubt about it. The slide was a huge success.

Harold, still smiling, looked across the green. The statue of Nathaniel Patten, a zealous missionary of the last century, much admired by Harold who had been instrumental in honouring the old gentleman on his hundredth anniversary, was plentifully daubed with snowy patches. The white cap on his head, and the snowy shawl across his shoulders were deposited naturally from above, but the spattered frock coat showed clearly the results of well-aimed snowballs.

Certainly, the teachers at Thrush Green school were going to have unusually lively pupils on this winter morning, thought Isobel.

At that moment, Betty Bell appeared, pushing her bicycle up the path with some difficulty. She had finished her ministrations at the school next door, remembering to carpet the lobby with newspapers as Agnes knew she would. For good measure she had surrounded the fire guard round the tortoise stove with more newspaper, to catch stray drips from wet clothing and, her duties there done, now approached the Shoosmiths' abode.

'Lord!' she puffed, blowing into the kitchen on a gale of cold air. 'What some weather, eh? Your front path wants doing, and that's a fact.'

'I'm just off to tackle it,' Harold assured her, putting down his cup, and going in search of his largest shovel.

There were others already at work when Harold emerged from his house. At The Two Pheasants, hard by the village school, Mr Jones the landlord was busy shovelling the snow away from the door.

His neighbour, Albert Piggott, watched him morosely, leaning heavily the while upon an upturned broom.

'Time you cleared your own patch,' pointed out Mr Jones, becoming annoyed at Albert's scrutiny.

'I shan't be doin' much,' growled Albert. 'Jest my bit round the door. That lazy Cooke article can dig over to the church. His arms is younger'n mine.'

'Strikes me, young Bob Cooke's doing the lot these days,' replied the landlord, straightening his aching back for a moment. 'Can't see you earn your wage, Albert.'

Albert forbore to answer, but shuffled a few paces nearer his grubby front door, and thrust the broom languidly this way and that in front of him.

Mr Jones muttered something uncomplimentary under his breath, seized his spade again, and set to with a will. It was a sore trial having Albert Piggott as next door neighbour, and he was already regretting his action in getting the miserable old sexton of St Andrew's to help with the beer crates in the evenings. Half the time he didn't turn up, and the other half he was too muzzy to do the job properly.

Ah well! His mother used to say: 'These little things are sent to try us.'

One thing was certain, Albert Piggott was the most unpopular man in Thrush Green.

Mr Jones scooped up the last shovelful, dumped it neatly on the pile at the corner, waved to Harold and went indoors, ready for opening time.

Across the green the distant sounds of other inhabitants at work carried clearly to Harold. Ella Bembridge was digging a way to her gate from her thatched cottage. She and Dimity Henstock had lived there for years until Charles had

whisked Dimity across to the rectory and now to the lovely vicarage at Lulling. A cigarette was clamped to her lower lip, and its blue smoke mingled with the clouds of breath around her.

Somewhere nearer, in the grounds of the most splendid of all the Thrush Green houses, Harold could hear the cheerful cries of children. It was probably Paul Young's half-term holiday, and it sounded as though he had a companion with him. A good deal of spade-clanging was going on, and even more laughter. Clearing the Youngs' drive was going to take some time, Harold surmised, but it was certainly being enjoyed.

He straightened his aching back and looked with pleasure at the clear blue sky. It made a breathtakingly lovely backdrop to the snowy landscape and the grey-golden buildings around the open space. A good spot to live, Harold told himself, for the umpteenth time. He never grew tired of the place.

It was lovely in all the seasons, possibly at its best in autumn, when the avenue of horsechestnut trees glowed with tawny foliage, and drifts of golden leaves crackled underfoot and whispered as the wind played with them.

But nevertheless, this morning's view of Thrush Green took some beating. Even the rough patch of ground left by the cruel removal of Charles's rectory was smoothly beautiful, and the stark shapes of the tombstones in St Andrew's graveyard were softened by snowy drapery.

Three more yards, thought Harold, eyeing his progress, and he would go in for a well-earned cup of coffee.

2 The Rector Goes About His Duties

LATER THAT day, in the sunny afternoon, the newly appointed vicar of Lulling and the more familiar rector of Thrush Green, Lulling Woods and Nidden, set out for Thrush Green.

All these important persons, as Pooh-Bah might say, were rolled into the one chubby frame of Charles Henstock. He drove his shabby car very carefully along the High Street, waving, as he made his royal progress, to a number of his parishioners. Occasionally a passing car would hoot, or flash its lights, but Charles Henstock contented himself with a wave of the hand.

'You see,' he explained to Dimity sitting beside him, 'I'm never quite sure what flashing lights mean. There was an excellent letter on the subject in one of the newspapers some time ago.'

'There's Bertha Lovelock!' exclaimed Dimity. Charles waved dutifully, and continued his story.

'The writer said – he was also a man of the cloth, by the way – that he couldn't make out if the driver was telling him his lights were on, or warning him that there was a police trap or an accident or flooding or some other disaster –'

'A police trap isn't a disaster,' objected Dimity. 'Mind that pigeon!'

'Or whether,' continued her husband unperturbed, 'the driver was simply saying: "Good morning, vicar."'

'There's another pigeon,' said Dimity. 'Sometimes I

think they're more foolhardy than pheasants about crossing the road.'

The rector changed gear to negotiate the short steep hill which led to Thrush Green. At the summit he pulled into the side of the road for Dimity to get out. She was going to see her old friend Ella Bembridge while Charles set about some sick visiting of his more northerly parishioners.

Dimity picked her way carefully across the snowy road and Charles watched her enter her old home, before driving on.

To his left St Andrew's loomed above its white church-yard. The door of The Two Pheasants was now closed, and Charles guessed that the landlord was having a well-earned snooze in his snug sitting room behind the bar. Smoke curled from most of the chimneys, and he could imagine the cheerful log fires of his friends. It would have been pleasant to call on Harold and Isobel, or Frank and Phyllida Hurst but he had duties to the sick, and his first call must be at the most beautiful house on Thrush Green, where the Youngs lived. Here he must make enquiries about Joan Young's father who lived with his wife in the converted stables. Charles feared that the old man was close to his end, and it would be best to find out first from his daughter if he was up to receiving visitors.

Charles sighed as he turned into the Youngs' gateway. As a staunch Christian he had no doubt of his old friend's future happiness in a life beyond this. But how he would be missed by those he left behind!

Meanwhile, Dimity sat by Ella's fireside and heard the latest news of Thrush Green. Robert Bassett's failing health was the saddest item, and already known to Dimity.

'And it looks as though Percy Hodge's new wife isn't at

all happy,' said Ella, puffing at one of her untidy cigarettes which she rolled herself in a slap-happy manner.

'Tell me more,' urged Dimity. It was extremely agreeable to hear all the latest gossip. She considered Charles a perfect husband, but he refused to impart those little snippets of information about his parishioners which his wife would have welcomed. Ella had always been one of the first to hear about her neighbours' affairs, and always enjoyed passing on her knowledge. Dimity realized how much she missed her confidences.

'Percy's fault, I gather. He will keep harking back to his first wife's virtues – particularly her cooking.'

'How very unfair!' cried Dimity. 'I mean, we all know that Gertie was a wonderful cook, but it's so stupid of Percy to expect Doris to be the same.'

'So John Lovell told him, I gather, when Percy called at the surgery to have his ears syringed. "Comparisons are odious", he quoted to him, but I don't suppose Percy took it

in. If he's not careful, his Doris will up and leave him, like Albert Piggott's Nelly did.'

'Oh, I do hope not,' said Dimity earnestly.

'Thank God I'm a spinster,' replied Ella. 'I really couldn't be doing with considering a man's feelings day in and day out. Let alone cooking and cleaning for him! As it is, I can make a real meal of a boiled egg and a slice of toast, and am spared spending the best part of the morning scraping vegetables and mucking about with meat.'

'Well, I quite enjoy cooking,' answered Dimity, 'as you know, and it's really a pleasure to cook for Charles, he's so appreciative.'

'As well he might be,' agreed Ella, 'after the terrible stuff that Scots housekeeper of his dished up. I shall never forget seeing an appalling dish of grey tripe with grey dried peas round it, and all swimming in thin grey gravy. She was carrying it in for poor Charles's lunch. My heart bled for him.'

'She married, you know, when she left Charles.'

'I pity her husband,' said Ella. 'Now he *would* have something to complain about, and that's a fact. By the way, I picked up a cookery book at our last jumble sale.'

'Anything useful in it?'

'Not much that we haven't tried, and a very irritating way of explaining things – far too devil-may-care for my taste. You know the sort of thing: "Toss in a handful of chopped walnuts", "Add a dash of tabasco, Worcester sauce, curry or any other personal favourite". I like to know how much of everything. All this airy-fairy stuff annoys me.'

'Quite,' agreed Dimity. 'After all, a handful would vary considerably from person to person, and what's a dash anyway? A teaspoonful or three drops?'

'What's more it gives all the recipes in those vile grammes – and I'm horrified to see that those nice tubs of margarine which one could count on being half a Christian pound are now marked as two hundred and fifty grammes.'

'I expect that's why the cookery book had been sent to the jumble sale,' said Dimity sagaciously. 'Frankly, I just use my old recipes, all full of lovely ozes.'

'We're too old a pair of dogs to learn new tricks,' agreed Ella. 'I must say I'm proud to use our old blue and white jug marked British Imperial Pint. I feel I know where I am.'

At that moment there was a knock on the door, and before Ella could answer it, a voice called:

'Can I come in? I'm taking off my wellingtons.'

'Connie, with the goats' milk,' exclaimed Ella, making her way into the hall. 'Come in by the fire. I didn't expect you to plough up here through this snow.'

Connie entered and greeted Dimity with a kiss.

'Heavens, it's good to see a fire,' she cried, holding out her hands to the blaze. 'I thought I'd come up in good time. It might snow again according to the weather man.'

'Don't suppose he knows any more than we do,' said Ella flatly, 'for all those satellite pictures they dote on, and the rest of the gimmicks. I reckon Albert Piggott does rather better as a weather prophet. His chest and joints are wonderful predictors of climatic conditions.'

'How's Dotty?' enquired Dimity.

'Very well, I'm glad to say. As long as she doesn't do anything silly such as wandering out in the snow to see if Dulcie's all right, and that kind of thing, she's in good trim. But you know dear old Aunt Dot – she likes her own way and I have to watch her.'

'Well, you do it very well, Connie,' said Ella. 'She's lucky to have you there.'

Ella went on to tell Connie about the latest news at Thrush Green, and how the inhabitants were coping with their particular snow problems. Dimity sat back in the old familiar armchair and studied Dotty Harmer's niece.

No one, she decided, could call Connie handsome, but she had fine eyes and her thick auburn hair showed very little grey. She must be in her forties now, strongly built, and with a determined look about her square chin. She needed strength of character to cope with her indomitable aunt, thought Dimity. It said much for her sweet disposition that she was obviously devoted to the trying old lady, and had given up her own home to come to her aid. It was to be hoped that Dotty appreciated Connie's attentions, but really poor Dotty grew more vague and eccentric as the years passed and Dimity sometimes wondered if her old friend really grasped what was happening around her.

'And how has your house stood up to the snow?' she asked.

'Oh, we're pretty snug,' answered Connie. 'There's nothing like a good thatched roof and thick walls for insulation. Thank goodness Aunt Dotty always kept the outside in good repair. The interior, of course, was another matter, but I'm gradually getting it straight. You'll be glad to know I've had a marvellous spring-clean of the pantry.'

'And about time too,' said Ella forthrightly. 'Why Dotty didn't succumb to food poisoning years ago beats me. Those witches' brews of home-made wine and preserves made from dubious plants were positively grisly. Dim and I knew better than to eat any of Dotty's concoctions, but the doctors around here know jolly well that there is a local indigestion known as "Dotty's Collywobbles" which the unwary suffer from if they sample your aunt's potions.'

Connie laughed, and Dimity thought how attractive she

was when animated. It made one realize how young she was after all.

'The first things to go were half a dozen fearful jars of fungi swimming in cloudy liquid,' she told them. 'Heaven alone knows what they were, but I took them down into Lulling Woods and tipped the contents into a deep hole, when Aunt Dot was having a nap. I didn't dare bury the stuff in the garden in case the hens scratched it up.'

'Yes, she gave me a jar,' said Ella. 'It went straight in the dustbin, but I believe she sent several pots to Lulling Church Bazaar. Luckily Mrs Bull knew about them, and no doubt disposed of them safely.'

'One certainly gets some extraordinary things sent in for the church fund raisers,' commented Dimity. 'Lady Mary sent six pairs of pink corsets, all rather grubby too which made it worse, and so *vast*, of course, that it was difficult to know what to do with them.'

Connie rose to go, and Ella accompanied her to the door.

'Talking of unwanted gifts,' said Ella, when she returned, 'would that spoilt cat of yours eat hare?'

'There's nothing Tabitha likes more,' Dimity replied. 'She used to get some when we lived here, but somehow nobody leaves a nice hare hanging on the door knob at Lulling vicarage as they did at Thrush Green.'

'Percy Hodge left it in even better shape,' said Ella, 'all skinned and jointed in a plastic bag. Enough for a large family, so come and take your pick, Dim.'

'I'm sorry Percy's not happy,' said Dimity, as Ella wrapped a generous portion of the farmer's largesse for her friend.

'Maybe they'll shake down together. Will you and Charles eat any of this?'

'Indeed we will! It will be a great treat.'

'Good. I should never get through a third of all this. Now shall we have a cup of tea, or wait for Charles?'

'Charles will have had at least six cups by now,' Dimity assured her old friend. 'So let's put on the kettle.'

At that moment Charles was sitting beside his old friend Robert Bassett, having refused all refreshment pressed upon him by hospitable Milly Bassett.

Robert was in his dressing gown sitting near the window with a rug over his knees. Outside, a bird table had been fixed to the window sill, and blue tits and greenfinches squabbled over a net of peanut kernels suspended there, while a bright-eyed robin, ignoring the commotion, pecked busily at some kitchen scraps.

'They must be grateful for all that sustenance,' observed Charles.

'Not half as grateful as I am to them,' responded Robert. 'They are a constant joy. I find I can't read for long, and the television tires my eyes after a time, but I can watch these little beauties for hours on end. Tell me, Charles, how are you enjoying the new living?'

The rector recognized this query as a deliberate attempt to divert attention from his own problems, and told the invalid how much he and Dimity enjoyed their new house and explained their modest plans for the garden.

Milly excused herself and hurried back to the kitchen where she was cooking a splendid Dundee cake. Charles guessed rightly that she was relieved to see her husband happily engaged in conversation, thus relieving her for a short while from her anxious surveillance.

For there was no doubt about it, as Charles knew well as he rambled on gently about his own affairs, that Robert had little time left to him. He had lost a great deal of weight. His

complexion had the waxen pallor of the desperately ill, and
the bones of his thin fingers showed clearly as he plucked
feebly at the rug. But his smile was as sweet as ever, and he
listened as courteously as he had always done to Charles's
remarks.

At last Charles rose, looking at his watch.

'I must be off, Robert, I've one or two other friends to
visit, and it gets dark so confoundedly early still. I'll call in
again if I may.'

'Before you go, I've something for you,' said Robert,
pointing to a large envelope on his desk.

Charles brought it to him, and his old friend withdrew a
beautiful leather-bound book of poems which he gave to
the rector.

'James Elroy Flecker,' said Robert. 'A poet I've always
loved, and as fond of this country as you and I have been. I
should like you to have it.'

Charles was deeply moved.

'I shall always treasure it,' he assured the sick man. 'As a
boy I learnt "The Old Ships" at school, and can still quote
from it. I share your admiration, Robert, and you couldn't
have given me anything more precious.'

He held the thin hand in his for a moment. It felt as frail as
a bird's frame.

'I must see Milly before I go,' he said, turning towards the
door. 'I'll come again, Robert.'

'You must come soon then,' called Robert after him, as
the rector made his way towards the kitchen, blinking tears
away before facing brave Milly.

It was past six o'clock before the rector turned his car
towards Ella's cottage where Dimity awaited him.

He was, as she had surmised, awash with many cups of

tea and had vague indigestion. Beside him lay the beautiful parting present from Robert in company with a large bag full of cooking apples which had been pressed upon him at his final visit in Nidden.

In some ways it had been a sad afternoon, thought the good rector, slowing down to let a pheasant stalk majestically across the lane, and yet there had been beauty too. He remembered Robert's loving look as he had presented him with the book, and the kindly welcome he had received at all the homes he had visited.

He gradually approached Thrush Green. The sun had set, and dusk was falling over the wintry scene.

' "Light thickens," ' said the rector aloud, ' "and the crow Makes wing to the rooky wood." '

He savoured the sonority of the phrase. What a comfort it was to have a retentive memory! He corrected himself quickly. His memory, he reminded himself, was certainly not retentive when it came to practical matters, as Dimity frequently told him. Where on earth, for instance, had he left the key to the vestry? And what had he done with that slip for the cleaners which Dimity had given him only that morning?

Nevertheless, he comforted himself, it was a never-failing joy to find a happy phrase surfacing to add to the pleasures of daily life.

He looked approvingly at the white landscape against a darkening sky. In the distance he caught a glimpse of Lulling Woods, black against a steely-grey background.

'Rooky, indeed!' said the rector aloud. Who but Shakespeare could have thought of a crow making wing to a rooky wood, thus adding blackness to blackness?

He drew up outside Ella's cottage. The light glowed from her windows, shining a welcome, but the good rector sat still for a moment or two remembering his afternoon.

He would visit Robert again within the next day or two. Meanwhile he proposed to read some of the poems, which they both loved, before he slept that night. He wanted his old friend to know how much this last gift had meant to him.

But now he had other duties. He emerged into the chilly owl-light, and hurried up the path to collect his wife.

3 Unknown at The Fuchsia Bush

THE SNOW lasted for a full week. For the first three days the pristine purity which had so delighted Charles Henstock continued to enchant most of the inhabitants of Lulling and Thrush Green. The trees glittered in the frosty sunshine. Walls and hedges, capped in white, reflected the radiance of the clear sky. Underfoot the snow crunched to hard ice, and skaters were out in force on the shallow reaches of the River Pleshey and local ponds.

But overnight the weather changed, and by the fourth day a slow thaw had begun.

Snow fell from the outstretched branches of the vicarage cedar tree with soft flumps and clouds of snow dust. It slithered from walls and hedges. It dropped dramatically from the roofs of the houses and shops in Lulling High Street, much to the disgust and discomfiture of those walking below about their proper occasions. Two respectable ladies, about to enter The Fuchsia Bush in search of morning coffee, were engulfed in a miniature avalanche which descended from the guttering, and were obliged to spend their coffee break hatless and coatless as these garments were dried on the café's radiators.

At Thrush Green, Mr Jones's ancient spaniel, dozing peacefully in its kennel, was completely covered and had to be rescued by its alarmed owners from a four-foot fall of snow off an outhouse roof.

In the playground next door little rivulets ran from under the slush, much to the children's pleasure and their teachers' annoyance. Shoes and socks were rapidly soaked, and hardened delinquents of six and seven years of age had to be taken to task for throwing the last of the snowballs at their smaller brethren.

Nathaniel Patten's mantle slipped from his shoulders. The chestnut trees shed their loads, and the cars threw up a shower of watery slush as they passed.

It was, as the landlord of The Two Pheasants remarked to his neighbour, 'a dam' uncomfortable spell of weather.'

'Might freeze,' Albert replied morosely, 'and then we'll all break our legs, I shouldn't wonder.'

'That's right!' commented Mr Jones. 'Cheer us all up!'

And he bustled back into the snugness of the bar.

On that same morning, Charles Henstock planned to visit Robert Bassett but decided that he would telephone Joan Young first to see if a visit would be welcome to the invalid. He had seemed so frail a few days before, and the rector could not help wondering if the doctor might have vetoed any such excitements as visitors.

The bell seemed to ring for an unconscionably long time, and the good rector was filled with the usual doubts of one in his situation. Should he put down the receiver? No doubt, if he did so, then Joan Young would arrive, panting from the garden, just in time to find the instrument silent. On the other hand, the poor girl might be prostrate with a splitting headache, and lying abed praying for the noise to stop, with her hands over her ears. Really, thought Charles, even the simplest operation is fraught with worry, and one could quite understand how nervous people succumbed to all sorts of dreadful mental strain.

He was about to return the telephone to its cradle when Joan spoke.

'My dear,' said the rector, 'I trust I haven't brought you from the garden?'

'No indeed,' she replied. She sounded breathless nevertheless. 'In fact I was about to ring you. About Father.'

A sudden chill gripped Charles.

'How is he?'

'I'm sorry to tell you, Charles, but he has gone. Mother found him only ten minutes ago.'

The rector murmured his sympathy.

'He spoke to my mother about six o'clock when she gave him some tea, and then said he would go off to sleep again.'

The voice, so well-controlled, suddenly broke.

'I'm going to ring off,' said Charles, gently taking command. 'You have enough to do now, but let me help in any way. Who is with you?'

'Ben and Molly are coping,' replied Joan, 'and have gone to fetch John.'

'I'll call again later,' said the rector, adding his sympathy again.

He found that his knees were uncommonly shaky as he made his way to his study. Poor Milly and the family! How Robert would be missed! And how regrettable that he himself had not called to see his old friend yesterday! But there it was. The old sad cry of 'Too late, too late!' with which most mourners scourge themselves, rose to the rector's mind with bitter poignancy.

But such remorse was fruitless. His duty now was to the living who had so much to face at a time when their distress was at its most acute. Thank goodness, thought Charles, that the young Curdles lived in the same house! Both Molly and Ben would be of practical help and inestimable comfort to the Youngs, and to Joan's sister Ruth who was married to Doctor Lovell, and lived nearby.

There was a great deal to be said for living in a close community, mused the good rector. Irritating though it was at times to find that one had little or no privacy, yet when death or disaster struck how comforting to have the support of friends and relations close at hand.

Sighing, Charles went to break the news to Dimity.

Within a few hours, the news of Robert Bassett's death was general knowledge. Although he had been in ill health for several years, as always the news of his going came as a shock to Thrush Green and Lulling.

His contemporaries remembered him well as a young man at Thrush Green. Joan and Edward Young's fine house had originally been Robert's, but he preferred to live in Ealing where he carried on his furniture business, only visiting his daughters and the lovely Cotswold house two or three times a year.

When at last he had been obliged to retire he and his wife Milly had no desire to turn out the Youngs, nor in fact did they want to cope with such a large establishment. It was then that Edward, a sound architect, had so successfully converted the old coach house in the garden into an attractive bungalow, and where Milly and Robert had spent the last few years very happily.

Winnie Bailey was one of the first to hear. She was the widow of Donald Bailey who had been the senior partner of the Thrush Green practice when young John Lovell had come to join him, had settled in successfully and later found Ruth Bassett for a wife.

It was John who broke the news to Winnie as he left the surgery to hurry across the green to his father-in-law.

Winnie watched his departure with a heavy heart. One of the saddest things about growing old was the inevitable loss of contemporaries. It was some comfort to know that Robert's widow was surrounded by her family at this sombre time, but nothing, as Winnie herself knew, could mitigate the loneliness of the partner left behind.

She went into the kitchen to tell Jenny, her maid and friend who lived in the same house. Jenny was busy breaking a handsome cauliflower into its separate florets at the sink when she was told the news.

To Winnie's alarm, her serene Jenny, who always seemed to face a crisis with exemplary placidity, burst into tears, and sat down heavily on the kitchen chair.

'But Jenny,' said her mistress, much bewildered, 'we all knew the poor man had very little time left. Why are you so upset?'

Jenny raised a wet and woebegone face.

'He was kind to me once. It was when I first came to Lulling as a little girl. I was sent to the big house with a message, and I was a bit scared. Mr Bassett answered the door, and must have seen I was frightened, and he took me round the garden and asked me all about where I was living and that.'

She gave a violent hiccup, and Winnie patted her back as though she were curing a baby of the wind.

'And he picked me a bunch of flowers – pinks and roses, I remember – to take back to the old people, and he gave me a shilling for myself. I never was so rich in my life. And best of all, you see, I had something to give my pa and ma which I'd never had before. They thought the world of those flowers, and I thought the world of Mr Bassett, and always did.'

A mighty sniff terminated the tale, but Winnie could see

that the telling of it had eased poor Jenny's grief and that now she would recover her habitual calm.

'That's a very fine memory to have of a very fine man,' she said gently. 'Typical of dear Robert.'

Jenny rose to her feet, and mopped her face vigorously.

'Well, now I must get back to the cooking. Poor old gentleman, but there – it's time the vegetables were put on.'

And Winnie, returning to her own duties could not help being reminded of one of the entries in James Woodforde's Diary which she had been reading.

'Found the old gentleman almost at his last gasp. Totally senseless with rattlings in his throat. Dinner today boiled beef and Rabbit rosted.'

Life is just such a jumble of tragedy and everyday chores. Robert himself would have appreciated warmly the confrontation of death and the preparation of Jenny's cauliflower, in the same hour.

The funeral was at St Andrew's church a week later. It was a still day, mild and grey, with only a few tattered shreds of snow under the hedges to remind the mourners of the bitter weather.

The rector took the service for his old friend and gave a short and simple address. The two hymns chosen by the family were Robert's favourites, 'Ye holy angels bright' and 'God be in my head'.

After the service, when the congregation had gone home and Robert rested alone beneath a canopy of bright flowers, Charles and Dimity went with Ella to her nearby cottage and had tea there. Dotty Harmer and her niece Connie had been persuaded to join them.

Naturally, most of those present were in a subdued mood, grateful for the comfort of a bright fire and a cup of tea among friends, on a sad occasion.

Dotty was the exception. She was at her most chirpy, chattering of her memories of Robert in his younger days, and scattering cake crumbs as she waved her claw-like hands about.

'He had a most dreadful old bicycle he kept here in the coach house. D'you remember, Connie? It had an acetylene lamp. So smelly. No, of course, dear, it was before. your time. He ran into my father's flower bed with it once. Father was *most upset*.'

'Oh dear!' commented Dimity nervously. Old Mr Harmer had been a fierce martinet, dreaded by all, and such an encounter must have had dire consequences.

'Of course,' went on Dotty, 'Robert had such charming manners, and was so truly contrite, that Father let him off with only a slight kick on the shin. *Very* good of Father, we all thought.'

Charles caught Ella's eye and looked away hastily.

'I liked the hymns, didn't you?' continued Dotty, wiping her fingers on the hem of her skirt. 'He was always musical, and I'm so glad he didn't ask for "ER-bide with me". So lugubrious, don't you think? I mean, if someone is bound straight for heaven, as I'm sure dear Robert is, then why not have something cheerful to speed him on his way?'

'May I have another cup of tea, Ella?' asked Charles, looking a little pinker than usual.

'Personally,' said the irrepressible Dotty, 'I should like the Hallelujah Chorus, though it does take some time to get through, of course, and one would need a full choir. But it's so *rousing*, isn't it? Triumphant, and yet sacred. Do bear it in mind for me, Connie dear. Or failing that I rather like a pretty little song called "I Like Life", but perhaps if one were lying there dead, as presumably one would be if the doctors had examined one efficiently, then to ask for life might be a little presumptuous, in the circumstances. What do you think, Charles?'

The rector put his cup down.

'I think, Dotty, that you should sit back quietly and enjoy Ella's excellent tea. We've all had a sad afternoon, and need a little rest, I'm quite sure.'

'Well,' said Dotty, 'speaking for myself I feel quite perky, but no doubt there is something in what you say.'

And after Charles's gentle chiding she sat back in her chair and sipped her tea like an obedient child, much to the relief of her companions.

The still grey days of February continued. The sky remained overcast. The leafless trees stood with no stirring of branches. It seemed as if all Nature slept.

The roads were damp. The hedges were beaded with minute drops, and even the birds seemed silent.

In Lulling High Street the pavements gleamed wetly. The pollarded lime trees, bristling with leafless twigs, were streaked with lines of moisture. The air was heavy, and Lulling folk looked across the water meadows of the nearby River Pleshey and longed for relief from this oppressive humidity.

' 'Tisn't natural,' said one waitress to another in The Fuchsia Bush. 'Not a bit like spring. And as for getting a polish on these tables, well, it's love's labour lost, I say.'

'Never mind, love,' responded her fellow worker, Gloria Williams, who was busy arranging iced buns in a glass cabinet and licking her fingers noisily the while. 'Be March in a day or two, coming in like a lion, no doubt, and we'll have all the old biddies coming in grumbling about their hair being messed up.'

Her companion, Rosa, flicked a duster idly over an improbable collection of plastic flowers with daffodils nuzzling red geraniums above some fiercely autumnal leaves, all set precariously in a tub which had once held margarine.

'I was thinking of giving the windows a clean,' she said, with a yawn. 'But there, old Mrs Peters isn't coming in today, and it don't hardly seem worth it.'

Mrs Peters was the present owner of The Fuchsia Bush, and was possessed of an energy which would galvanise any but such obdurate employees as those at the café into action. When she was present, even the lethargic waitresses were stirred into semi-activity. In her absence, they reverted to their usual apathy.

'I wouldn't trouble,' agreed her colleague. 'Not this weather. Get all smeary, wouldn't they? You take it easy, dear. We'll have the elevenses lot in any minute now, and we'll be fair rushed off our feet.'

The two sat down at a table at the back of the empty room, and Rosa began to tell Gloria about the disco she had attended the night before when the door bell gave its mighty ping, and in came an elderly man. Rosa sighed.

'Here we go, then. I'll take him, dear. You do the next.'

She allowed the stranger to settle at a table near the window where he had a good view of the High Street, and had time to buff her nails on her apron while he studied the menu.

Slowly she approached.

'What can I get you?'

'Some coffee, please. Oh, and one of those iced buns.'

'White or black?'

The stranger look temporarily nonplussed.

'Surely you will bring me a pot of coffee and one of hot milk?'

'It's usually just a cup.'

'Well, today will you please bring me a pot of each, as I have asked you.'

His eyes were very blue, Rosa noted, and flashed when he was cross. Proper old martinet, she reckoned. A general or admiral or something awkward like that, and used to having his own way, that was sure.

'It'll be extra,' she shrugged.

'I've no doubt I can stand the expense,' he said shortly. 'And I'm in a hurry, so look sharp.'

Rosa ambled into the kitchen at the rear.

'Got a right one in there,' she informed the kitchen staff. 'Wants a pot of coffee and one of hot milk. I ask you!'

She cast her eyes aloft as if seeking divine aid for such recalcitrance.

Old Mrs Jefferson, chief cook for many years at The Fuchsia Bush, and a staunch upholder of long-forgotten principles of service, gave one of her famous snorts.

'Then get what he's asked for. It ain't your place to query a customer's order. Do as you're told, and keep a civil tongue in your head.'

'You don't have to face the customers,' grumbled Rosa.

'I have in my time,' reminded Mrs Jefferson, 'and given satisfaction too, my girl, which is a lot more than anyone can say about you. Now, get your tray ready, and see if you can manage a smile on that ugly mug of yours. Enough to turn the milk sour looking like that.'

She whisked back and forth from stove to the central table, nimble as ever despite her impressive bulk.

Rosa took the tray without a word, but if looks could have killed, Mrs Jefferson would have been a substantial corpse on the kitchen floor.

★

Half an hour or so later, the stranger emerged from The Fuchsia Bush into the muggy air of Lulling High Street.

The shoppers were in action now, and the tall figure had to circumvent perambulators, dogs on leads, and worst of all, two ladies having a lengthy gossip with their baskets on wheels spread behind them across the width of the pavement.

'Excuse me!' said the man firmly, pushing aside one of the baskets with a well-polished brogue.

'Really!' exclaimed one of the ladies. 'What are people coming to? It's a pity if we can't stop to say a civil word to our friends!'

But she waited until the stranger was out of earshot, before making these protestations.

Her companion was gazing after the upright figure making his way up the slight incline towards the market place.

'I believe I've seen him before,' she mused. 'Years ago.'

'Well, I shouldn't bother to resume the acquaintanceship,' replied her friend. 'A very thrusting sort of individual, I should think.'

They settled back into their former positions and continued their interrupted discussion.

Miss Violet Lovelock was in the market place comparing the price of leeks on each of the vegetable stalls.

It was really outrageous how expensive even the lowliest vegetables were these days, she thought. Perhaps three of Dawson's thick leeks would make enough soup for two meals for the three of them. Plenty of the leek water, of course, and some salt and pepper should eke things out.

She was just putting her parcel in her basket, and endeavouring to avert her eyes from page three of the newspaper in which the leeks were wrapped – what was the

world coming to! – when she noticed the figure striding vigorously uphill across the road.

Miss Violet gazed with concentration. She knew that walk. Who was he? If only her sight were keener, but she feared that her sisters were quite right in urging her to get her spectacles changed. Now a lorry was in the way. Now he had stopped to look in Barlow's window, and had his back to her. If only she could place him! There was something familiar about that straight back. Now who could it be?

The figure moved on, and suddenly opened the door of the solicitors, Twitter and Venables. In a trice he had vanished into the murk of that establishment, leaving Miss Violet to ruminate on her way home.

Perhaps she had been mistaken. Perhaps it was a complete stranger going into dear Justin Venables' office on business.

Her sight really was getting worse, and it made it quite easy to make mistakes when people were at a distance. She would think no more about it.

And yet – there was *something*! And that something had given her a thrill of pleasure, as though some long-forgotten happiness had been stirred into life again, on that quiet grey morning in the damp Lulling street.

4 Rumours At Thrush Green

MARCH ARRIVED, but there was nothing lion-like about its coming.

The same grey stillness enveloped Lulling and Thrush Green. The same listlessness enveloped the inhabitants. Everyone longed for the clouds to lift, for a great wind to rush gustily through the trees, for the streets to be blown dry and for spirits to feel exhilaration again.

At Lulling vicarage Charles was having a most uncomfortable interview with one of his keenest parishioners. Mrs Thurgood was the widow of a wealthy provision merchant who had supplied a great many first-class Cotswold grocers with such exotic articles as coffee beans, tea, spices, dried fruits and preserved fruits, jars of ginger, toothsome pâtés and a host of other elegant comestibles.

His fleet of dark blue vans, chastely inscribed in gold lettering, were a common sight in the district, and Mrs Thurgood, carrying on the tradition of her husband, was a generous donor to all the church finances, and boasted that she never missed a service.

Anthony Bull had been her idea of the perfect vicar. 'The sort of fellow,' she had been heard to say, 'that one can invite quite safely to the house, no matter who is staying.' She approved of his distinguished looks, his charm of manner and the content of his sermons. She liked the ritual, the robes, the genuflecting, the sonorous chanting, the plethora of descants and the use of the seven-fold Amen. He was, in her eyes, completely satisfactory, and she mourned his promotion to a Kensington living.

She was also making it quite clear that she found Charles Henstock much inferior in every way to his predecessor.

'I can't believe,' she was telling Charles, 'that dear Mr Bull didn't mention this business of new kneelers for the Lady Chapel.'

'He had a great deal to think of, you know,' said Charles, 'before his move. It probably slipped his memory.'

'I doubt it,' replied Mrs Thurgood. 'I spoke to him a few weeks before his departure pointing out the need for a complete new set. He said, I remember, that he would mention it to you, as obviously you would be in charge when the work was undertaken.'

And who could blame Anthony Bull for shelving the problem, thought the rector? But now, it seemed, the birds had come home to roost, and it had become his problem.

'Do we really need new kneelers?' began Charles. 'The present ones seem very attractive, and I fear that we must guard against undue expense.'

'*Of course* we need them! And I made it quite clear to Mr Bull from the outset, that I would be happy to pay for all the materials. It's just a case of getting the Mothers' Union, and the Ladies' Guild, and the Church Flower Ladies to take on the work – one kneeler apiece should be all that is needed – and to get your permission to go ahead.'

At the mention of all the potential kneeler-makers, many of whom Charles found profoundly intimidating, he found his mind turning to the hosts of Midian who prowled and prowled around.

'And, of course,' went on his formidable visitor, 'it would be best to have one person leading the way.'

Like a bull-dozer, thought Charles unhappily.

'To co-ordinate the whole scheme,' said Mrs Thurgood. 'For one thing we must think about Design and Colour.'

'But surely, each lady would choose her own pattern?'

'Good gracious, no! Naturally the main colour must be blue. Soft furnishings in Lady Chapels are traditionally blue. And one must have the kneelers of uniform size. And frankly, I think that they should all be of the same design. Luckily, my daughter Janet, who is exceptionally gifted and has studied Design, Tapestry Work and Embroidery at Art School, has drawn up a charming pattern on squared paper, ready for the project.'

Charles began to feel besieged. The preliminary skirmishes were over. Now the heavy guns were in action.

He looked out at the misty garden, the beaded grass and the cedar tree, darker than ever with moisture. That glimpse of placid unchanging nature gave him the strength to counter-attack.

'It's plain that you have given much thought to the matter,' said Charles kindly. 'And it is most generous of you to offer to face the expense. I shall talk to Dimity about it – she is always so practical – and have a word with my church-wardens. Perhaps I may ring you in a day or two?'

Even the redoubtable Mrs Thurgood realized that she had advanced as far as was possible on the present occasion. Now was the moment to halt and remuster her strength for future assaults.

'Very well,' she agreed, rising from the vicarage sofa. 'Everything is absolutely ready as soon as you give the word. I know,' she added meaningly, as she preceded the vicar of Lulling into the hall, 'that it was a matter very dear to Mr Bull's heart. How we miss him!'

This parting thrust was successfully parried by the genuine sweetness of Charles's smile.

'We do indeed, Mrs Thurgood,' he said. 'But Lulling's loss was Kensington's gain, and I hear he is exceptionally happy in his new parish.'

He watched Mrs Thurgood's ramrod-straight back departing down the drive, and sighed.

The Mothers' Union! The Ladies' Guild! The Church Flower Ladies!

Could he ever hope to gain a victory against such a monstrous regiment of women?

It was Ella Bembridge, Dotty's old friend, who first discovered the identity of the tall stranger in Lulling. Like so many ladies who live alone, Ella had the uncommon knack of assimilating local gossip and, what was even better, of remembering it. It was not that she actively ferreted out information as many of the Thrush Green and Lulling ladies were wont to do. Such obvious seekers after gossip were well-known in the community, and those who met them were on their guard and curbed their tongues.

But Ella was invariably engaged in one of her many crafts, clacking her handloom, knitting or crocheting at incredible speed, or simply rolling one of her deplorable cigarettes, and so appeared to the retailer of local news to be attending principally to the matter in hand. Consequently, much was divulged, and Ella's keen mind retained it.

'Did you know that the Venables have got a visitor?' she asked Charles and Dimity when she called in for the parish magazine one morning.

'Anyone we know?' asked Dimity.

'I shouldn't think so. He's been overseas most of his life, but he was born and brought up here, and went to the grammar school when Dotty's father was headmaster.'

'Poor boy!' exclaimed Dimity. Mr Harmer's idea of corporal punishment would have brought him before any present day court on a charge of battery and assault, if not grievous bodily harm, and the tales of elderly old boys, even though understandably exaggerated, were enough to curdle the blood.

'Kit Armitage. That's his name,' went on Ella, stuffing the parish magazine between a head of celery and her library book in the rather lop-sided basket of her own making. 'I expect Dotty will remember him, and the Lovelocks, of course, but before our time here.'

'Is he staying long?'

'I don't think so. He's looking for a small place of his own now that he's retired. Justin's always dealt with the family's legal affairs, and they've kept in touch over the years, and I gather he's just having a week or so with them until he gets settled.'

'Of course, now that Justin has retired he must have

plenty of spare time to entertain,' observed the rector. 'I sometimes wonder if he would consent to coming on the Parochial Church Council. He would be such an asset with his grasp of legal and financial affairs.'

'Try him,' advised Ella. 'Besides he might back you up on such knotty problems as the new kneelers.'

'And how on earth do you know about the new kneelers?' asked Charles, looking at Dimity in bewilderment.

'Not from your wife,' responded Ella robustly. 'I've never met such a model of discretion. But Frances Thurgood button-holed me in the butcher's this week, and hoped I would "use my good offices", as she put it, to persuade you to agree.'

'Really!' the rector expostulated.

'Don't worry,' continued Ella. 'I wouldn't support Frances Thurgood on any of her projects, on principle. Of all the bossy, scheming, devious bullies I have met, she takes the biscuit.'

'Ella, please!' protested Charles, holding up a plump hand. 'I don't like to hear you speak so ill of anyone.'

'You wouldn't,' agreed Ella. 'You're far too tolerant. And if you really want me to speak ill, I can do a lot better than that.'

'Not now,' broke in Dimity. 'Sit down, dear, and have a cigarette.'

Ella allowed herself to be persuaded, took a chair, and then produced the battered tobacco tin which was her private cigarette-making factory.

'Don't you give way to her, Charles,' she said, when she had at last got the cigarette going and was wreathed in blue smoke. 'Let her win this round and she'll have you licked for many to come. As for this dreadful plan of using Janet's ghastly design, well, nip it in the bud, is my advice. Have you ever seen any of that girl's work?'

'No,' said Charles and Dimity together.

'Well, you've been spared a very horrific experience. She had a show of her drawings and paintings in the Corn Exchange last autumn. Enough to put your teeth on edge, believe me. Half the time you wondered if they were the right way up, and the other half you were sorry if they were. And all with such pretentious titles! The Reckoning, Meditation, Aspirations, A Theme of Beauty, Transcendental Awakening – all that sort of twaddle. And nothing under eighty quid! As you might imagine, there were mighty few red sales stickers about.'

'She did go to Art College, I understand,' said Dimity timidly.

'I should take that as an excuse rather than a recommendation,' replied Ella. 'No, Charles. Just you watch it! Smite her hip and what-ever-it-is, before she does it to you. And if Justin Venables will come and support you, I should get all the help he can give you. Or perhaps this new chap, Christopher Armitage, will turn out to be a pillar of the Church if he settles here.'

'I certainly miss Harold Shoosmith by my side,' admitted Charles. 'He's still such a help at Thrush Green, but so far I don't seem to have found anyone quite so supporting at Lulling.'

'Keep hoping,' said Ella, stubbing out her untidy cigarette, and collecting her things. 'Must be off. I promised to sit in with Dotty this afternoon, as Connie's off to have her hair permed.'

On the doorstep, she paused and looked skyward.

'Smells different, Charles. Has the wind turned round?'

They both gazed towards St John's weather-vane.

'It has indeed,' cried the rector. 'Let's hope we get a

change in this depressing weather. We need something to raise our spirits.'

'Cheer up, Charles,' said Ella, smiting him quite painfully on the shoulder. 'You'll win through whatever the weather. But beware of Frances Thurgood!'

She stumped off towards the High Street on her way to Thrush Green. Dear old Charles! She hoped he would stand firm about those dam' kneelers. And not for worlds would she ever let that saintly man know of the beastly, condescending, cruel remarks which that cat Frances had made about him in her hearing.

Within twenty-four hours the grey clouds had lifted, the welcome sun shone again, and the March wind scoured the streets of Lulling.

Dead leaves frisked about the gutters like kittens. Inn signs creaked, saplings swayed, and the housewives of Lulling and Thrush Green watched with relief the lines of flapping washing billowing in the gardens.

At Thrush Green school the lethargy of the last few weeks had made way for the usual boisterous high spirits which wind invariably engendered. Grateful though little Miss Fogerty and her headmistress were for the change in the weather, nevertheless it brought its problems.

The children were noisy and excited. Doors banged, papers flew from desks, windows burst open, and general disorder prevailed. At break the children rushed screaming around the playground, pushing and romping like so many crazy puppies, clothes flattened against bodies, and hair on end.

Miss Fogerty was quite used to such behaviour. On duty in the playground, a mug of tea in hand, she watched the chaos about her with a benevolent eye, but alert to any particular recklessness which might lead to injury. John Todd, for instance, temporary aeroplane though he was, had no need to zoom quite so menacingly round the unsuspecting infants nearby. Arms outstretched, a mad gleam in his eye, and a terrible puttering noise emerging from his mouth, he constituted a considerable danger to his fellows, and Agnes Fogerty went at once to chide him.

It was because of this, and her subsequent attention to other malefactors crazed with March euphoria, that she failed to notice the two men who were pacing round the empty plot left by the vanished Thrush Green rectory, where Charles and Dimity had been so happy.

It was her companion, Dorothy Watson, who noted their activities and mentioned it when school had finished for the day and the two friends were restoring themselves with a cup of tea and shortbread fingers in the school house.

Even in here the wind made itself felt, singing through the key hole and stirring the curtains. But compared with the upheaval at school, it was remarkably peaceful, and anyway very pleasant to see the branches tossing in the garden, and the grass silvering as the breeze combed it.

'They were surveyors, I imagine,' said Dorothy. 'They had one of those great tape measures in a leather case. I think one works for the council. It's strange we haven't heard anything.'

'We will,' Agnes promised her. 'You know Thrush Green. The news gets round in no time. And if you managed to see them, Dorothy, dear, I'm quite sure plenty of other people did too. More shortbread?'

Miss Fogerty was quite right. Albert Piggott and his neighbour Mr Jones, landlord of The Two Pheasants, had also noticed the two men at work.

'Council chaps,' said Mr Jones. 'I did hear from Perce Hodge that the council had bought the site.'

'What for?' asked Albert, toying with his half-pint of bitter. 'And how does Perce know? 'E never goes nowhere to find out. That missus of his keeps him knuckled down, I hear.'

'You wants to watch your tongue about Percy's Doris,' warned the landlord. 'It don't do to come between husband and wife, and their private life's their own, I reckon.'

'What's come over you, turning so righteous?' asked Albert. 'You was the first to blab about my Nelly when she left me for that dratted oilman. One thing, he'll have learnt his mistake by now, I don't doubt. And nothing's private in Thrush Green, as you knows, and I do too. So come on, tell us what Perce said about the council.'

Mr Jones polished a tumbler carefully, huffed inside it, and polished it again before replying.

'Going to build old people's homes, so he said. Heard it from his cousin who cleans the council offices.'

Albert digested this news with a mouthful of beer to settle it.

'Ah! I wonder! By rights it should have another rectory on it. It's church land, ain't it?'

'Not now, boy. The church sold it to the council, and it's my bet they're looking over plans for these homes and going to choose the cheapest. I bet Mr Young's put in a plan. He fair hated that old place, and he always said he'd like to see something worth looking at on the site.'

'Bet that'll be a fine old eye-sore, if his own new offices are anything to go by. I'd a done better myself. No roof hardly, and the windows hanging off of the guttering, and brick as black as your hat. Makes a proper mess of Lulling High Street, I reckons,' said Albert sourly.

At that moment young Ben Curdle, his son-in-law, came in with a basket full of empty bottles.

'Morning, Dad,' he nodded. 'What you having?'

Albert brightened, and pushed his empty glass forward.

'Been talking about these new homes the council's going to build over yonder,' he said. 'I was just wondering who's going to live in 'em.'

'Well, you might be one,' said Ben.

Albert bridled.

'What would I need with a council place?' he asked indignantly. 'I got me own nice little cottage, paid for by the church. I'm not all that old anyway!'

'You will be soon,' replied Ben, with maddening calm. 'And it won't be long before young Cooke is doing all the church caretaking – he does most of it now as far as I can see. Then he'll want a place. Yours would suit him fine one day.'

Albert grew red with wrath, and began to bluster.

'See here, Ben, I still pulls my weight. Why, only yesterday I had all the mats up and swilled over the aisle. Took me best part of two hours, that did.'

'That's what I mean,' said Ben. 'It should only take half an hour at the most. You're gettin' past it, Dad, and you'll have to face it. If you could get one of these new homes, you'd be quids in. I bet there'd be a warden to look after you, and that'd save my Molly working her fingers to the bone for you.'

He picked up his empty basket, nodded pleasantly to the landlord and departed.

'Well I'm blowed!' puffed Albert in disgust. 'That's a fine way of goin' on, ain't it? Telling me I'm too old to work, and practically handin' over my house to that young lay-about Cooke. Me livin' in an old people's home indeed! I'd watch it.'

Mr Jones let him rumble on crossly. He wiped the counter with a red-checked cloth and then lent across it conspiratorially.

'See here, Albert. You're looking ahead a bit. No one's said anything about you losing your house, and while you're still working it remains yours.'

Albert looked slightly mollified.

'And what's more,' went on his companion, draping the damp cloth over the beer handles to dry, 'no one knows for sure if old people's homes are going up there. Someone once said it might be a clinic or some such.'

'Or a brewery?' queried Albert. 'Now that would be a real good idea, wouldn't it?'

He swilled down the remainder of his glass and hobbled quite briskly to the door.

5 A Visit To Tom Hardy

ONE BLUE and white day towards the end of March, the rector made his way towards a remote cottage near the River Pleshey.

He walked by the path bordering the river, holding on his hat every now and again as the boisterous wind tried to tear it from his head.

The gentle murmuring of the water was lost in the noise of the wind around him. The pollarded willows along the banks were bristling with young twigs, and the golden-green leaves were beginning to unfurl.

Here and there an ancient willow, spared the woodcutter's attention, trailed branches in the river. As the wind whipped them the long twigs flailed the water creating little whirlpools and eddies.

A moorhen fled squawking as the rector passed by, its feet making a sequinned track on the surface of the stream. A water vole crossed nearby leaving an arrow-shaped wake as it forged towards the safety of the bank.

The rector had an observant eye for such details. They added to the joy of his walk which he had undertaken for just such refreshment. He had felt the need for a little solitude, for time to relish the lovely natural scenes about him, free from the intrusion of fellow humans.

He noted the crinkled bark of the willow trunks, the criss-cross pattern softened by grey-green lichen. He smelt the pungency of water-mint growing in the muddy shallows at the brink of the Pleshey. He heard the plop of small animals making for watery cover as he approached, and he saw the great galleons of white clouds sailing superbly across the blue sky above the water meadows, and felt the wind on his face.

He revelled in his senses which brought to him such richness, and thanked God that he still had health and strength to enjoy all five. This morning walk acted as balm to Charles's spirits, for despite his serene appearance and his gentle courtesy to everyone, he was a secret worrier, and at the moment there was plenty to perplex him.

He had only been at Lulling for a few months and already he knew that he fell short in many ways of the expectations of his new parishioners. It grieved him.

It grieved him, not because he was a vain man eager for the approbation of his fellows, but because he seemed to be causing anxiety to others. Mrs Thurgood's obvious disdain was comparatively easy to bear. Charles was perceptive enough to realize that her adoration of Anthony Bull made her consider any successor inadequate. But she was not alone in her criticism. It was this that perturbed him.

He had known from the start that to follow someone as magnetically outstanding as Anthony Bull would not be easy. He had been a man who engendered strong feelings, particularly in women. Charles recognised that there would be robust loyalty for his predecessor, and he considered it a laudable thing among his flock. What was hard to bear was the simple fact that anyone who succeeded Anthony was bound to be different, and that that particular fact was being ignored by some of his followers.

He had heard comments on his inadequacy, some obviously intended to wound. Several devout ladies had reproached him delicately about the simplicity of his services compared with the more extravagant ritual of Anthony's reign. He did his best to explain his beliefs. Comparisons might be odious, but he had to face them. For all the pin-pricks, the petty humiliations, the unnecessary injustices done to him, yet Charles never wavered in his own admiration of Anthony Bull nor in the forbearance with which he faced his critics.

His chief unhappiness was caused by the fact that at least three families had now started to support a neighbouring vicar. This he found extremely upsetting. Only half an hour earlier, outside The Fuchsia Bush on his way to the river, he had run into one of his deserters, Albert Beverley.

'I was hoping to see you,' the rector had said cheerfully. 'We haven't seen much of each other lately.'

Albert Beverley looked about him unhappily.

'Well, you know how it is. The weeks slip by, don't they?'

'Time certainly flies,' agreed the rector. 'Perhaps I shall see you and the family –?'

'Ah!' said Albert hastily, 'must get on. I've promised to meet the wife in here. Late now, I'm afraid. Nice to have seen you.'

And he bolted into the haven of The Fuchsia Bush where, it was quite apparent, no wife was waiting.

It was incidents like this which were so distressing. 'The slings and arrows of outrageous fortune' he could bear for himself, but it was the Church which mattered.

Charles suddenly stood stock still and gazed across the river.

'That's the real trouble,' he said aloud, much to the surprise of a thrush briskly tapping out a snail from its shell on a handy flint. 'It's the Church that matters! I am failing the Church!'

He sighed deeply, clutched his hat, and continued on his errand.

The thrush gobbled down its succulent breakfast, and also went about its daily business.

On that same March morning Justin Venables sat in his usual seat in front of the well-worn desk at Twitter and Venables.

Although he had had his seventieth birthday, Justin was still known in Lulling as 'Young Mr Venables' to distinguish him from his illustrious father, Harvey Venables, who had founded the firm with Basil Twitter when both young men had returned from World War One.

The partnership had flourished, so much so that a third partner, called Adrian Treadgold, had been appointed. It was soon apparent that this latest addition was not of the same solid qualities as Basil Twitter and Harvey Venables, and when he blotted his copybook by running away with the wife of a well-to-do landowner, who was also a much respected client of the firm, then Adrian Treadgold's name was removed from the brass plate, and from all the office stationery.

Young Justin had served with his father until the latter's death. When he attained the age of seventy he made it clear that he was retiring. The whole of Lulling regretted his departure, and the office itself begged him to keep in touch. He was persuaded to keep on a few very old and valued clients, and to this end he was available at the office on Tuesday of each week.

'And don't expect me to do more,' he had told his staff severely. 'You boys are now in your forties and fifties and quite old enough to know your job. I want time for my fishing.'

On this particular Tuesday morning he sat contemplating a cast-iron ash tray bearing the words 'Long Live Victoria 1837–1897' and a colossal inkstand bearing a silver disc which told the world at large that it had been presented to Harvey Venables on the occasion of his silver wedding.

Justin was so used to these historic pieces that he barely noticed them. What he was more interested in was the wall clock which said ten minutes to eleven. His client was already five minutes late, and Justin valued punctuality.

Among the few favoured clients of advanced age whom Justin still attended was Dotty Harmer. Some years earlier he had defended her successfully on a charge of careless driving. He was fond of his eccentric old friend, and glad that he had helped to prove her innocence on that occasion. Nevertheless, wild horses would never have dragged him into any vehicle driven by Dotty. He was relieved when he had heard that she was now without a car, and that her niece Connie acted as chauffeur whenever she was needed.

It was Connie that he awaited now. When she arrived, he would ask Muriel in the outer office, to bring them coffee. He was glad that he had allowed himself to be persuaded to spend this one day a week in his old chair. He did not mind admitting that he missed the office routine, and the company of his staff, and particularly the faithful Muriel who had been with the firm for almost as many years as he had, and knew exactly how he liked his tea and his coffee and kept him supplied with shortbread of her own making. Why, he thought suddenly, she must have made pounds of the stuff over the years! He had never thought of it before. He must make a point of mentioning it to her. She would value such civility, good faithful girl.

It was also some relief, he secretly admitted, to get out of the house regularly and on legitimate business. Much as he appreciated his freedom nowadays, and his escape from the stern limits imposed by the clock and his desk diary, yet there was a certain aimlessness about mornings at home which had become something of a problem to a man accustomed to a rigid timetable.

And then, it was quite apparent that he was something of a nuisance to his wife. She was used to having the house to herself from eight forty-five every morning. The newspaper used to be hers when it was pushed through the letter box at nine o'clock. Now he grabbed it, as his right, and she had pointed this out to him only that week.

Then there were those little visits from neighbours, and the cups of coffee and gossip which he found irksome. Yes, there was no doubt about it, retirement forced one to make adjustments, and he readily admitted that his dear wife probably found difficulties quite as great as his own, in this new situation. Ah well, thank heaven for Tuesdays, he thought gratefully!

The hands of the clock now stood at five to eleven, and Justin was about to check with Muriel about the time of Connie Harmer's appointment when the door opened, and Connie stood, pink and breathless, on the threshold, with Muriel.

'Oh, Mr Venables, I'm so very sorry I'm late –' she began.

'Think nothing of it,' replied Justin. 'Come and sit down, my dear Miss Harmer. Coffee please, Muriel.'

Two miles away, Charles Henstock waited on the doorstep of Tom Hardy's cottage, and admired the tidiness of his little garden.

It had been a water-keeper's house once, but Tom had taken it over when the water board had decided to dispose of the property. Not many of the tenants had been satisfied with the amenities offered, and the board did not feel that the expense of adequate plumbing, new wiring and extensive structural repairs could be undertaken. The waterkeeper who looked after the next stretch of the river owned a car, and with an increase in salary was glad to take on the extra work. Tom Hardy, a widower in his late fifties, had been pleased to buy the property for a fairly low sum.

He had once run a haulage business, but had sold it when he came to live at Keeper's Cottage. He was a jack-of-all trades, remaining in touch with many of his business associates, and willing to turn his hand to driving a heavy vehicle, painting and decorating, doing odd-job gardening and even giving a hand with sheep-shearing in the early summer.

He was held in high regard by the inhabitants of Lulling and Thrush Green who appreciated his old-fashioned virtues of patience, honesty and helpfulness. Among his various trades was the felling and chopping of trees, and it was in his role of a supplier of logs that Charles came to see him.

He heard footsteps approaching round the side of the house, and Tom appeared holding a dead rabbit dangling by the legs.

'Come round the back, sir,' said Tom. 'I thought there must be someone about. My old Polly growled, but she's past bothering about stirring herself these days.'

'I can't think why I knocked at the front door,' replied the rector. 'I usually come to the back one, but I was thinking of something else.'

'Sunday's sermon, maybe?' Tom smiled, his blue eyes looking sideways at his visitor.

He led the way into the kitchen, and motioned Charles to a sturdy wooden armchair by the table.

'Glass of my home-made beer?' asked Tom.

'Thank you. A small one would be very welcome.'

Tom vanished into a larder which ran the length of the room, and the rector looked about him.

It was a man's room, no doubt about that. Over the mantelpiece, above the kitchen range, was a gun rack holding three guns. By the side of the fire-place some large coat pegs supported a belt of cartridges, a riding crop, pieces of leather harness and a fishing gaff, and propped in a corner were a shepherd's crook and a thumb stick cut from a fine hazel sapling.

On the mantelpiece itself stood a tobacco jar, a large box of matches, a tin labelled TEA and another labelled SUGAR, and on the adjacent dresser, in front of the willow-pattern plates, stood an old-style circular knife cleaner, a wooden box labelled SALT and a basket of eggs.

There was not a flower or a plant to be seen, not even a bunch of herbs hanging up to dry. The kitchen table was bare, though scrubbed very clean. A woman, thought the rector, would have had a cloth on it, and probably a plant standing atop, but there was something attractive about this sparsely accoutred mannish room. He decided that it must be because everything visible was strictly functional, plainly useful, unadorned. There was a workaday atmosphere here, as honest and unassuming as its owner.

Charles thought of his own drawing room at Lulling vicarage. It was a charming room, beautifully proportioned and filled with all the objects which he and Dimity treasured. There were cushions, pelmets, ornaments of china, brass and silver. There were vases of flowers, pictures, a tapestry fire screen and innumerable rugs.

It was a gracious room, a woman's room, and he loved it. But sitting here, among these stark surroundings, on his hard wooden chair, caressing its well-worn arms and noting that the only picture provided was a corn-chandler's almanack by the door, his own drawing room seemed frivolously cluttered, and these simple surroundings chimed better with his present mood.

Tom returned with two tankards.

'Like to come in the parlour?' he asked, as though suddenly aware of his surroundings.

'No, thank you, Tom,' said the rector. 'I like this room very well.'

'I live here most of the time,' said Tom. 'Mind you, I give the parlour a clean every now and again, and keep the window ajar. But it's full of fal-de-lals, Margaret's best china in a cabinet, and the bird cage she used to keep her budgies in, and the family bible – all that sort of Sunday stuff.'

'Sunday stuff?'

'Well, a few books, you know. The kind of thing you looked at after church on Sundays.'

He laughed rather shame-facedly.

'Not as I go now, as you well know, sir. I'm what I call lapsed C. of E. when I'm asked what religion I am. Still, I could say the Creed to you now, and the Twenty-third Psalm, and sing most of the usual hymns, if need be. It's just I don't feel the need for going to church. I used to go with Margaret. She enjoyed Mr Bull's services, but to tell you the truth, I found him a bit too high-falutin', if you know what I mean?'

A warm pang of happiness made the rector's heart beat more quickly. As quickly, he chided himself for this involuntary response to comfort.

'He's very much missed, I know,' said Charles steadily. He put his tankard carefully on to the bare table top. 'I miss him myself, I don't mind admitting. But what I called for, Tom, was to order some logs and to ask you if you have any idea how many we should need. I believe you supplied Mr Bull in his time?'

'Well, they always kept plenty of fires going, but they'd the two maids living in so that was one extra fire for them. And they liked the hall one going in really cold weather. I don't think you'd need as much as Mr Bull wanted. I'd say two good loads would see you through.'

'I think you used to deliver two to the old rectory at Thrush Green, if I remember aright. The present house is considerably bigger, Tom.'

'And a sight warmer, sir. That old place was pesky cold always, and caught all the winds God sent, specially the north-east. No, your present place is better built, and sheltered too. The church keeps a lot off you in the way of weather. Acts as a protection, you might say.'

The same warm feeling of comfort engulfed Charles. He rose to go.

'I'll take your advice, Tom. Two loads whenever you can manage it, and the old coach house is waiting for the logs. I swept it out myself yesterday.'

'Right!' said Tom, accompanying his guest to the back door. 'And if need be, I'll top you up after Christmas.'

A Welsh collie dog, grey round the muzzle and with one opaque eye, nuzzled the rector's ankles as he gained the path. The rector patted the silky flanks.

'She's a good old girl,' said Tom fondly. 'Rare company! Don't look much, like me and my house, but she suits me.'

'That's all that matters,' the rector assured him.

The wind was behind him as he went homeward, thrusting

him so forcefully that now and again he was nudged into a few running steps.

He found himself exhilarated by the boisterous wind. His spirits, so low on the outward journey, had revived. Could it be the exercise and fresh air which had worked this small miracle? Or could the good fellowship of honest Tom, and the glimpse of his simple and uncomplicated way of living, have put his own worries into perspective?

Whatever the reason, Charles felt better able to face his problems. It reaffirmed his belief in sticking to his principles, to do right by all his flock to the best of his ability, to foster patience and forbearance, and to ignore the pinpricks of petty malice.

He remembered suddenly that someone – he rather thought that it was A. P. Herbert of blessed memory – said that he was sustained by four words:

Fear nothing! Thank God!

The first two words took care of the unknown future. The last two covered past mercies received.

The rector turned the four words over in his mind, and was strengthened and comforted.

In Justin's office Connie was about to make her departure. Dotty's business, concerning the deeds of the cottage at Lulling Woods, was over, the coffee drunk, and Justin was ushering her to the door.

'Did you ever meet Christopher Armitage?' he asked her. 'Kit, he's called more generally. I know your aunt would remember him. He was at school when her father was headmaster.'

'And he survived?' laughed Connie.

'Yes, indeed. A resilient fellow, and excellent company. He's just retired and looking about for a house here.'

'No, I haven't come across him, I'm afraid.'

'Well, he's based with us for a little while, but at the moment he is looking up relatives and old friends before getting down to serious house-hunting. We expect him back in a week or two. No doubt he'll call to see your aunt before long.'

'That will be nice,' said Connie.

They had now reached the open front door. The wind had blown in a few dead leaves from the lime trees. They skittered about the tiled floor like small crabs.

'Well, thank you again,' said Connie, holding out her hand. 'Come and see us when you can. We both enjoy visitors.'

Justin watched her hasten down the street, a trim athletic

figure. Dotty was lucky to have her, he thought.

He bent to pick up the dead leaves and put them carefully in the waste paper basket when he returned to his office.

He suddenly remembered the shortbread, and rang for Muriel.

'Yes, Mr Venables?' she asked deferentially.

'Muriel, I should have said this many years ago. The shortbread is always delicious. Miss Harmer told me to tell you how much she enjoyed it this morning, as I have too hundreds and hundreds of times. Much appreciated, Muriel, believe me.'

'Oh sir!' faltered Muriel, turning pink. 'Thank you. I'm so glad –'

She broke off and hurried from the room, and straight to the privacy of the staff lavatory where she mopped her tears.

Why was it, she thought fiercely, that one could stand any amount of scolding and censure without a qualm, and yet dissolve into tears at a few words of kindness?

She tidied her hair, stuffed her damp handkerchief up her sleeve, and after a colossal sniff, returned to her duties with a gladsome mind.

6   Spring Fevers

THE MISSES Lovelock were delighted to hear that Kit Armitage had returned.

'I thought I recognised that back,' said Violet triumphantly. 'So upright, still so straight and soldierly! He always had a most impressive carriage.'

Miss Ada looked at her younger sister with faint dislike.

'I can't recall Kit's back being anything very different from any of the other young men's.'

'Oh, I always admired his stance when we played tennis,' said Violet. 'He always threw the ball a tremendous height in the air when he served. D'you remember, Bertha?'

Bertha nodded. Pencil in hand she was engrossed in the crossword, but her cheeks were a little flushed. There was no doubt about it, the return of Christopher Armitage was causing a stir in this particular household.

'He was always very athletic,' observed Ada. 'Wasn't he Victor Ludorum one year at the Grammar School? And once he turned twenty cartwheels at a tennis party here. Someone said he couldn't – Justin maybe – and I remember he put down his glass and took off his jacket, and went over and over all round the lawn.'

'I suspected at the time that he had partaken of too much punch. If you remember we let that maid we had at the time mix up a second batch, and she was very free with the gin.'

'Kit was never the worse for drink,' protested Miss

Violet. 'Just high spirits, on that occasion, I feel sure.'

'Well, I don't suppose he turns many cartwheels nowadays,' said Bertha. 'Nor Dotty either. What a dreadful affair that was!'

'She only turned *two*,' Ada pointed out, 'and it was Kit who dared her to. Besides, her bloomers were perfectly respectable and substantial, which was a blessing, I must say, in the circumstances.'

'Well, we were all young then,' said Violet indulgently, 'and what a lot of fun we had in the old days! It will be good to see Kit again and revive happy memories.'

'We must invite him to lunch when he returns,' agreed Ada. 'What a pity he lost his wife so long ago! She was a pretty girl, I remember.'

'I always thought she was rather fast,' commented Miss Bertha. 'A typical Londoner, and she certainly came without her gloves to Sung Eucharist once.'

'Perhaps she forgot them,' said Violet.

'A lady,' replied Bertha severely, 'never forgets her gloves.'

And thus rebuked, her sister fell silent.

The winds of March, which Shakespeare's daffodils enjoyed, was not welcome to Albert Piggott at Thrush Green.

For one thing, they blew an unconscionable number of leaves into the church porch of St Andrew's and needed to be swept out by Albert himself.

When young Cooke had taken on most of the church duties of a heavier nature, digging graves, tending the coke furnace and so on, it had been arranged that Albert would be responsible for sweeping the church floor and the porch. When a really stiff breeze came along, no matter from which quarter of the globe, the leaves managed to eddy in drifts against the church door, under the stone benches which flanked the porch, and often into the church itself. Albert found it all very trying.

March winds also made him cough. Albert's bronchial equipment had always been sub-standard, even Doctor Lovell admitted that, and Albert's habitual dolour exaggerated his condition. He was not given to suffering in silence, and intended to let the landlord of The Two Pheasants have a detailed account of his respiratory ailments as soon as he went in there for his midday meal of a pork pie, pickles and beer.

But that was not all that he had to worry about on this particular morning. For once, Willie Marchant the postman, had brought him a letter. It was hand written, and Albert opened it with caution.

The message was short. It was signed 'Charlie Wright'

and Albert's face registered disgust, as well as its habitual gloom, as he read.

Dear Albert,
    Nelly has had a bad turn and is in hospital here. Thought you ought to know as you are her next-of-kin.
Charlie Wright

' "Next of kin" indeed!' said Albert aloud. 'And a fat lot of good that is!' Didn't he take her on? Didn't this dratted oil man, this wife-stealer, have first claim on Nelly?

He thrust the letter into his pocket and went across to deal with the dead leaves which were as troublesome as Nelly herself. He felt no stirrings of pity for his ailing wife. She'd chosen her bed, hadn't she? Well, she must lie in it. Let this Charlie do the coping. It was no business of his. He would ignore the letter.

But he found that he could not ignore the matter completely. As he swept morosely, coughing occasionally, and taking a rest every now and again on one or other of the stone benches in the porch, he began to wonder about Charlie's message. Did the fact that he had informed him that he was next-of-kin mean that Nelly was likely to snuff it? In which case, did it mean that any property belonging to her would then come to him?

It was one thing to let the oil man who had lured away his Nelly have the responsibility of looking after her 'in sickness and in health', as it said in the marriage service – not that Nelly and this Charlie had bothered with such niceties – but quite a different kettle of fish if the dratted fellow came into Nelly's bits and pieces, simply because he didn't write back as, he supposed glumly, a husband should.

Sitting, resting his head on the broom handle, Albert pondered this problem. True, Nelly had never had much in the way of possessions, but there had been a gold wrist watch and a brooch from Italy she was fond of, and come to think of it, there was a Post Office savings book that she kept mighty quiet about in her handbag.

On the other hand, if it meant going all the way to Brighton to see her in hospital, he was inclined to forfeit her assets and let the pair of them sort out their troubles. Why should he bother about them? A fat lot they'd troubled about him, that was for sure!

He brushed a spider from his knee and began to sweep it, with the leaves, into the corner of the porch. Although he told himself that he would take no action over the letter, he still suffered a small nagging doubt.

Perhaps old Jones could give him some advice? Two heads were better than one, they said. Over his pub dinner he would mention it, in a casual way, to the landlord, and see what transpired. No need to rush his fences, and if he had to reply after all, then Molly could give him a hand with the writing.

Somewhat comforted he fetched a shovel and bucket to collect the leaves, and even chirruped to a robin who had come to investigate the activity.

On the Saturday morning following the arrival of Albert's letter, little Miss Fogerty lay prone on her bedroom floor at the school house, and conscientiously went through the exercises prescribed by Doctor Lovell.

He had been sympathetic about her aching joints some months previously, and had forborn to tell her automatically to lose a stone in weight as he did to three-quarters of his patients suffering from anything from gout to gallbladder troubles. Miss Fogerty, who could not weigh much over six and a half stone, was exempt from this ritual prescription, but was given some tablets to help alleviate the pain, and a sheet which set out some simple exercises for strengthening muscles.

Agnes Fogerty did not like to tell her medical adviser that the tablets tended to make her head swim, and that she had cut down the dose privately to half. The exercises, she believed, were certainly strengthening her legs, although they seemed to strain something in her back at the same time.

However, she was philosophical about this unwelcome side effect, and after adjusting her lisle stockings, she gazed at the ceiling, and began to raise and lower each leg in turn.

It was extraordinary how similar that damp patch was to the map of Wales! A lovely country, and one she hoped to visit again when at last she and Dorothy retired. She counted to ten, and then resumed the exercise.

Such a pity that retirement had needed to be postponed! Perhaps if she had been at Barton now the good sea air would have put paid to all these aches and pains.

Time for bicycling, and very strenuous it was too. It was all very well for Doctor Lovell, half her age and athletic too, to loll back in his chair at the surgery and issue his instructions, but really it was no joke when one was in one's sixties and with kneecaps cracking like pistol shots!

Puffing heavily, little Miss Fogerty lay still and surveyed the carpet under the bed. Betty Bell kept things beautifully – no dust at all, and only one hair grip which she had lost only two days ago. It was quite interesting seeing the world from a different angle, and rather pleasant lying on the carpet. How nice to be a cat!

She pulled herself together hastily, and set herself to cycle another two minutes before tackling her standing routine.

There, that was done! She scrambled to her feet with the help of the bedstead, and stood quite still until her head had stopped spinning. Then she went close to the wall and kept one steadying hand on it while she rose and fell on her toes. Doctor Lovell had said earnestly that he wanted to restore suppleness, as far as was possible, so that she could run again quite easily.

Agnes had not liked to tell the dear man that she had not run anywhere for the last ten years, and had no intention of starting again now, but she was fond of her adviser and respected his faith in her possible prowess.

She did her exercises zealously, studying a still life in water colours executed by one of Dorothy's college friends. It depicted a bowl of fruit with a few vegetables lying beside it, and Agnes was not wholly enamoured of it. Certainly, the grapes were superbly done, and the bananas were recognisable, of course, so yellow and curved, as they were, it would be hard to disguise them, but the carrots looked anaemic and those green things which must be artichoke heads were not the right green.

Dipping briskly from left foot to right, Agnes recalled her own efforts at vegetable painting. Cabbages, she remembered, had responded wonderfully to a mixture of veridian green, a spot of crimson lake and a little Chinese white. The result had been a most successful soft colour, and her art teacher had congratulated her on the effect. Very gratifying it had been.

Agnes felt that her legs had suffered quite enough, and began to rotate her arms gently. She wandered to the window, and surveyed the little world of Thrush Green as she worked away.

A stranger was walking purposefully across the grass

towards the Youngs' house. He was tall and soldierly. He had no hat and his hair was thick and silvery.

'That must be young Mr Venables' friend,' thought Agnes, now shrugging her shoulders up and down as Exercise Six required. 'What a nice-looking fellow! No arthritis there, I'm sure!'

She finished her twentieth shrug conscientiously, folded the exercise list away in a drawer, tidied her hair and went downstairs to tell Dorothy about the Youngs' visitor.

Kit Armitage was warmly welcomed by Joan and Edward Young and the sherry glasses were soon filled.

After some exchange of news, Kit said how very sorry he had been to hear of the death of Robert Bassett.

'Of course, he was a good deal older than I am, but I was quite often invited to play tennis here and he was always so excessively kind. No bad hand at lobs and volleys either, if I remember rightly.'

'He loved all games, and was very quick on his feet,' agreed Edward. 'I used to dread being asked to partner him. He could beat me hollow at tennis, and although he was the most considerate of partners, I always felt mightily inferior. I was courting Joan at the time and very conscious of the poor figure I was cutting.'

Joan laughed.

'I was so sorry for you, and pity being akin to love I'm sure it helped your cause.'

'And your mother?' asked Kit.

'Pretty shaken, and can't make up her mind if it would be better to stay on in the little house, or move in with Ruth up the road. I tell her not to make any decisions yet. It's too soon after Father's death to make plans.'

'Very wise. Now tell me about the other Thrush Green

friends. I gather Dotty is still fighting fit.'

'I don't know about that, but she's jolly well looked after by her niece Connie. Do call and see them. Dotty remembers you well.'

'I'm looking forward to seeing her again.'

He asked after Albert Piggott, the Misses Lovelock, and was told about the disastrous fire which had robbed Charles and Dimity of their home.

'And what's going to be there instead?' he asked.

'Eight homes for old people,' Edward told him. 'I've just put in my plan. We want something easy on the eye this time.'

'I could do with an old people's home myself,' observed Kit. 'Let me know if you hear of a small place anywhere near Lulling or Thrush Green. I'm getting down in earnest now to some house-hunting.'

They took him round the garden and showed him the attractive little house which Edward had designed and converted from the old stable. Mrs Bassett was out, and he promised to call on her another time.

'And whose is this?' he enquired, eyeing the gipsy caravan which had once been the home of Mrs Curdle, Ben's grandmother.

Joan told him about the old lady's death, the sad but necessary sale of the fair, and how glad they were to have Ben and Molly living in the flat at the top of the house.

'Mrs Curdle!' exclaimed Kit. 'May the first! My goodness, that takes me back. What a day that was every year! We used to look forward to that fair day for weeks.'

'We all did,' said Joan. 'It's lovely to have the caravan here as a reminder. Sometimes Ben's children have a tea party in there with their friends. I don't think Mrs Curdle would have let them make as much noise as we allow them.'

They walked to the gate, and Kit looked at his watch.

'I'll call and see Dotty another time, but do you think Winnie Bailey would remember me?'

'Try her and see,' advised Joan, and they watched him step out across the grass in the direction of the doctor's.

'If your mother does decide to live with Ruth,' said Edward, as they returned to the house, 'I wonder if Kit would want the stable cottage? He'd be a considerate neighbour, that's certain.'

'I've been thinking about it too,' said Joan, 'but I feel we should offer it to Ben and Molly before anyone else. The flat was ideal when they only had George to consider, but now there are two children they are pretty cramped up there. Besides, they need a garden of their own, and those stairs are quite tiring, although Molly never complains.'

'You're right, of course. I hope your mother decides to stay on. She's near enough for us to keep an eye on her, but she can still feel independent with all her own things around her. Let's shelve the problem until further notice.'

And so they left the matter.

Kit found Winnie Bailey in the garden picking daffodils for Ella Bembridge who was with her.

After introductions, Winnie tried to persuade him into the house, but he pleaded shortness of time and promised to call again.

They accompanied him to the gate.

'And we hear you hope to settle here,' said Winnie. 'It will be lovely to have you among us. Do you play bridge still?'

'Yes, and just as badly, but I'll make up a four whenever you like. But not just yet. I'm busy looking for a little house. Two up and two down sort of thing – well, perhaps *three* up and three down, on second thoughts – but something I can cope with alone. Any ideas?'

'None at the moment,' said Winnie slowly. She turned to Ella.

'There's that place near the Cookes along the Nidden road,' said Ella. 'But I doubt if you'd want to be anywhere near that family. And someone told me that there's a flat going over The Fuchsia Bush in Lulling High Street.'

'Terribly noisy,' observed Winnie.

'I think I'd like a little garden,' said Kit, at the same moment.

Anyway, the ladies assured him, they would ask around and let him know if anything cropped up.

'I've got my name down with several agents, of course,' said Kit, 'but I wouldn't mind betting I get something through my friends eventually.'

They waved goodbye to him, and returned to the house to collect the daffodils from the shelter of the porch.

'Tell you what,' said Ella, uttering one of her favourite phrases, 'I'll mention it to Charles and Dimity. Between them they quarter four parishes, and if we can't find something suitable for that nice man, I'll eat my hat.'

Albert Piggott found little comfort in Mr Jones's advice about Nelly's illness.

Having read the letter, which emerged much crumpled from Albert's pocket, he reacted forthrightly.

'If Nelly's in hospital then you should go and see her,' was his edict. 'Oh, I know all about her leaving you, and the rows you had, but that's in the past, Albert, and she's still your wife, you know. You get down to this hospital and see her. It's your duty to stand by her.'

Albert was taken aback by such straight talking.

'I don't know about my duty,' he responded with some heat. 'What about her duty to her lawful wedded husband, eh? What I'm concerned about is this Charlie. I bet he's got his eye on Nelly's bits and pieces, and why should he have 'em?'

Mr Jones looked at him with disgust.

'And you've got your eye on them too, I take it? You makes me puke, Albert, that you do. There's this poor soul – your own flesh and blood –'

'And plenty there was of it too,' interjected Albert morosely, recalling his wife's vast bulk.

'Flesh and blood,' continued the landlord unperturbed, 'dying, from what this chap says, and you think of nothing but what you might get out of it. Finish your beer, Albert, and clear out, will you? I'm fed up with this business. You asked my advice and this is it. Ring up this chap, find out where Nelly is, and get down there pronto to see her.'

At that moment, two men entered the bar and he turned to serve them, still flushed with anger at Albert's behaviour.

Albert took advantage of the interruption to creep away to his house next door.

There was cold comfort there, but at least it was more congenial today than The Two Pheasants.

7 Albert Piggott Under Pressure

THE AFFAIR of the Lady Chapel kneelers still caused the good rector some unhappy twinges, but nothing more had been said directly to him by Mrs Thurgood.

Could she have decided against pursuing the matter? It seemed unlikely. There was a ruthless tenacity about the woman which Charles recognised only too well. He quailed before it, and chided himself for cowardice, but this self-flagellation did not mitigate his fears.

He had a horrid feeling that Mrs Thurgood was simply biding her time before returning to the attack. With Dimity beside him one afternoon, they had examined the present kneelers minutely, and had put aside any which appeared to be the worse for wear. Naturally, Mrs Thurgood's own kneeler was one of the shabbiest as she was such an outstandingly regular church-goer, and about six or eight others would benefit from some attention. But on the whole, Dimity and Charles agreed, the rest of the kneelers were perfectly capable of fulfilling their function for several years.

Comforted by this discovery, Charles felt that he could withstand any onslaught from the doughty Frances Thurgood. It was certainly rather unnerving to find that the weeks slid by without any further manifestations of the lady's pugnacity. What lay behind this silence? Had she decided to give up the fight? Had she simply forgotten about the kneelers? Had she, perhaps, suddenly regretted her offer to pay for the work?

Charles wondered if he would ever learn the answers to these questions. He had not long to wait.

One bright morning he collected the letters from the hall mat and carried them to the breakfast table where Dimity was already buttering her toast. There were half a dozen or so envelopes, but one was immediately noteworthy for its excellent quality and imposing seal at the back.

'From the bishop,' said Charles, opening it first.

Dimity, watching him closely, saw his expression turn from pleasure to dismay. Having read the bishop's letter, he then turned to another enclosed with it, and the dismay upon his chubby countenance was now tinged with indignation.

'Well, *really!*' protested Charles, handing over the letters. 'Now what do you make of that?'

Dimity read rapidly. The bishop's note was kindly and concise. It said that he had received the enclosed letter from Mrs Thurgood to which he had replied. He said that he had every confidence in Charles's decision and urged him not to

worry unduly about a matter which was really very trivial. He sent his regards to Dimity and hoped to see them both very soon.

Frances Thurgood's letter was belligerent in comparison. She set forth her own generosity, her anxiety to see the Lady Chapel furnished 'in a God-like manner', and hinted at the regrettable attitude taken up by Anthony Bull's successor both in his services and his dealings with parishioners. She trusted that the bishop would see fit to remind the present incumbent of his duties.

'The *cat!*' fumed Dimity, throwing the letter across the table. 'To go behind your back like that! It is absolutely unforgivable, Charles! What will you do?'

'Nothing in a hurry,' said her husband equably. 'I may say something I should regret later, and I don't want the dear bishop to be badgered any further with complaints about me.'

'You are far too forgiving,' said Dimity.

'I don't know about that.' He picked up the bishop's letter, and read it again.

'You know, Dimity, it is really uncommonly nice of him to write so warmly. And in his own hand too!'

'He's hardly likely to write in anybody else's,' retorted Dimity, with unusual tartness. She still smarted from the effect of Mrs Thurgood's outrageous behaviour, and was irritated too by Charles's deference, one might almost say *awe*, in his handling of the bishop's letter. In her opinion, Charles was quite as worthy as the bishop himself – probably a better man altogether when you considered his modesty and selflessness – and Dimity felt herself glowing with mingled righteous indignation and wifely devotion.

'Well, I only hope I don't encounter Frances Thurgood in the next day or two,' she exclaimed. 'I don't think I could remain silent about such appalling behaviour.'

The rector looked alarmed.

'Oh, my dear, please don't fan the flames! The bishop is absolutely right to call this a trivial matter. I will speak to her privately before the week is out, but I beg you to say nothing, if you love me.'

He looked so pink and agitated that Dimity's wrath faded, and she bent across the table to kiss his cheek.

'I will do exactly as you say,' she promised him.

Meanwhile, Albert Piggott had problems of his own.

After his rebuff at the hands of Mr Jones, the landlord, he had almost decided to ignore Charlie's letter, and leave Nelly's future in the hands of the gods.

But he reckoned without the loquacity of The Two Pheasants. It so happened that Ben Curdle called in for a pint soon after his father-in-law had departed.

The landlord, still full of indignation at Albert's callousness, told Ben the story. Ben returned to his flat at the top of the Youngs' house to consult Molly on the matter, and that evening they went together to face the old man.

He was surlier than ever, and obstinate with it.

'She's been no wife to me,' he asserted. 'Why should I put myself out for her?'

'Don't talk so daft!' said his daughter. 'She looked after you all the time she was here, and kept the place lovely. And cooked a treat! And what thanks did she get?'

'She had me company. And me money,' growled Albert.

'You listen to me, dad,' said Ben quietly. 'If anything happens to her you're going to regret it. And what's more, all Thrush Green is going to chuck it in your face. She's your wife, whatever she's done. You'd best get down there as fast as you can.'

'And how am I going to get to Brighton, may I ask? And who pays the fare?'

'We've been looking up ways and means. I can put you and your case on the morning coach at Lulling. It goes right up to Victoria Coach Station, and there's plenty of coaches direct from there to Brighton. You'd be with Nelly in a matter of hours.'

Albert began to look cornered.

'And Ben and I will pay the fare,' Molly promised him. 'We've talked it over, haven't we, Ben?'

Her husband nodded loyally, and Albert looked more hopeful.

'Well, I don't say as it might not be the right thing to do,' he admitted cautiously, 'but she's a fair old trollop, as well you know, and I don't reckon she deserves to see me again.'

Molly privately thought that her father's remark could be construed in two ways, but prudently remained silent.

'That's settled then,' said Ben, standing up. 'I'll pick you up in the van at a quarter past eight tomorrow morning, on my way to work. The coach sets off at eight-thirty, so you'll be all right.'

'And I'll come over tonight and pack one or two things for you,' added Molly swiftly. 'You may want to stay for a while.'

'That'll be the day,' commented Albert bitterly.

But he knew when he was beaten.

In common with most small communities, news in Thrush Green and Lulling has always spread with the rapidity of a forest fire.

Sharp eyes that morning had seen Albert waiting at the coach stop. He was actually wearing a tie as well as his best dark blue suit, the one in which he had married Nelly at St

Andrew's. At his feet stood a small case.

Obviously, he was off on his travels, and where would that be? News of Nelly's illness had already gone the rounds, and it did not need much guesswork on the part of his observers to settle his destination.

The coach stop was immediately outside The Fuchsia Bush, and Mrs Peters, the owner of this establishment, noticed Albert as she drove up to open the café. Ten minutes later Gloria Williams arrived on foot, and soon after that her co-worker Rosa entered their place of work.

The coach was late, and Albert was shifting impatiently from one foot to the other.

'No doubt Nelly's took a turn for the worse,' surmised Rosa. 'I did hear she was in the intensive.'

'What's that when it's at home?' queried Gloria, licking her fingers and arranging a curl over one eyebrow.

'It's where they put you when it's touch and go,' Rosa explained. 'You're all wired up to a television thing for the nurses to watch.'

'And Nelly's that bad?'

'I expect so,' said Rosa with evident satisfaction. 'Can't see old Smiley there bothering to go and see her if she was just in an ordinary ward.'

'My mum said no one wasn't allowed to see people when they was wired up like you say.'

Rosa was somewhat put out by this sudden display of medical knowledge from a junior.

'Oh! Know it all, do you?' she enquired, with heavy sarcasm. 'Perhaps you can tell me –'

But at this moment, Mrs Peters came hurrying through from her swift inspection of the kitchen, and the two girls broke off their discussion to collect their overalls and to appear moderately active.

'Come along, girls,' cried their bustling employer. 'No time for gossip! The tables need dusting, and one of you must hurry along to Abbot's. We're nearly out of butter.'

Gloria cast a resigned look at her colleague behind Mrs Peter's back, and at that moment the London coach drew up with a dreadful squealing of brakes.

The door opened automatically. Albert picked up his case and mounted the steps. Within a minute he was on his way, all his movements having been watched by the three ladies behind the window of The Fuchsia Bush.

Betty Bell was full of the drama when she blew into the Shoosmiths' house at Thrush Green 'to put them to rights'.

'Fancy our Albert making such a trip! I bet he wouldn't have gone if he'd been left to himself though. They say Mr Jones gave him the rough side of his tongue, and Ben and Molly put the pressure on too. I'd dearly like to be a fly on the ceiling when he sees his Nelly in hospital. What's the betting he takes her some flowers? Or a bunch of grapes? I don't think! The mean old devil! Want your study done over?'

Harold looked helplessly at his wife. She came swiftly to the rescue, as always.

'Bedrooms today, Betty. I did the study yesterday.'

'Righty-o! I'll lug the vacuum up.'

She made for the kitchen, but lingered in the doorway.

'They say she's pretty bad, you know. Trouble with her breathing. Well, with all that fat and her being so short in the neck it's not surprising. My auntie was the same. Never had a cold but what it was bronchitis. Doctor Lovell took her off butter but it never did any good. Now it's all this fibre nonsense. Everyone comes out of that surgery being told to eat bran these days. Last year it was no animals fats, and the year before that no sugar. I s'pose we'll all be on hay or silage this time next year. Funny folk, doctors, I reckon.'

'Who told you that Mrs Piggott was seriously ill?' said Isobel, trying to stem the tirade against the medical profession.

'Why, Percy Hodge! He was just coming out of The Two Pheasants as I was leaving the school yesterday. Been in to get his courage up to face that Doris of his, I don't doubt. Now, there's a fine how-do-you-do. She's real sharp with poor old Perce. He has to take his shoes off outside the back door, and then she hands him a clothes brush to have a clean-up in case he's got any bits of straw and that on him. You'd hardly credit it, would you? And she once a barmaid.'

'But Nelly –' broke in Isobel.

'Ah yes! Well, Perce said Mr Jones had told him he'd read a letter of Albert's that said she was at her last gasp.'

'Oh dear!'

'One thing, I bet she ain't calling for Albert, ill though she is. And I wonder what she'll say when the old misery turns up at her bedside? Enough to give her a prolapse.'

'I think it's "relapse",' said Harold.

'That as well, I shouldn't wonder,' conceded Betty. 'I'll get that vacuum cleaner. Standing here listening to you running on won't buy the baby a new frock, will it?'

She vanished through the door, and the Shoosmiths exchanged conspiratorial glances.

'I think I could do with a second cup of coffee,' said Harold handing over his cup.

'I'll join you,' said his wife.

April was at its loveliest that year, the first spring that Charles and Dimity had enjoyed in their new home at Lulling.

Charles woke early one April morning and lay quietly watching the changing sky. The first apricot warmth faded slowly to pink and then to a clear shade of lemon yellow.

Charles watched the young leaves fluttering in silhouette against their changing background. A dove cooed. A black-bird poured forth a liquid stream of bird music, and the metallic call of a nearby wren added to the dawn chorus.

As the day brightened into silvery light the birds became more active, swooping from trees to earth, from hedge to further hedge, in their search for food and nesting material. The air seemed full of their activity, and the flutter of wings and the varied cries brought the morning to life.

Charles lay beside his sleeping wife savouring this joyousness of spring. Truly, his lot had been cast in pleasant places, he thought, as he watched the sun burnishing the eastern side of the ancient cedar tree.

It was good to have a quiet contemplative time now and again. He recalled one of Wordsworth's sonnets learnt long ago at school:

The world is too much with us: late and soon,
Getting and spending, we lay waste our powers:
Little we see in Nature that is ours;
We have given our hearts away, a sordid boon!

His own day, Charles knew only too well, was a succession of activities which kept him busy mentally and bodily. Somehow one was always looking ahead, planning the next move, trying to cut down time. And in all this bustle the present was lost. The daisy opened, closed and died. The chaffinch threaded the last shred of moss into its nest before sitting. The sun reached the point in the heavens when the weathercock turned to gold. And all these wonders passed unremarked, because the clock on the mantelpiece gave stern reminder of the service at three-thirty, the visit to a sick parishioner at five o'clock, and the meeting of the Parochial Church Council at eight sharp.

Charles Henstock was the first to honour his duties towards God and his neighbours. But what a bonus it was, he told himself as he stretched his toes luxuriously in the warmth of the bed, to have these precious moments of just *being*, of becoming aware of all the other lives impinging on one's own, and of having time to give thanks for such revelation.

He sat up, being careful not to disturb his wife, and gazed out of the window. There was a heavy dew. It looked more like September than April. The grass shimmered and glittered in the low rays of the rising sun. Each little spear, it seemed to Charles, bore a shining droplet. How many thousands would there be, he wondered, clustered beneath the trees, spreading far and wide, almost to the church itself?

Surrounded by leaves! All sorts of shapes and sizes, large and small, green and gold, smooth and rough, some aromatic, some not, but all breathing entities, as far as the eye could see!

He found the thought strangely moving and comforting. It put his own life into perspective. It made him more

sharply aware of his modest place amidst such a wealth of
living things. The trees he looked upon now would still be
there when he himself had gone. And that little jewelled
chaffinch, rose-breasted and blue-capped, which fluttered
at the window, would have become a lacework of small
ivory bones long before he himself took the same way
home.

Dimity stirred.

'Are you all right?' she asked drowsily.

'Everything's all right,' Charles assured her truthfully.

One breezy spring afternoon Connie emerged from Dotty's
cottage, milk-can in one hand and Flossie's lead in the other,
and made her way to Thrush Green to deliver Ella Bembridge's daily quota of goat's milk.

Albert Piggott had proved surprisingly capable at dealing
with Dulcie's bounty while her aunt had been laid up, but
once Connie had settled in she assured him that she could
manage the animals.

'Well, I don't mind givin' a hand when you're pushed,'
said Albert. 'Makes a change from humping a broom round
the church or tidying the grave-yard, and old Dulce and me
gets on pretty fairish. Goats has got more sense than people,
I reckons.'

Connie thanked him sincerely. She knew that by nature
he was a gloomy soul, and that he had strangely blossomed
in his new role as animal minder. She assured him that she
might well need his services if a domestic emergency arose,
and he seemed content.

It was as well that she had not relied upon him daily, she
thought, following Flossie along the footpath, for she had
just heard about his departure to Brighton to visit his wife.
As things were, she found looking after Dotty and the many

animals well within her capabilities, and enjoyed renewing her friendships in Thrush Green. But just occasionally, when the sun was setting over Lulling Woods and that wistful time between daylight and dark spread its shadows, she mourned the cottage she had left behind in Somerset, and the familiar shapes of hills and trees around it. But it was a momentary sadness, and Connie was able to dismiss it bravely. Aunt Dotty had always been good to her and Connie knew that she was sole heir to her little estate. She was glad to be able to give her a hand now that she needed it. Certainly, no one could have been kinder or more grateful than her eccentric aunt, and what were known in the neighbourhood as 'Dotty's funny little ways' gave Connie no cause for alarm. She was quite used to them, and in any case the affection she felt for this unusual relative was strong enough to over-ride any fears.

Flossie quickened her pace when they reached Thrush Green, and Connie found herself running to keep up. Luckily, the lid of the old-fashioned milk can was well-fitting, but she could hear the liquid splashing about inside.

The children were having games in the playground, and Connie could hear them chanting: *I sent a letter to my love*, while little Miss Fogerty watched carefully from outside the circle to make sure that all the rules of the game were properly kept.

The path to Ella's front door was lined with velvety wallflowers, wine-dark, gold and cream. The scent was delicious, and even Flossie stood still, nose upraised, as if enjoying their fragrance.

No one was in. Connie went into the garden to see if Ella were there, but both back and front doors were locked, and the windows tight shut. Obviously, Ella was out for some time, and now she came to think of it, Connie recalled that she had said something about going to that excellent shop in Ship Street, Oxford, to buy tapestry wools.

'Well, Floss,' said Connie, 'we must just leave the milk in the porch. No biscuit for you today, old girl. We'll see if we can find one at home.'

Flossie was reluctant to leave Ella's abode. It was rarely that she had to return without having consumed one of Ella's wholesome digestive biscuits, but she was a philosophical animal, and at last consented to accompany Connie homeward.

They crossed the green, and now the children were playing 'Twos and Threes', still in their circle, and still being watched indulgently by little Agnes Fogerty.

Connie and Flossie soon entered the narrow footpath beside Albert Piggott's cottage. His windows too were shut, and Connie wondered how he was faring on his travels.

As they emerged into the field leading to Dotty's, Connie became aware of footsteps behind her. She glanced back and saw a tall stranger, with silvery hair, striding along purposefully.

Connie quickened her step. The path was narrow, and unless she stopped to let him pass, there was really nothing else to do. She did not want to be obliged to carry on a conversation with a complete stranger simply because the path forced them to walk closely together.

To her surprise, the footsteps behind her quickened too, and a voice hailed her.

'I say, don't run away! Aren't you Miss Harmer? Miss Connie Harmer?'

She turned to face the oncomer. He really had a fine turn of speed for a man of his age, and a remarkably well-cut tweed jacket and shining brogue shoes.

'My word, you go at a good pace!' he said, smiling at her. 'I'm Kit Armitage, and I was about to call and pay my respects to my old friend Dotty. That is, if she would be willing to see me. How is she?'

'She's getting on well, and will be all the better for a visit from you,' said Connie, holding out her hand.

8   Albert Makes A Journey

ALBERT PIGGOTT arrived at Victoria Coach Station later in the morning, and his first port of call was a café.

Breakfast time seemed a long way behind him. He sat at a table and waited for someone to serve him.

He was not a lover of London. True, he had only visited the capital about five or six times in his life, and had always thought it noisy and dirty. If anything, it seemed noisier and dirtier than ever.

'Self-service here, love,' said a large woman setting down a tray on his table.

Albert looked bewildered.

'You fetch your own, see? Get a tray and pick out what you want off of the bits and pieces. You get your drink at the end.'

'Thanks,' said Albert, picking up his case.

'You can leave that with me, love. I shan't pinch it.'

Albert shuffled off, collected the tray and, copying the rest of the queue, selected a currant bun and a plastic cup of coffee.

'I takes sugar,' he said to the girl behind the hissing machine.

'On the table,' she told him impatiently. Albert drifted off.

The woman at his table was busy with a large piece of chocolate cake and a cup of tea.

She nodded to him, but he was relieved to find that she seemed quite content to continue her meal in silence. His case was exactly as he left it.

He had over an hour to wait, and killed time over the coffee and a newspaper someone had left on the next table. The woman had departed, without speaking again, long before Albert had finished the sports' pages. It seemed odd to him that one could share a table and yet not pass a common word. Not like Thrush Green, he thought with a pang!

He looked at the crowd about him. He might have been a fly on the ceiling for all the notice they took of him – or anyone else, for that matter. What a way to live!

At length, he picked up his case and set out to track down the bus which would take him to his destination. He was tired already, and looked forward to having a nap as soon as his case was safely stowed on the rack, and he had found a seat.

It was nearly four o'clock when Albert finally arrived at the hospital. The coach had been late in starting, and various road works had delayed them. The hospital was some distance from the town centre and involved a tedious bus journey. Albert, who had grown increasingly anxious about this whole project, now began to wonder just how Nelly would greet him.

He was directed up many flights of stone stairs and along miles of corridors before arriving at Nelly's ward. Other visitors surged along with him, bearing bunches of flowers, boxes of eggs and bundles of clean nighties. Albert began to wonder if he should have splashed out on one of the small bunches of violets being sold at the gate, but it was too late to bother about it now.

He saw Nelly as soon as he entered the long ward. She was easily the largest and most gaudily dressed of the ladies present, and her hair was even brighter than he remembered it.

But there was no smile to match the hair. An expression of intense hostility greeted him, and the ominous words:

'And who told you to come, may I ask?'

Albert put his case by the bedside locker and sat down upon a hard chair.

'Your chap,' he said, still breathless from the stairs and corridors.

'What, my Charlie?'

'That's right. Said you was at death's door, and I was to come.'

'Well, you can go back again for all I care,' said Nelly, pulling her bright pink bed jacket across her splendid bust. 'I told you I never wanted to see you again.'

Albert was silent. For one thing there seemed to be no

answer to such remarks, and in any case he was dog-tired.

After some minutes of uneasy silence, Nelly relented a little.

'Well, now you're here you might tell me about that dead and alive hole Thrush Green.'

'It's just the same,' said Albert.

'And them old Lovelocks? Wizened old trout. Never known love, and not many locks between 'em.'

'Don't see much of Lulling folk.'

There was another pause. By the next bed a crowd of exuberant Pakistanis were passing round photographs of a family wedding. They seemed to have plenty to say.

'Well, what are you in for?' said Albert, stirring himself at last. 'Going to be in here long?'

'Another few days. Something to do with my gall bladder, they say, but it's my belief they haven't got a clue. One thing I do know. The food's something chronic. I wouldn't offer it to a dog.'

'Ah!' said Albert, relapsing into silence again.

'You aren't going all the way back tonight, are you?'

'Hadn't thought about it.'

'Well, you'd better think now. You'll never get a coach or train from London as'll get you to Thrush Green today. I'd stay overnight if I was you.'

'Where, may I ask? I ain't sharing a bed with Charlie!' Albert was stung into sarcasm, and the thought of having to spend good money on a night's lodging. It was something he had not thought about seriously, despite the pyjamas and face flannel carefully packed by Molly, 'just in case'.

Nelly bridled.

'Charlie don't want your company, believe me. He comes along after work, by the way, so if you don't want to see him, you'll have to look slippy.'

Albert bent down for his case.

'Brought me a box of chocolates?' asked Nelly, eyes bright with anticipation.

Albert had a sudden brain wave.

'Didn't think they'd allow it, but I've got today's paper.' He took out the copy which he had picked up at Victoria.

'Better than nothing, I suppose,' said Nelly. 'Have a word with Sister as you go out. She knows somewhere to stay around here. Won't break the bank either, I gather.'

Albert stood up.

'Well, I hope you'll go on all right.'

'I suppose I ought to say "thank you for coming", but to tell the truth, Albert, I'm blowed if I know why you did. Still, who knows, I might pop back to Thrush Green for a bit of convalescence. How'd you like that? We had some good times now and again after all, didn't we?'

She giggled as she reached for the paper.

Albert wondered if he should kiss her goodbye, but decided that the circumstances did not warrant it. He raised his hand in farewell, and set off down the ward.

At the end he looked back. Nelly was already immersed in the paper.

'Mrs Desmond sometimes obliges,' the nurse had said, and had directéd him some quarter of a mile from the hospital gates.

It was already beginning to get overcast, and the tall Victorian house looked particularly gloomy.

He mounted the steps and rang the bell. A buxom woman with grey curly hair opened the door.

'The hospital people –' began Albert.

'Ah! You're looking for a bed for the night. Come in!'

Albert followed her into a bleak hall with black and white

tiles on the floor. A massive fern in a brass pot dominated the scene.

Mrs Desmond mounted the stairs and Albert followed in her wake. The carpet was thick and the banisters shining. A strong smell of furniture polish pervaded the place. It was apparent that the owner was house-proud.

'I keep two bedrooms ready for people like yourself,' said Mrs Desmond. 'The hospital works in with me. I don't do meals, except breakfast, and that's Continental.'

Albert wondered if that meant frogs' legs or any other French nonsense.

'But there's a fish and chip shop down the road, or if you want anything rather classier for supper there's a "Little Chef" nearer the sea front. Here's the room.'

She opened a door and stood back for Albert to enter. The room was sparsely furnished, but the linoleum on the floor, and the brass handles on the dressing table, gleamed with daily care.

A gas fire stood in the hearth, its rows of little skulls awaiting ignition. Mrs Desmond waved towards it.

'It takes tenpenny pieces if you want some heat.'

I bet it does, thought Albert grimly. But the bed looked comfortable, and he was dropping with fatigue.

'How much?' he said shortly.

'Seven pounds, for bed and breakfast. Continental, as I said.'

'What's that mean?'

'Tea-or-coffee-rolls-and-butter-and-marmalade,' recited Mrs Desmond. 'And now if you'll excuse me I must go down to the kitchen. I've a piece of bacon on the boil. Are you staying?'

'Yes, please,' replied Albert.

'It's easier if you pay now,' said his new landlady. 'Then

you're free to go any time in the morning.'

Albert took out a greasy wallet and extracted seven one pound notes. It seemed a monstrous sum to him. Mrs Desmond took it and stuffed it into her cardigan pocket.

'We lock the front door at eleven-thirty sharp,' she said. 'Give me a call if you need anything. The water's hot if you want a wash.'

She vanished along the landing, and Albert sank down in the wicker chair and contemplated the miniature Golgotha of the gas fire.

Seven pounds! What a day! It seemed to have gone on for ever. And what good had been done? Dam' all, as far as he could see. Sheer waste of time and money, and as like as not Nelly might turn up again at Thrush Green. One tiff with Charlie could easily send her back to her lawful wedded husband. The thought was too horrific to face.

Albert shivered. A few drops of rain spattered at the window, and the room was cold and dark.

A box of matches stood on the mantel shelf and Albert turned the gas tap. There was a welcome hissing noise. The fire popped into life as he applied the light, and the rows of skulls glowed with welcome heat.

Obviously, someone else's tenpenny piece had not run out.

It was the brightest spot of Albert's day.

Later he went out in search of a meal. The fish and chip shop was crowded with young people in studded leather coats, with here and there a head-band or earrings. The deafening noise from a juke-box was a further deterrent for Albert.

The 'Little Chef' was infinitely superior. There were even some flowers on the tables, and the girls were young and pretty.

Albert demolished a plate of bacon and eggs, with baked beans and tomatoes, and a crusty roll to mop up the liquid. He sat back to enjoy a large cup of strong tea with four spoonfuls of sugar in it. Life certainly appeared brighter. His purse was lighter, but he remembered that Molly and Ben had given him two fivers as well as paying his fare. One way and another, he'd be all right.

He wandered back to Mrs Desmond's by way of the sea front, and paused to lean on the sea wall. He had never been over-fond of the sea. Too wet and cold and restless. And too much of it anyway. Give him some nice fields and woods, any day, all round him, not half the view taken up with this heaving monster.

He stayed there for some time until he found his eyes were closing of their own accord.

He roused himself, threaded his way through the streets to Mrs Desmond's, had a perfunctory wash in the corner basin, and undressed.

He clambered into the spotless bed. It creaked alarmingly, but Albert did not care.

Within five minutes he was deep in the sleep of the utterly exhausted.

Nelly's gibe about the Misses Lovelocks' complete ignorance of love was far from the mark.

They had been attractive young women in their time, and the straight-cut boyish fashions of the twenties had suited their sparse figures very well.

Ada and Bertha were some years older than Violet, but all played tennis together at their own home in Lulling High Street, or at friends' and neighbours'.

Justin Venables and his brothers, Dotty Harmer and her brother, had been some of their contemporaries and tennis partners. Ada had been engaged for some months to Justin's elder brother, but he had gone to India and met someone else. The engagement was broken off, but there was soon another admirer to take his place, although marriage, yet again, evaded Ada.

Violet was easily the prettiest of the sisters in their youth. She may not have had the same deadly back-hand of her sister Ada, or the smashing volley of her sister Bertha, but her eyelashes were definitely longer, her hair curlier and her legs more shapely than her sisters!

It was she who nurtured a secret passion for Kit Armitage, then unattached and at his most handsome. The two elder sisters were inclined to be derogatory about her affection.

'Don't throw yourself at him so blatantly,' said Ada primly. 'No man wants to be pursued. You only make yourself cheap.'

'He won't thank you for making him look silly in front of the others,' added Bertha. 'If he wants to be more friendly then he will make the running.'

Violet said little, but privately thought that Ada and Bertha were prompted by feelings of jealousy rather than sisterly concern. Kit Armitage was easily the most glamorous of their circle, and long after he had left England and then found a wife abroad, Violet kept a warm place for him in her heart.

His reappearance had stirred her affections into life again. True, they were both old people now, but was it not possible, thought Violet, that they might find a great deal in common? Kit was now a widower. Might he not be in need of an understanding companion, much his age?

She was careful to conceal these slender hopes from her two sisters, but with memories of Violet's earlier infatuation the older two ladies were on their guard.

However, all agreed that such an old friend should be welcomed again to Lulling, and much thought went into the best way to entertain him.

'A tea-party seems rather *feminine*,' announced Ada, 'and I don't think we are up to a formal dinner party, what with cleaning all the silver, and getting Mrs Fox in for the evening to wait at table.'

'Besides the expense,' pointed out Bertha.

'Besides the expense,' agreed Ada.

Violet held her tongue.

'So it boils down to lunch,' said Ada. 'I suggest we ask Justin and his wife, now he has retired, and Winnie Bailey.'

'It makes rather a monstrous regiment of women,' protested Bertha, 'with the three of us.'

Ada considered the problem.

'Well, I really can't think of any unattached men whom we could invite. Men are so thoughtless in the way they die

before their poor wives. For every widower or bachelor in Thrush Green and Lulling there must be half a dozen lone women. It really is trying!'

Violet now ventured to speak.

'He won't expect us to have even numbers. After all, he knows our circumstances. If Justin and Lily are here to keep us all company, I think it will make a very nice little party. And you know that six fit very comfortably round our dining room table.'

Her sisters looked at her with approbation.

'You are quite right, dear. Let's leave it at six, and I'll send out invitations today. We might think of an easy meal to serve too. Cold, do you think?'

'Definitely cold,' said Bertha. 'And people can help themselves. Salad, of course, though lettuces are a terrible price at the moment.'

'We have our home-made green tomato chutney,' replied Ada brightening, 'and those spiced pears are perfectly good if we lift off the mildew at the top.'

'We should have baked potatoes then,' said Violet, asserting herself. 'And soup first. It looks more welcoming, and our dining room can be very cold, as you know.'

'As you wish, dear,' said Ada with some hauteur. 'Frankly, I see no need for a *feast*, but if you like to make yourself responsible for the soup course and give an eye to the baked potatoes in the second, I see no reason to object. Gentlemen do seem to need more than we do.'

'Then I think we should have a fruit tart for pudding,' went on Violet, encouraged by her success. 'A hot apple tart is always popular.'

'I thought of doing one of my cold shapes,' put in Bertha. 'Made with some of our bottled gooseberries it could be quite acceptable.'

'We'll have that as well,' said Violet firmly. 'We shall need a choice.'

Her two sisters exchanged glances. Was Violet going to be silly all over again? And at her age?

Flinging caution to the winds, Violet entered the fray again.

'And we must order some cream,' she added. Ada and Bertha drew in their breath sharply. The expense!

'*Double* cream!' added their renegade sister, pink and reckless.

What was the world coming to?

9 Dotty Harmer Has Visitors

THE INHABITANTS of Thrush Green awoke on May the first to a morning of such pearly beauty that they remembered, with a lift of the heart, that the loveliest of months had begun.

But there were some among them whose exhilaration was tempered with a certain sadness. These were the people who remembered, with poignant clarity, that May the first, for many years, meant the excitement of old Mrs Curdle's famous fair.

Ben Curdle, her grandson, had particular cause to recall it as he cycled by the green to work on that glistening morning.

It was he who had been forced to sell the business a few years earlier and to leave the nomadic life, which he had always known, for a settled existence at Thrush Green with Molly and the two children.

He did not regret the change. It was a decision which had to be made. The fair was running down after Mrs Curdle's death, beaten by more sophisticated pleasures such as television and bingo.

Ben knew that he was fortunate to sell when he did. The price had been a good one. Molly was glad to be near her father, miserable old curmudgeon that he was, thought Ben privately, and young George Curdle had settled well at Thrush Green village school. The Youngs were the kindest of landlords, and Ben enjoyed the work he had found as a mechanic in the local firm of agricultural engineers.

Nevertheless, as he mounted his bicycle that May morning he felt a pang of nostalgia. He remembered the clopping of hoofs as the old horse-drawn caravan had threaded its way through the deep lanes of southern England. He recalled the thrill of finding satin-skinned mushrooms in the dewy grass, and the smell of them cooking with bacon on Gran's minute stove. He could hear now the small intimate sounds of early morning, the birdsong, the snuffle of the horse at its nosebag, the rattle of the frying pan. Later, the noises would turn to the clamour of the fair; men shouting, swingboats creaking, the raucous music from the roundabouts and the shrill cries of excited children.

And through it all, running like a linking theme through this orchestration, was the low and sometimes harsh voice of his beloved grandmother. She had been a despot, a benevolent one to Ben, but not to any of her employees who shirked hard work.

She was on duty every hour, and expected the same unswerving loyalty from all who travelled with her. It was one of the qualities which had given Curdle's Fair its name for complete reliability. If the Fair was due to arrive on a certain date, then without fail it would be there. Ben could remember floods, breakdowns to the waggons, sudden illnesses and once, between High Wycombe and Marlow, a wicked storm which had sent a jagged fork of lightning upon one man, Jem Murphy, who was leading his frightened horse, and who had to be taken to hospital suffering from shock and burns.

Even so, the Fair had arrived punctually at its next destination, Ben remembered with pride.

Ah! It had been a good life, and a good training for a boy! Old Gran had taught him right from wrong and had set him standards of behaviour which were now standing him in good stead. He could only hope that he could pass on those standards to his own children.

He took a deep breath of fresh morning air, and pedalled energetically towards his work.

No good looking back, he told himself. Times changed, and perhaps for the better. He would buy Molly a box of chocolates on his way home to celebrate the first of May. She would understand.

An hour or two later Winnie Bailey and Jenny, her friend and maid, were recalling Mrs Curdle and the Fair.

'To tell you the truth, Jenny,' said Winnie, busily rolling out pastry at the kitchen table, 'I was about to throw out those bunches of artificial flowers that have been gathering dust on the top shelf of the landing cupboard, but I couldn't bring myself to do it.'

'I should hope not,' replied Jenny. 'Why, Mrs Curdle made them with her own hands! And I bet if you put them in the dustbin George Fry'd pick 'em out and return them to you. He'd know, as a dustman, just where everything came from. You wouldn't get rid of Mrs Curdle's flowers as easy as that!'

'I think I should have burned them,' confessed Winnie. 'They're made of fine wood-shavings, you know. But it wasn't that which held me back. It was just that I remembered how dear old Mrs Curdle looked when she handed over a new bunch every first of May. They'll just have to stay there, I'm afraid. But I wonder what the person will think when he or she comes to clear up this house when I'm gone!'

'No sense in talking like that,' said Jenny sturdily. She mopped the draining board briskly. 'You've years ahead of you yet.'

'I hope so. Especially when it's a morning like this. We'll get our little jobs done quickly today, Jenny, and make sure we get out in the sunshine. I'm going to take some magazines to Miss Harmer this afternoon.'

'Well, I wouldn't stop to tea,' advised Jenny. 'I hear she's taken to making her own bread.'

'Thank you for warning me,' said Winnie.

Winnie Bailey was not the only one making for Dotty Harmer's house near Lulling Woods.

Stepping briskly up the hill to Thrush Green was Kit Armitage, a carrier bag swinging in his hand. He was some ten minutes behind Dr Bailey's widow, and admired, as she so recently had done, the gauzy green of the young leaves in the avenue on Thrush Green, and the pyramids of tight lilac buds to be seen in the gardens.

A robin accompanied him along the path leading from the green to the fields where Dotty's cottage lay snugly embedded. The bird bobbed ahead of him on the dry stone wall, bowing and chirruping. Was he trying to distract his attention from some nearby nest, Kit wondered?

It was good to have this little companion. Kit admired the smooth plumage, the flaming breast, the bead-bright eyes. He, or perhaps she, thought Kit, as somewhere he remembered reading that male and female looked alike, was a fine specimen, and he fell to wondering if a clutch of small pink-spotted eggs was hidden nearby, and hoped that all would turn into splendid replicas of the bird before him.

Dotty's cottage came in sight. He appreciated the way that the grey thatched roof faded into the folds of land around it. Dotty's garden was extensive, and it was adjoined by a paddock of almost two acres. No wonder Dotty in her time had been able to give her love of animals full scope. Ponies, donkeys, goats, pigs and sheep had at one time or another had the paddock as their home, and a small pond at the end of the garden had been a playground for endless generations of ducks and geese.

Nowadays the pond was used by only ten or so ducks. Dulcie, the goat, lived in solitary splendour in the paddock, and had the sturdy goat-house for her sole use. Not that she often deigned to sleep inside. Dulcie preferred the roof of the shed even in snowy weather. She was just as contrary as any other of her species.

A small pebble had found its way into Kit's shoe, and he was obliged to lean against the stone wall and unlace his shoe. Standing there, on one leg, he surveyed Dotty's little estate with an admiring eye.

There was no doubt about it, the house and its acre or two made a very pretty picture. It was what estate agents would call 'a desirable property'. It was remarkably quiet tucked away from Thrush Green, and yet had an entrance on to a side road which led into Lulling and villages further west.

There was a small orchard near the house, just beginning to come into leaf. Soon, Kit surmised, there would be a pink and white froth of blossom to add to the general enchantment.

As he watched, a figure emerged from the door, carrying a bright orange plastic bowl. Although Kit could not see them, he heard the frenzied squawking of hens hurrying towards their meal.

He recognised the figure as his newfound friend Connie, and obviously she was giving the hens an early supper. Perhaps she was going out later, he thought, bending down to lace his shoe. Surely hens were fed about dusk? Not that he was an expert on such matters, he was the first to admit.

But he hoped suddenly that Connie was expecting to go out. Much as he admired dear crazy old Dotty, he was sorry for this gallant niece who seemed to have very little fun, but who never complained of the lack of it. From the few times he had met her, Connie appeared to him to be completely selfless, and yet at the same time refreshingly free from the solemnity which so often accompanied that saint-like quality.

He liked her laughter, her strong sense of the ridiculous. He liked her gentleness with her odd charge. He liked the way she appreciated the books and records he lent her, and he was sure that those in the carrier bag, now resting on a fine clump of coltsfoot by the wall, would be enthusiastically welcomed.

Altogether, he thought, stamping his foot to make sure the shoe was as it should be, he just liked Connie.

He strode along the path, happy to think that he would be in her company for the next hour or so.

Albert Piggott, upstairs in his bedroom, had noted the passing of Winnie Bailey and then Kit Armitage along the lane that ran beside his cottage.

He was in the act of trying to fit a piece of cardboard into one of the window-panes. A sudden gust of wind had wrenched the window from its shaky fastening one night, and one pane had shattered.

Albert was getting tired of the moaning noise and the fearful draught when he was abed, and at last had decided to do something about it. By rights, he should inform the rector who would see that a proper glazier did the job, and the church would pay the bill, for Albert's cottage was church property.

'But by the time I've been all through that rigmarole,' grumbled Albert to his cronies at The Two Pheasants, 'I'd be down with the pneumonia, and in me grave, dug with me own hands, I don't doubt.'

'Won't hurt you to patch it up,' said the landlord heartlessly. 'See you all right for a bit until the rector can find a proper man for the job.'

'You saying I'm not a proper man?' queried Albert nastily. 'I can keep my place up together as well as the next.'

'Well, it don't look like it did when your Nelly was there,' asserted Mr Jones, unrepentant.

Albert had choked into his beer mug at the mention of his wife's name, and had departed very soon afterwards.

'Proper touchy, old Albert,' said one man to another. 'Don't dare mention his Nelly, that's for sure.'

It was immediately following this conversation that Albert had started his repair work. Now, cardboard still in hand, he crossed the small landing to the back bedroom, now unused, to follow the progress of the travellers towards Lulling Woods.

'Ah!' said Albert to the cat which had followed him upstairs. 'Off to see old Dotty, I'll be bound. I wish 'em joy of her tea table if they stay that long.'

He stood for a few moments watching the scene, and then returned to his own bedroom which looked out upon St Andrew's church. It was there that he and Nelly had wed, worse luck!

A tremor shook him as he thought of the awful possibility of his wife returning. What was the position, he wondered? If she'd left him of her own free will then surely he would not be obliged to have her back? He supposed that, in the eyes of the law, he was still married to the wicked old besom, for that's what she was, he told himself, edging the cardboard gingerly over the damaged glass.

If only it did not cost good money he would go to one of those solicitor fellows like Justin Venables and ask for advice. But then he might suggest a divorce, and though it would be nice to be free again, there'd be the hell of a lot of gossip about it at The Two Pheasants, and the rector might give him a talking-to and tell him to forgive and forget and all that stuff.

Women were kittle-kattle, thought Albert morosely, giving a sharp tap to an awkward corner. A man was better off without them. He wanted no more truck with Nelly, and if she was so bold as to come to Thrush Green again he'd run her out of town, that he would!

Emboldened by this sudden blaze of spirit he gave the cardboard a last shove. There was a sickening crack, and a moment later, the distant tinkle of shattered glass hitting the pavement. At the same time, the cardboard buckled and fell inward upon the grimy bedroom floor.

A stiff breeze blew into the room stirring the net curtains.

'Lord love us!' shouted Albert. 'It's enough to drive a man barmy!'

He stumbled towards the stairs, the cat fleeing from his wrath before him.

He wrenched open the front door, and nearly fell over a diminutive figure about to post a note about the school jumble sale through the letter box. One of Miss Fogerty's more trustworthy pupils gazed at Albert with round blue eyes.

'Mr Piggott, sir! Your top window's bin and fell out,' he announced importantly.

Albert's reply was terse and to the point. When the small boy repeated it to his mother, later that day, he was sent into the scullery to wash out his mouth at the sink, poor child.

At Dotty's cottage the two visitors were prevailed upon to stay to tea.

Kit had accepted the invitation with alacrity. Winnie had begun to demur, Jenny's warnings still in mind.

As if she read her thoughts, Connie said: 'It's all very simple. Just some scones I've just taken out of the oven, and a pot of honey that Dimity gave me.'

'I can't resist hot scones and honey,' said Winnie, settling back in her chair.

She turned to Dotty.

'And are you eating well now? I expect Connie plies you with all sorts of goodies.'

'I've a better appetite now that I can get into the garden,' said Dotty. 'There are some beautiful young nettles in the paddock that I should cook if I could get there, but Connie says the spinach from the freezer has more vitamins, so we had that today.'

'Is that the stuff Popeye the Sailor-man used to eat in our youth?' asked Kit. 'He was welcome, from the look of it.'

Connie laughed.

'Very strengthening, you know. But tell me all the news from your end of Lulling. How are Charles and Dimity?'

'Working too hard as usual, and Charles is still worrying about those confounded kneelers. Some battle-axe —' he stopped suddenly. 'Not a friend of yours, I hope? I'm still putting my foot in it, forgetting how everyone is related in these parts.'

'If you mean Frances Thurgood,' replied Connie with spirit, 'I don't think she has many friends. Not in this house anyway. Aunt Dotty can't bear her ever since she caught her putting poison down by her garage. She said she had rats, but Aunt Dotty ticked her off about other animals picking up the stuff, and there was a right royal battle.'

'How did Dotty come across this scene?'

'She'd been invited to lunch, I gather, but after telling Frances what she thought of her, she stumped off. There's a lot of her father in Dotty, you know.'

'A very strong character,' agreed Kit, looking across the room at the two women engaged in animated chatter. 'You don't find her too demanding?' he asked diffidently.

'I can't deny that she can be very self-willed,' replied Connie, in a low voice, 'but she is very dear to me, and I'd never leave her. We get on well, and I think she realises that she must have someone at hand, and she would rather have me than anyone else. It's a very pleasant place to live in.'

'I just wondered if you would ever be free to come out with me one evening? I know Charles and Dimity want to ask you too, but to be frank, they asked me to see how you were placed with Dotty-sitters.'

'Betty Bell has obliged, as they say, and although I hesitate to do it too often, I should love to have an evening off some time.'

'Then we'll arrange it,' said Kit cheerfully, and followed his hostess into the kitchen to help her by carrying in the tea things.

Later that night, Lulling Woods and the surrounding fields lay silvered under a full moon.

Connie, in bed, was happily tired. It was good to look forward to a change of scene in the company of kindly Kit Armitage. Aunt Dotty had enjoyed her impromptu tea party, and she felt all the better for the company.

She plumped up her pillow, turned on her side, and was asleep in five minutes.

Next door, Dotty lay awake, but she too was content with her day. It was strange, she thought, surveying her bony hands spread out on the moon-lit quilt, how pleasant life was even though her movements were so restricted.

If anyone had told her a year ago, that she would not be able to walk much farther than the length of her garden, she would have been shocked to the core. But now that it had happened she found that there were compensations.

She studied her small confines with more attention to

pleasurable detail. Only this morning she had enjoyed looking at the thrum-eyed and pin-eyed primroses beneath the hedge. She had noted the tight buds of the lilac and the stiff green spears of the iris leaves.

The comings and goings of the garden birds meant more to her now than the flocks of lapwings and rooks which she used to watch on her travels farther afield. The antics of a bumble bee at the window engaged her attention as sharply as Flossie's chasing across Thrush Green had in earlier days.

And there was as much joy to be had from the surprise visit of two old friends, as from all the dozens one used to meet at social gatherings. One had much to be thankful for, thought Dotty.

There was no doubt about it. God tempered the wind to the shorn lamb, as her old father would say. And despite the lack of Mrs Curdle's Fair, she thought inconsequently, it had been a good first of May.

She pulled the bed clothes around her bony shoulders, and went contentedly to sleep.

10   Mrs Thurgood Fights Again

CHARLES HENSTOCK's suspicions that the redoubtable Mrs Thurgood would return to her
onslaught on the Lady Chapel kneelers were well-
founded.

He had seen very little of the lady for several weeks, and
had noted the empty pew with some misgivings. Had she
taken umbrage and left his church? If so, which one was she
now attending? And had he failed in his duty towards this
parishioner?

His questions were answered when he heard that Mrs
Thurgood and her artistic daughter were enjoying a tour of
Italy, 'taking in,' as one of his congregation put it, 'Rome,
Florence and Venice.' It sounded rather indigestible to
Charles who preferred his culture in book form whilst
sitting peacefully in his study.

Nevertheless, he was relieved to hear that the lady had
not swept in dudgeon from St John's for ever. Perhaps she
would return from her travels with a more informed sense
of beauty, and would realise that the kneelers looked very
well as they were in their ancient setting.

On the other hand, thought Charles with a pang of alarm,
the daughter might have decided to copy some hangings of
the Doge or the Borgias and was already returning with a
folio of designs ready sketched out on graph paper.

Charles chided himself at this point. He was letting Mrs
Thurgood dominate his thoughts, and all to no good. It was

no use allowing his imagination to run away with him. No doubt, she would return much refreshed, and in a more amenable state of mind. He resolved to do nothing until Mrs Thurgood raised the matter herself. After all, he and Dimity had given time and attention to the problem, and he knew he was on firm ground.

But these kindly and rational notions were swept away one sunny May afternoon, when the rector was alone in the vestry checking one of the church registers in response to an overseas correspondent who had asked for details of his grandparents' marriage.

It was the sort of job that Charles enjoyed, and he was happily turning the pages at the vestry table, when he became conscious of voices.

Two women were obviously visiting the church and were now in the Lady Chapel. Charles decided to let them continue their tour while he went on with his investigations. If their visit was protracted he proposed to emerge and welcome them, showing them some of the more unusual features of his beautiful church.

But suddenly, the voices became much clearer.

'I shan't leave it at that, you know,' said one woman stoutly. 'You can see for yourself the state they're in. It would never have done for dear Anthony.'

With horror, Charles realised that his adversary was back. Should he declare himself, or hope that they would soon go away?

Before he had time to make a decision, the younger woman spoke.

'You're quite right, mother. But then what can you expect from this Henstock fellow? No idea of how to run things.'

'I agree. No standards at all. A vulgar little man, and a

wife to match. Just take a look at this one, dear. Very badly frayed.'

Charles Henstock closed the register, coughed loudly, and made his way past the organ into the Lady Chapel. To be called 'a vulgar little man' did not upset him. But to hear his adored Dimity spoken of in such scathing terms was more than he could bear.

Nevertheless, his demeanour was calm as he confronted the two women.

Apart from a sharp indrawn breath from Mrs Thurgood, and a certain reddening of her daughter Janet's complexion, the ladies appeared free from any guilty reactions.

'We are just back from Italy,' announced Mrs Thurgood, 'and we are going through the kneelers again. What neglect! The sooner they are replaced the better.'

'Dimity and I spent a good deal of time inspecting them too,' said Charles gently. 'We put aside some half-dozen which we thought needed repair.'

'*Repair?*' boomed Mrs Thurgood. 'They need more than *repair*! This church has never been the same since dear Mr Bull left us. And I said as much when I wrote to the Bishop.'

'I know,' replied Charles. 'I saw the letter.'

At that, even Mrs Thurgood's boldness wavered, but she contented herself with a snort of disgust.

'I don't intend to discuss the matter now in this holy place,' Charles pointed out, 'but if you and Miss Thurgood –'

'Mizz,' broke in Janet. 'I prefer to be known as Mizz, spelled M and S.'

'I beg your pardon?'

'Capital M, small S,' explained Janet.

'Oh!' said the rector, now enlightened, 'like "*manuscript*".'

'Not in the least like "*manuscript*",' exclaimed Mrs Thurgood. 'But to get back to the point.'

'I was about to say,' said Charles, 'that it would be a good idea to step across to the vicarage to discuss this matter. I have a few papers to put together in the vestry, and then I hope you will accompany me there.'

'Have we time, mother?' asked the manuscript.

'Yes, indeed,' said Mrs Thurgood firmly. 'This is something of outstanding importance.'

Within ten minutes, the three were closeted in Charles's study, and the battle began.

Charles, the kindest of men, nevertheless had a streak of steel in him. When his duty had to be done, nothing could make him shirk it.

There were many parishioners who, having mistaken Charles's gentleness for weakness, could remember the shock they had received on facing their rector's uncompromising attitude to wrong-doing. That pink chubby face and kindly smile hid the strongest sense of right and wrong, and when it came to the point Charles feared no man on a matter of principle.

He sat behind his desk, a crucifix on the wall behind him, a beautiful silver and ivory present from Harold and Isobel Shoosmith to replace the one lost in the Thrush Green fire. The Thurgood ladies sat before him on wooden upright chairs of a somewhat penitential pattern, although to Charles, a man of simple tastes, they seemed perfectly suitable for his study.

'Please let me know what worries you, Mrs Thurgood,' began Charles. 'I thought that we had already settled this affair of the kneelers.'

'You know quite well we haven't,' replied Mrs Thurgood forthrightly. 'I take it as an insult, a rebuff, a slap in the face –'

'What is?' interjected the rector.

'This turning down of my offer to bear the expense of replacing the kneelers.'

'We are not unmindful of your generosity,' said Charles, 'but my wife and I, and the Bishop too, see no reason for a wholesale replacement. As I said, a few need mending, but the others will last for several years. We should all be deeply grateful if you could undertake the repair work, but we do not want to see you put to needless expense.'

'Humph!' snorted the lady, 'I'm willing to face the expense, and I certainly don't think it "*needless*". The fact is, Mr Henstock, the church is being run down. The singing

leaves much to be desired, the vestments are shabby, the flowers are not arranged with a quarter of the skill that Mrs Bull brought to the job, and the services are *distinctly low*! I tremble to think what dear Anthony Bull would think should he ever return.'

'I have always had the highest regard for my predecessor,' answered Charles equably. 'He was a devout and conscientious churchman, but his ways were different from mine. I am the first to recognise it. Nevertheless, I am, I trust, equally devout, and attentive to my parochial duties, and the Bishop, I am glad to say, approves of my conduct.'

'You are going to lose your congregation, believe me,' warned Mrs Thurgood. 'There is a great deal of gossip and discontent. Am I to understand then, that you refuse to let me replace the kneelers?'

'That is so. It is quite unnecessary.'

Mrs Thurgood arose and her daugher followed suit.

'Then in that case, sir, we have no alternative but to leave your company and your church.'

She swept towards the door, and Charles was only just in time to open it for her. He accompanied the two ladies to the front door in silence, bowed them out politely, and returned to his study.

He went to the window and took a deep breath of scented air. Tabitha, the cat, was sprawled on her back in the border, comfortably flattening some pinks and warming her stomach in the sunshine.

'I suppose one could say that the powers of evil won that skirmish,' he said, addressing the cat, 'but somehow I feel that right has triumphed, in the whole battle.'

The Misses Lovelocks' lunch party in honour of Kit Armitage took place a few days after Charles Henstock's confrontation with the Thurgood ladies.

Preparations had been lengthy and heart-searching. Violet, still determined to provide something rather better than the usual fare found at the house, had been studying half a dozen recipes for asparagus soup with considerable anxiety. The asparagus bed was already sprouting well in the shelter of the garden wall, and Violet examined it daily.

As she had rashly suggested a fruit tart as well as the 'cold shape' which her sisters considered obligatory at any luncheon, she also had to look out some bottled plums and make some pastry. She had secretly wondered if she could buy some ready-made frozen pastry, and use it while her sisters were out of the kitchen, but even Violet's stout heart quailed at the thought of being discovered in such deceit. She must just do the best she could, she told herself, and if it happened to get a little overdone, as her pastry sometimes did, she would shake plenty of caster sugar over it and put up with Ada's rebukes.

The main course was the one which gave the ladies the most concern.

'Pork is out,' announced Bertha. 'Justin simply can't digest it, I know for a fact.'

'Pork is not in season anyway,' Ada said loftily. 'Not the right thing for a summer luncheon at all.'

'What about chicken?' said Violet.

'One seems to have chicken whenever one goes out to lunch,' observed Bertha.

'Because everyone likes it,' said Violet. 'It's light and easily digested.'

'And cheap,' added Bertha thoughtfully.

'Yes indeed,' said Ada brightening. 'It's certainly cheaper than most meat.'

The three ladies pondered over this happy attribute of

chicken in silence. It appealed strongly.

'And it is extremely tasty when cold,' said Ada. 'Shall we slice it in the kitchen and let people help themselves?'

Violet, still strong in her intention to do right by Kit Armitage, was emboldened to say:

'I think we should have *two* chickens, or else a nice piece of cold gammon to go with it.'

Ada and Bertha exchanged glances. What was Violet coming to? It really seemed as if she were as infatuated as she had been all those years ago. What else could have driven her to suggest such unnecessary lavishness? *Two* chickens indeed!

'The men can have a leg apiece,' said Ada brusquely.

'They'll want breast as well,' argued Violet obstinately. 'And they may need second helpings.'

'*Second helpings?*' echoed Bertha, aghast at the thought.

'Men get hungry,' said Violet, sticking to her guns. 'And in any case, we can eat up anything left for the rest of the week.'

'But *two* chickens!' exclaimed Ada. 'I really don't know –'

'And the carcases will make excellent stock,' persisted Violet.

Silence fell again upon the agitated ladies. It was Ada who broke it at last.

'Perhaps a piece of gammon might be a good idea,' she conceded eventually. 'It always looks so pink and pretty garnished with parsley. Yes, *one* chicken, not more than three pounds in weight, should do us all very well if there is boiled bacon to supplement it.'

'Collar or fore-quarter,' said Bertha, 'is much cheaper, you know.'

'Gammon cuts *much* more economically,' Violet put in swiftly.

And there the matter rested.

Kit Armitage, his old friends Mr and Mrs Venables and the three Lovelock sisters fitted very comfortably round the old ladies' beautiful dining table.

In a way it was a pity, thought Justin, who knew a good deal about antique furniture, that its beauty was hidden by an exquisitely laundered damask tablecloth, but his hostesses were of the generation which gave much attention to the drapery of tables, and he had to admit that the pristine whiteness showed up the sparkling glass and old silver very satisfactorily.

Thanks to Violet's persistence the meal was unusually generous by Lovelock standards, and everyone tucked in heartily.

The conversation turned to affairs at Thrush Green and, in particular, to Kit's difficulty in finding suitable property to buy.

'I should really prefer to be high up,' he said. 'Somewhere around Thrush Green would suit me very well, and I'm getting a little bored at The Fleece, kind though they are.'

'You know you can always come back to us,' said Justin.

'Yes, indeed,' echoed his wife valiantly, trying to ignore the unworthy thoughts of extra catering, bed-making, and general entertaining which loomed darkly.

'You've done more than your share for the wanderer,' said Kit, 'and very grateful I am, as you know.'

'What about Mrs Bassett's house?' suggested Ada. 'Has she decided yet to go to Ruth's?'

'I know Joan and Edward are waiting to hear,' said Violet. 'And then, I believe, they propose to offer it to the young Curdles.'

Kit turned to her.

'I'm so glad you told me, because I was wondering if I dare approach them about it, and it might have been awkward for them. Now I shall keep quiet.'

His smile made Violet's heart turn over. It was good to think she had helped him.

'Won't you have another helping of plum tart?' she asked.

'Yes, please. It's quite the best tart I've tasted for years,' he told her. And Violet's happiness was complete.

At the other side of the table Bertha leant across.

'Have you tried Mrs Jenner? The Henstocks had a flat there when the rectory burnt down. It's along the Nidden road. Very light and airy, but you'd have to do for yourself, of course.'

'I believe Charles mentioned it, but there was someone in it at that time. Still, many thanks for the idea. I'll follow it up.'

'Cousins of mine,' said Justin, 'have a mill house farther up the Pleshey, but it has six bedrooms and several out-houses and is horribly damp. They are selling.'

'I don't blame them,' replied Kit, smiling. 'But I think six bedrooms are more than I need.'

'I know poor Isobel Shoosmith scoured the area for months looking for a little place,' put in Ada. 'In the end she married dear Harold, so that solved her problems.'

'Well, I hope mine will be as happily resolved,' said Kit. 'Now, who knows anything about these old people's homes which are going up at Thrush Green? I heard that Edward's plan was successful, and the builders have made a start.'

'I should put your name down for one,' observed Justin. 'You can't start too early for that sort of thing.'

A week passed before Kit decided to call at Mrs Jenner's.

Connie had told him that she was pretty sure that her flat was now free. A service couple on leave had had it last, some distant cousins of Mrs Jenner's, so Connie had heard.

Charles and Dimity were enthusiastic about the idea, recalling with pleasure their happy few months there. He heard too, in the roundabout way of all village communication, that Mrs Bassett was now definitely going to make her home with her younger daughter Ruth, the wife of Doctor Lovell, and that Molly and Ben Curdle were to move into the stable house as soon as it had been redecorated.

It seemed to Kit, as he walked along the road to Nidden, that summer had really arrived. A heat haze hung over the valley where Lulling drowsed in the afternoon sunshine. He paused to look down the pathway which led to Connie and Dotty's house, and caught a glimpse of the buttercup-filled meadow which surrounded their garden.

The hawthorn hedge, which bordered the dusty lane, bristled with fresh red sprigs and was laced with sticky young goosegrass clambering up it from the ditch below. A number of black and white cows were clustered by a farm gate and surveyed him pensively from black eyes beneath a fringe of eyelashes. Their jaws worked rhythmically as they chewed the cud, and Kit thought how soporific it all was, the slow movements, the gentle heat on one's back, the fragrance of bruised grass and the distant hills veiled in a blue haze.

For two pins he would have settled himself under a hedge, and had a snooze, but he dismissed the temptation and went dutifully onward.

He found the house, a pleasant square Georgian building which had once been a farmhouse, and knocked at the door. A red admiral butterfly opened and shut its wings on the path beside him, and everywhere was very quiet.

He began to wonder if anyone were at home, or if perhaps he should have gone round to the back door, when he heard sounds within and Mrs Jenner stood before him with a middle-aged man beside her.

'Mrs Jenner? I'm Kit Armitage. The rector suggested you might be able to help me.'

'Please come in,' said Mrs Jenner.

'Well, I'll be off,' said the man.

'Please don't hurry away on my behalf,' began Kit.

'I was just off anyway,' said the man. He waved a general farewell and made for the gate.

'I hope I didn't interrupt,' said Kit, following his hostess into the hall.

'My brother,' explained Mrs Jenner. 'He farms next door. Percy Hodge. Perhaps you've heard of him?'

'I think maybe the rector may have mentioned him.'

'He's going through a bad time at the moment,' confided Mrs Jenner, leading the way upstairs. 'His wife is giving him trouble.'

'I'm sorry to hear that,' said Kit, surprised at such confidences from a stranger.

'Second wife, you know. Not a patch on the first. And a bit flighty between you and me.'

She threw open the door of the main room upstairs, and Kit, like the Henstocks before him, felt a glow of pleasure. Sun streamed through the large sash windows. The fruit trees were in bud below, and the scent of late narcissi from clumps in the orchard wafted about the room.

'What a lovely room!' exclaimed Kit.

'It is nice,' agreed Mrs Jenner equably. 'Gets all the sun that's going. Come and see the bedrooms. One is quite big, next to this room, and there's a smaller one at the back.'

She showed Kit everywhere, even opening cupboards and drawers. Everything shone and Kit wondered if he would ever be able to keep the place in the apple-pie order now before him.

In the kitchen he made a confession.

'I'm not much of a hand at cooking, I'm afraid, Mrs Jenner. I've lived abroad a great deal and been rather spoilt in that direction.'

Mrs Jenner surveyed him kindly and then smiled.

'I could cook you something most evenings, if you like,' she offered. 'Wouldn't be anything special, you understand, and not on Tuesdays or Thursdays when I go to Choral and Bingo, but we could come to some arrangement, I feel sure.'

Kit, much touched, began to thank her. But she cut him short.

'Any friend of the Henstocks is a friend of mine, Mr Armitage. That man is a born saint, and I've just been telling Perce to go and have a talk with him about his married troubles.'

Poor Charles, thought Kit. Still, no doubt he was accustomed to such problems.

'Well,' he began diffidently, 'if you'll have me, Mrs Jenner?'

'With all the pleasure in the world,' said his new landlady.

11 Problems At Thrush Green

AS THE weeks passed, and high summer embraced Lulling and Thrush Green, Albert Piggott's fears of the return of his Nelly grew less painful.

He regretted the journey to see her. It had been a complete waste of time and money, in his opinion, and it looked as though that confounded Charlie Wright still reigned supreme in his wife's fickle heart.

She must have been out of hospital for weeks now, he told himself with some relief, and that silly threat of hers to spend her convalescence at Thrush Green could safely be ignored.

In fact, Albert was living in a fool's paradise, and things were far from harmonious at Nelly's present address.

It was true that the lady had recovered with remarkable rapidity from the operation, although the surgeon had been quite ferocious about Nelly's superfluous fat and had practically ordered her to lose three stones in weight as soon as she had come round from the anaesthetic. He gave her to understand that it was only his consummate skill which had enabled him to get to the vital parts on this occasion.

Nelly, too weak to argue, agreed to take home a diet sheet which she had no intention of reading, and there the matter rested.

Charlie had called regularly at the hospital, and Nelly had looked forward eagerly to returning home. She could hardly wait to get back to a bed without a horrible piece of plastic sheeting over the mattress, and to some windows which she could have open all night instead of enduring the enveloping hot stuffiness of the ward throughout the hours of darkness.

Charlie took her home and she went straight to bed. In the days that followed, she got up for a few hours and enjoyed cooking Charlie's evening meal and cleaning the house again.

In the midst of her relief at being at large again, she hardly noticed that Charlie was somewhat subdued.

He came home later than usual too, and one evening smelt strongly of chypre perfume. It was a cloying scent that Nelly had always disliked, being an eau-de-Cologne woman herself, and she was alert at once. However, she had the sense to say nothing.

When Charlie had driven to work the next day in his oil van, Nelly began a systematic search through Charlie's drawers and the small desk where he kept his papers. She found nothing, but the smell of the chypre was faintly on the air when she came to the wardrobe.

Only Charlie's clothes hung there. Nelly had appropriated the bedroom cupboard on her arrival, and had little occasion to open the wardrobe. When she did, on this day, she went swiftly through all the pockets, and found a crumpled note in the jacket of his best blue serge suit. It said:

'Will be at the usual 6.30. If you can't make it, give the Grand a ring. 2946.

Best love –
Gladys'

Nelly knew at once who was this correspondent. Gladys and her husband Norman were a couple who lived on the other side of town and whom they met frequently at various pubs where small, but incredibly noisy, bands played, and the customers joined in hearty singing which grew louder as the air grew bluer with cigarette smoke and dubious stories.

It came back to Nelly now, that chypre was the perfume which always engulfed Gladys. Her mouth grew grim as she folded the note and put it into her handbag as evidence of Charlie's misdoings.

Strangely enough, although she was angry at this deceit, she felt sorrier for Norman than she did for herself. He was a poor fool, she had always thought, no match for his boisterous wife with her thick lipstick and over-blacked eyelashes. Still, despite being something of an old stick, Nelly had found him very polite and always thoughtful for his wife's welfare. It was a rotten trick to play on poor old Norman, to carry on with Charlie like this.

Not that she imagined that Gladys was solely to blame. Nelly knew her Charlie's winning ways all too well. Six of one and half a dozen of the other, she told herself, whirling furiously about the house with a duster.

She would tackle him the minute he had finished the plate of bacon and liver prepared for him. No point in wasting that. Food was important to Nelly. And as soon as he'd apologised properly she would let him understand that it was never to occur again. She would leave it to him to inform Gladys that all was off. And naturally, there could be no more convivial evenings at the pub with that pair. No, forgive and forget would be the best way to tackle this problem, she decided, but Charlie must eat humble pie first.

The possibility of any other reaction on Charlie's part did not occur to Nelly, strangely enough. It was all the more shocking that evening when the note was smoothed out beside Charlie's empty plate, and Nelly stood, arms akimbo, awaiting his apologies and explanations.

'Oh, tumbled to it at last, have you?' said Charlie, grinning maddeningly. 'Well, now you know, what are you going to do about it?'

Nelly's wrath rose.

'It's what *you* are going to do about it that matters! You can tell that Jezebel to clear off pronto.'

'And suppose I don't intend to?'

'Then you can do without me.'

'Too right I can,' responded Charlie with spirit. 'I reckon I took you in when you'd fallen out with that misery Albert, and now it's time you went back.'

Nelly was flabbergasted. For two minutes she stood there, the superfluous fat so denigrated by her surgeon, quivering with rage and shock. Things were not turning out at all well. She decided to change her tactics.

'And what if I tell Norman what's going on behind his back?'

'You needn't try. He knows all right, and he won't stand in Gladys's way.'

'But what about me?' Nelly wailed, becoming tearful. 'What about all I've done for you, looking after this place, and cooking meal after meal? Haven't you got a shred of decent feeling left?'

'Now look here,' said Charlie pushing her down into a chair and facing her across the table. 'Let's get this straight. You came here of your own accord. Well, I was sorry for you, and let you come. Now it's my turn to want a change. Gladys is coming here any day now, so you've got notice to quit.'

'But where shall I go?' cried Nelly, now sobbing noisily.

'You know I haven't got no money, and there's no one round here I know well enough to take me in.'

'Look, girl! You've got Albert. He's still your husband. You may not get on like a house on fire, but my advice to you is to go back, and try and make a go of it this time. I warn you, there's no room for you here now. Gladys and I are going to marry as soon as we can. Norman's agreeable – well, perhaps *agreeable* ain't the right word – but he says it suits him.'

At this, Nelly put her head down upon the table by the greasy liver-and-bacon plate, and howled alarmingly.

Charlie, a kindly man at heart, patted the massive heaving shoulders comfortingly.

'Oh, come on! Don't take on so! You knew it wouldn't last. You go and have a good wash and go to bed early. You'll feel better then, and I'll bring you a nice cup of tea in bed. How's that?'

After some minutes, Nelly rose, snuffling heavily, and made her way to the bathroom. She was speechless with shock at the way things had turned out, and numbed with misery.

True to his word, Charlie brought in a cup of tea. He was wearing his outdoor jacket.

'I'm off to Gladys's. See you first thing before I go off to work.'

'Oh Charlie!' wailed Nelly, the tears beginning again.

'Cheer up,' said her faithless lover. 'I'll give you a hand with your packing tomorrow.'

And he vanished before Nelly had time to answer.

Nelly was not alone in her matrimonial troubles. Percy Hodge was equally unhappy. His second wife, Doris, who had seemed the ideal companion when he had wooed her at

The Drovers' Arms at Lulling Woods, had changed considerably after becoming his wife.

He thought of his dear Gertie, now dead some three years. What a hand with pastry! What a manager on the five pounds a week he had allowed her for housekeeping! How he missed her.

Well, they said: 'Marry in haste and repent at leisure.' Not that he had rushed into this second marriage. He had courted Mrs Bailey's Jenny long enough before approaching Doris, but she'd refused him. Strange, thought Percy, straightening his back from hoeing between the rows of peas. You would have thought she would have been pleased to exchange domestic service for married bliss, and after all, he was still an attractive chap, he believed, otherwise why had Doris snatched at his offer?

Women were odd creatures. The smell of pastry burning floated from the back door. His Doris was no hand at cooking, that was a fact. When he thought of the meals that Gertie used to cook, and the stuff that his present wife put before him, he grieved afresh. If only he had been able to persuade Jenny to share his hearth and home!

There was no doubt about it. Marriage to Doris had been a sore mistake. Without the company of The Drovers' Arms crowd, she had grown peevish. Occasionally, she took herself off to Bingo with his sister Mrs Jenner, but that was only because she was pressed to go.

There were constant rows, mainly about money. As Percy told her often enough, Gertie had managed for years on five pounds a week, and he did not see why Doris could not do the same. Farmers weren't made of money, he had said only that morning.

And what answer had he had? A stream of abuse which had shocked him. She must have picked up such language from The Drovers' Arms. Not from Ted and Bessie Allen, who had run it for years now, but there were some pretty rough types that came into the public bar of an evening and were too free with their expressions. Percy had been forced to walk out of the kitchen in the face of such a verbal assault.

The thing was what to do about it all? They couldn't go on like this. Let's face it, he had tried time and time again to make the woman see reason, but she simply enjoyed being awkward. Why, she'd even asked for a *private allowance*! Percy shuddered at the very remembrance.

When he had pointed out the rank impossibility of such a measure, she had said that, in that case, she proposed to look for work and if it were far from Thrush Green that would suit her very well.

On that belligerent note the two had parted. Percy had gone into the garden and Doris had set about the pastry with such ferocity that Percy foresaw an even tougher meal than ever ahead.

Ah well, he sighed! Time alone would tell how things would work out. If only it had been Jenny in his kitchen!

Someone had said those two words 'If only' were the saddest in the language.

Percy, resting on his hoe, agreed wholeheartedly.

Little Agnes Fogerty was sitting in a deckchair in the garden of the school house, relishing the warmth of the June sunshine.

School was over, and Dorothy Watson was in the kitchen preparing their simple tea, which they proposed to have outdoors.

Miss Fogerty was looking forward to her cup of tea and one biscuit, with more than usual relish. She was on a strict diet, and quite frankly, she felt all the worse for it.

Loyal though she was to dear Doctor Lovell, she could not help feeling that it was a pity he ever went on that course about the Place of Diet in Arthritis and Allied Diseases. He had talked of nothing else since his return, and those of his patients who had creaked and hobbled about Thrush Green for years, were now enduring a most uncomfortable time.

All meat was banned, all white bread, and sugar of any colour whatsoever. Anything made with flour was out, and dairy products were forbidden.

'It doesn't leave much,' Miss Fogerty had protested, but was quickly told about the advantages of fruit and vegetables, on which, it appeared, she would have to exist for the foreseeable future.

'Boiled water only for the first two days,' John Lovell had said, his eyes alight with a fanatical gleam. 'Then citrus fruits for three days, and after that perhaps a small apple. Then we can get you on to vegetables, particularly pulses. Pulses are absolutely essential to counteract any acid in the system.'

'But I shall be absolutely bursting with acid if I'm on citrus fruit for days,' exclaimed Agnes. 'I really cannot take lemon juice or grapefruit in any quantity. Even oranges upset me.'

Doctor Lovell, in the thrall of his latest obsession, hardly listened. Consequently, poor Agnes had braved the boiled water for two days and was now struggling through the three devoted to citrus fruits. Frankly, she was starving, and dizzy with weakness.

Doctor Lovell was going to be forgotten while she drank a cup of tea, complete with forbidden milk, and munched the digestive biscuit which Dorothy had insisted she should eat.

'I should take that diet of John Lovell's with a pinch of

salt,' she said, arriving with the tea tray, and setting it down on a stool between them.

'Salt's forbidden,' said Agnes.

'What isn't?' replied Dorothy tartly, pouring the tea.

'How marvellous that smells,' said little Miss Fogerty. Her small stomach gave a thunderous rumble, as she reached for her cup and the tempting biscuit.

'It should taste even better than it smells,' Dorothy assured her with a smile.

' "Forbidden fruits are sweet," ' quoted Agnes.

'I wouldn't mind betting,' said Dorothy, 'that John Lovell is settling down to buttered toast and doughnuts at this very minute.'

'Oh *don't!*' begged Agnes in anguish.

And Dorothy apologised.

Charles Henstock was also in his garden on that warm June day.

The grounds of Lulling vicarage were extensive, and by tradition had always been opened for any parish activity.

They were not as immaculate these days as they had been when Anthony Bull and his wife had employed a man full time to keep the place aglow with flowers and the lawns velvety smooth.

The same man came now, but Caleb was getting old, and he only attended to the garden on one day a week.

He combined this work with his job as sexton to St John's, and on the whole did his chores very well if rather slowly. Charles and he were fond of each other, and Caleb found his new master far less demanding than the old one.

They were working together on a long border when Charles heard the wrought-iron gate clang and saw his old friend Harold Shoosmith from Thrush Green approaching.

'Harold!' cried the rector, dusting his palms down the side of his trousers. 'How good to see you! Come and sit down in the shade.'

They retired to a garden seat under the ancient cedar tree.

Harold waved to Caleb in the distance.

'Am I interrupting anything?'

'No, no. We were just tidying up. Caleb's having a bonfire this evening in the churchyard, and we thought our little bits could go on it.'

'This is bliss,' said Harold leaning back. 'Wish my news were too.'

'Oh dear!' said Charles. 'Trouble in Thrush Green?'

He thought sadly that really he had enough of that commodity in Lulling alone, let alone his other three parishes. Mrs Thurgood and her daughter had never appeared again in his church, and one or two other ladies seem to have taken her part, and were not attending St John's. Could he be failing in his duties? He was most unhappy about it.

'Well, I think you should know that the Hodges are pretty acrimonious, and as far as I can see there's going to be a break-up in that marriage.'

'I do hope not,' said the rector alarmed. 'Percy will keep harking back to his first wife. I told him, at the time, he must look ahead not backward. I don't think that poor little Doris has had a chance.'

'Poor little Doris,' Harold observed, 'is somewhat of a virago.' He had knocked about the world rather more than the good rector, and was well acquainted with the diversity of human nature.

'Really? I've always found her a nice little thing.'

'She probably is with you. She's not with Percy.'

'I'll try to have a word with them. Separately, I think.'

'A good idea. They ought to be able to make a go of it. Otherwise I foresee that he'll be badgering Jenny again.'

'But he's *married* now!' cried the rector.

'Infidelity has been known,' pointed out his friend. 'Not that Jenny would encourage him, but on the other hand why should she be pestered?'

'Quite. I will try and call on Percy in the next day or two.'

He watched Caleb wheel the barrow towards the churchyard. It was very peaceful under the tree. A bee investigated a clover flower which had escaped the mower, and a thrush ran about the border with an eye cocked for any passing worm.

' "And only man is vile," ' sighed the rector.

'It does seem so, on a day like this,' agreed Harold.

'And how's dear Isobel?'

'Shopping. I'm picking her up in a quarter of an hour

outside The Fuchsia Bush. Oh, and there's another thing, I should mention.'

'And what's that?'

'Nelly Piggott's back.'

'Oh no! Not again!' cried Charles. 'Whatever will Albert say?'

'I shouldn't enquire,' advised Harold. 'I hear he's absolutely furious, but she's refusing to go, and if it comes to a physical battle I'd back Nelly any day. Weight alone would settle that.'

Charles shook his head sadly.

'Another call to make, I can see.'

The two men sat in silence for a few minutes, but the peace was soon broken by the return of Caleb, hurrying towards them.

'Sir! Come quick, sir! Someone's been at the poor box. It's all smashed in, and not a penny to be seen.'

'My God!' said Harold. 'We'd better get the police. Shall I ring them for you?'

'Please do,' said Charles. 'I'll go over to the church with Caleb to see if anything else has been touched.'

And the two friends hurried in opposite directions.

That evening Dimity looked across at Charles who lay, with his eyes closed, in the armchair.

'Do you know, my dear, it is the longest day today?'

'I'm not at all surprised,' said Charles.

12 A Question Of Housing

KIT ARMITAGE, happily settled at Mrs Jenner's, was still searching vainly for a suitable house of his own.

He realized that his present conditions were so pleasant that he was in danger of giving up the search altogether. It was good to have no responsibilities except such minor ones as getting his hair cut, paying his bills and cooking his own breakfast.

He had time to wander about the summer countryside looking up old friends. His Thrush Green neighbours were ever welcoming, and he called often upon Dotty and Connie.

He was on his way there one afternoon when he saw Edward Young looking over the old people's homes which were being constructed to his specification.

Kit walked over to talk to him.

'How is it going?'

'With any luck, we'll have them ready by Christmas,' responded Edward. 'What do you think of them?'

He smiled fondly at the muddle of planks, bricks, cement-mixers, wheelbarrows, drain-pipes and bulging sacks which littered the site. To Kit's untutored eye it simply looked an unholy mess.

'How many homes will there be?' he asked, playing for safety.

'Eight in all. Five along this south-facing aspect, and

three at right angles. You can see by the footings.'

Kit tried to look appreciative.

'Later, of course, we may add three or four more, changing this L shape to an open E, so to speak.'

'Ah, yes,' replied Kit, nodding sagely.

'But that all depends on the money, of course. It really does look splendid, doesn't it? Such an improvement on that awful rectory. My blood pressure went up every time I looked at it. Now we shall be able to look out on these eight little one-storey poppets.'

He smiled fondly upon the chaos surrounding him, and Kit envied him the inward eye which transformed this muddle into a vista of domestic beauty.

'Got your name down for one?' asked Edward jocularly.

'I'm seriously thinking of it,' replied Kit. 'I'm not getting much farther with my efforts.'

'I'd forget them for a bit,' advised his friend, stepping over a squashed bucket as he accompanied Kit to the safety of Thrush Green's grass. 'Go and have a break somewhere.'

'As a matter of fact,' Kit told him, 'I may well do that. An old school friend has invited me to a spell of fishing, and I'm sorely tempted.'

'An excellent idea! This weather's too good to waste on duties.'

He waved goodbye, and Kit noticed that he returned to his own duties with the greatest enthusiasm.

Connie agreed with Edward when Kit told her later.

'Something will turn up, probably when you are least expecting it,' she told him. 'Go and enjoy this break. It sounds just what you need, and you know you can always come back to Mrs Jenner. I gather you are her star lodger to date.'

'She's certainly my star landlady,' said Kit. 'Well, I'll look forward to seeing you both on my return.'

'Those Armitages were always charming,' said Dotty, when Kit had departed. 'His mother was a raving beauty. Such a pity the boy doesn't take after her.'

'I think Kit is very handsome himself,' said Connie defensively.

Dotty looked at her with unusual shrewdness.

'Yes, you probably do, dear. They say that beauty is in the eye of the beholder. And as a *young* man he was very much sought after. Those Lovelock girls made a dead set at him, and Justin's wife would have had him if he would have had her, if you follow me, but he was not keen – anyone could see that – and so she settled for Justin. A nice fellow, but very much second-best, we all thought.'

Connie did not reply. She could hardly imagine Dotty and the Lovelocks and the Venables as young people, and in any case, they all seemed so very much *older* than dear Kit.

The phrase 'dear Kit' echoed in her mind, and she was honest enough to admit now that he was indeed, in her own estimation, very much 'dear Kit'.

She checked her thoughts sharply. This would not do. She had dear old Aunt Dotty to think about, and that was quite enough to engage her attention at the moment.

Some two or three days later Connie and the faithful Flossie met Ella Bembridge on Thrush Green. Both women were going to post letters at the box on the corner near Tullivers, and Connie was carrying the milk can.

'Glad I've seen you,' hailed Ella. 'I've got a glut of early lettuces and was about to bring you some and save you a journey with the milk. Have you got a minute to spare?'

'I've got plenty of minutes to spare,' smiled Connie. 'Life

at Thrush Green is delightfully leisurely, I find.'

They walked back to Ella's snug cottage to collect the lettuces. A fine row of tight little Tom Thumb variety stood ready to be picked. Connie voiced her admiration.

'Best sort to grow,' Ella told her, moving along the row, and puffing as she bent double to her task.

'Quick growing, and all heart. That's how I like 'em, nice and crisp. And not too big for a woman alone like me. Five do you?'

She straightened up, the pale green rosettes clutched together in her two hands.

'Can you spare all those?' said Connie. 'Really two would be ample.'

'Take 'em! Take 'em!' replied Ella, stuffing them in the girl's arms. 'You might get somebody calling in at supper time. Kit Armitage, say.'

Connie was a little taken aback at this assumption that Kit was a regular visitor, and was stumped for words.

'I forgot,' went on Ella, 'he's just gone off to Wales to fish with the Olivers. Have you met them? They come up here occasionally to see the Lovelocks.'

'No, I don't know them. I've heard Kit mention Peter Oliver but I haven't met his wife.'

'He hasn't got one. It's his sister he lives with – or rather she's living with Peter since her husband died. Pretty woman. She'll be married again before she can turn round, you mark my words.'

She led the way to the garden seat, and began to roll one of her untidy cigarettes. Connie sat nursing the lapful of lettuces, and Flossie settled with a sigh, in the shade.

'We all thought she might be tempted by Kit Armitage. I gather she was a gorgeous looking girl in her youth. A proper raving beauty.'

'So was Kit's mother, I gather from Aunt Dotty.'

'Yes, I believe she was, but I never knew her, of course. Thrush Green seems to produce quite a few raving beauties. Perhaps Kit's gone down to see if she's just as attractive.'

Ella puffed away blissfully. Connie felt suddenly irritated, and longed to be on her own.'

'Well, I must get back,' she said, rising briskly. 'Many thanks for the lettuces. I know Aunt Dotty will be delighted.'

She set off for the gate, and Ella accompanied her. Flossie straggled behind, disappointed at the brevity of her rest.

'Give her my love,' called Ella to Connie's departing back. Really, the girl walked at an enormous pace!

Connie, unusually disturbed, made her way swiftly past Albert's cottage and gained the comfort of the lonely lane.

'To my mind,' she told the lagging Flossie, 'there are far

too many raving beauties connected with Thrush Green.
And alas, I'm not one of them!'

Nelly Piggott, busy scrubbing Albert's badly stained
wooden draining board with hot soda water, watched
Connie as she passed the window.

'Dotty's niece,' she told the cat, 'and single what's more.
Some women have all the luck!'

She paused for a moment from her labours, and sat down
on a kitchen chair to get back her breath. Say what you like
about doctors, thought Nelly, they may do a good job on
one bit of you, but that anaesthetic and the stitches and
whatnot fair played up the rest of you. She felt as weak as a
baby these days.

Albert was out. He was over in St Andrew's, supposed to
be tidying up, but Nelly guessed correctly that he was
simply keeping out of her way. Give him his due he'd
behaved remarkably well considering the shock she had
given him on her return.

The house had been empty when she had arrived in the
early evening, and Albert was next door at The Two
Pheasants.

Swiftly she had unpacked, putting her things in the spare
bedroom, and making up the bed with the deplorable linen
from the landing cupboard, before Albert's return.

Downstairs she washed up the mounds of dirty crockery
and cooking pans, and put some pork sausages in the frying
pan over a low heat. Who knows? Their fragrance might
mitigate her husband's fury. To tell the truth, Nelly was
remarkably apprehensive about this meeting. If Albert took
it into his head to push her out and lock the door, there was
little she could do.

She had a few pounds in her purse, and that was all,

hardly enough to give her a bed for the night and certainly not enough to keep her going for a week. Her heart jumped when she heard Albert at the door, but she stood and faced him steadily in the last rays of the evening sun.

It was quite apparent that he was fuddled with drink.

'What you doin' 'ere?' he growled, his speech slurred.

Nelly decided to speak the truth.

'I've left Charlie. He don't want me any more.'

'Don't blame 'im,' said Alert, making unsteadily towards a chair. 'Can't say I want you neither.'

Nelly advanced towards the sausages and turned up the heat. She began stabbing the sausages with a fork, and they hissed cheerfully.

She was very near to tears. It had been a long day, and she was exhausted with travelling, worry, and the after-effects of her operation.

'Just cooked us a bit of supper,' she said. 'I know you like sausages, and I've had nothing all day.'

She was surprised at Albert's lack of response. She had fully expected a stream of abuse, and perhaps physical violence. This moody sulkiness was unexpected. She did not know if it boded ill or good.

The fact was that Albert was too dazed with drink to take it all in. He was also ravenously hungry, he realized, and the thought of pork sausages, cooked to a turn by Nelly, had a mellowing effect.

They ate them at the kitchen table. Little conversation passed between them until Albert had mopped the grease from his plate with a crust of bread, and then leant back to survey his wife.

'You ain't stoppin' you know,' he told her. 'Sausages or no sausages.'

'Just tonight,' pleaded Nelly. 'I'm all in, and that's the

truth. Let's talk about it in the morning. I've made up the bed in the back room.'

'So I should hope,' said Albert nastily.

Nelly packed the dirty dishes in the sink and filled them with water.

'I'll do those in the morning,' she said wearily. 'I'm off to bed now, Albert.'

'And don't *snore*,' shouted Albert after her, as she mounted the stairs.

Ever since then an uneasy truce had been the order of the day.

Nelly had remained subdued, conscious that she was at Thrush Green on sufferance. She cleaned the house from top to bottom, cooked for the two of them, and took gentle walks in the neighbourhood mainly to keep out of Albert's way.

He, for his part, was secretly relieved to have his meals cooked and his house cleaned. As long as Nelly behaved with her present politeness he was prepared to let her stay.

Of course, he put a good front on his attitude when teased by his cronies in The Two Pheasants.

'Let her try any of her old tricks,' he told them, 'and she knows she's shown the door. But she's been in hospital and I'm not one to turn an invalid out, as well you know.'

His listeners certainly knew him well, and guessed correctly that the present state of affairs suited Albert nicely. No one in Thrush Green thought otherwise, and many went so far as to say that he was a lucky man to have his wife back.

Betty Bell was the most outspoken.

'I don't know how that Nelly Piggott can face coming back to that pig-hole of a place! She must've been hard up to come to stay with Albert. He's in clover, all right. Lovely smell of stew as I passed. Keeping him sweet, I suppose. How she can!'

'Well,' said Harold Shoosmith, putting down his cup, 'I suppose it's best for them both. Perhaps they'll make a go of it this time. I've always rather liked Nelly Piggott.'

'Good heavens!' exclaimed Isobel. 'Why?'

'I rather admire plump women,' smiled Harold, looking at his wife's slim figure.

'I'll do my best to put on a stone,' she told him.

Across the green, Winnie Bailey discussed the matter with Jenny.

'D'you think it will last?'

'It might this time,' answered Jenny. 'They're both that much older, and neither of 'em too well. If Nelly got a job, they might settle down quite comfortably together. But she'd need to get out of that house for part of the day, and earn some money of her own.'

'You've been giving it some thought,' observed Winnie.

'Well, to tell the truth, I've been thinking about Doris and Percy. She's in such a state she's threatening to leave him. I met her in Lulling yesterday and we walked back together.'

'Does she want a job?'

'Not really. I think if Percy was a chap who went out to work regular, like Ben Curdle, and wasn't just a farmer in and out of the house and under your feet all day, she'd settle all right. I told her to get something herself, and have a change of surroundings, but there's not a lot of work going, as you know.'

'What about Ted and Bessie Allen at The Drovers' Arms? She seemed to enjoy her time there.'

'She told me she'd asked them, but they're well suited and I think they're a bit chary of coming between husband and wife. It would be all over Thrush Green and Lulling if they took sides, wouldn't it?'

And Winnie Bailey agreed.

Dimity Henstock was walking from Lulling vicarage to St John's while Winnie and Jenny were happily discussing Doris Hodge's affairs.

She carried a trug filled with roses, pinks and peonies having offered to arrange the flowers whilst several of the regular flower ladies of the church were disporting themselves on holiday.

The sun was warm. The church clock showed her that she had plenty of time to spare. Lunch was cold today, and she succumbed to the silent welcome of a garden seat placed in the shelter of the south side of the church.

She placed the basket under the seat, in the shade, and prepared to enjoy her solitude.

Not that one felt alone in a churchyard, she told herself. She had never understood the feeling of fear which so many people confessed to about churchyards. After all, one was so often among old friends who were at rest beneath their grassy mounds.

She read the inscriptions near at hand. 'Eulalia Phipps', for instance. Now there was a name to enchant one! And it was good to know that she had been a devoted wife and loving mother to her nine sorrowing children.

Close by was Amos Enderby enclosed in iron railings and with the top of his tomb a little askew. He had been a Justice of the Peace, a Benefactor to the Town and a Much Respected Citizen. He had died of a Seizure at the age of forty-eight to the Great Distress of his Family and Friends.

The only sad thing, Dimity mused, was the thought of all the talents buried in Lulling's earth. Over there, was the grave of Lucy Bennet whom she well remembered as a superb needlewoman and cook. Her grandchildren had always been exquisitely dressed in handmade frocks with intricate smocking, topped by knitted cardigans made by their loving grandmother.

And nearby was Tom Carter who had been renowned for his skill in layering a hedge. While close beside him rested his old friend Dick who had been a fine cabinet maker. His work stood in many a Lulling home as a reminder of his craftmanship.

What a wealth of skills lay buried here, thought Dimity. She feared that her own accomplishments were small in comparison. She was really no hand at flower-arranging, for instance, when she thought of the expertise of the local Guild of Flower Ladies.

Reminded of her duties, she pulled out the trug and made her way towards the cool shadows of the church. Perhaps, though, she comforted herself, she might be remembered, if not as a loving mother of nine children, then surely as a devoted wife?

Taking heart, she set off to collect suitable vases for her modest arrangements.

On the next Sunday Charles Henstock celebrated Holy Communion at eight o'clock at his old church in Thrush Green.

The attendance was small, but this was usual. Most people came to matins at ten-thirty, and only a few of the faithful came to the eight o'clock service. Isobel and Harold were among them, and Charles went back with them to the corner house for a cup of coffee.

'I can't tell you how relieved I am to hear that Albert and his wife seem to have settled down again together. I very much dislike having to interfere in domestic matters, as you know.'

'Early days yet,' commented Harold, 'but we're all keeping our fingers crossed. I don't think Percy Hodge is faring so well though.'

'Oh dear,' said Charles, setting down his cup. 'I'm sorry to hear that. I haven't called, partly because I rather shirked it, and also because that old saying "Least said, soonest mended" is often quite right.'

'We heard yesterday that Doris has gone to stay with a sister. Of course, it may be just a genuine visit, but the old boys at The Two Pheasants reckon she's gone for good.'

'You shouldn't listen to gossip,' declared Isobel. 'And you know how things get exaggerated, especially after a pint or two.'

'It might be a good thing,' said Charles thoughtfully, 'if Doris has this little break. She may come back in a happier state of mind.'

'You were always an optimist, Charles,' smiled Harold. 'Have some more coffee while it's hot.'

13 A Job At The Fuchsia Bush

ON WEDNESDAYS Lulling was at its busiest. It was market day, and people from the surrounding villages joined the local residents in their hunt for bargains.

For many people it was the only day of the week when a local bus ran. There were threats too of even that meagre service being abandoned, and for those without cars it was a bleak outlook.

Lulling market is set up early each Wednesday morning hard by the ancient Butter Cross where a miniature square gives room for a number of stalls. As the market has grown over the centuries, a few stalls have been allowed to straggle up the road towards St John's church, and the pens where sheep used to be kept have been moved to a quieter place near the Corn Exchange, making more space for stall holders.

Traffic congestion on market day is quite a problem, and the prudent driver leaves his car in one of the many public house car parks or in the new car park situated behind The Fuchsia Bush in the High Street. Woe betide those foolish enough to park near the market square! Joe Higgins, the local traffic warden, has an eye like a hawk, and enjoys nothing more than slapping a ticket on a windscreen in the course of his duties.

Local people had always found it worth their while to

visit the weekly market. The produce was always fresh, and there were all sorts of choice things to be found, particularly on the Women's Institute stall where home-made cakes, jams and honey, stood beside trays of fresh brown eggs and baskets of apples and plums. Such rare treasures as yellow quinces, field mushrooms or a greenhouse melon can be found at the appropriate season, cheek by jowl with more homely fare such as crisp cabbages and great marrows striped like tigers.

Some of the stalls sported gay canvas awnings, yellow, green and red, greatly adding to the colourful scene. Sometimes an old lady, with dozens of balloons for sale, sat on a chair at the corner nearest to the Butter Cross. The fat balloons of every possible shape and colour, bobbed above her grey head, tugging at their strings as the wind caught them and squeaking as they rubbed against each other. Naturally, she was the magnet for hordes of children, and it was an exhilarating sight on 'Balloon Lady's Day' to see single balloons bobbing along the High Street, clutched in young hands, or tied to the handles of prams or bicycles.

The public houses did brisk business on market days. As well as extra beer and spirits there were many more dishes to choose from on a Wednesday menu, and trade flourished. Here old friends met to exchange news or to do business, and most people returned home from the market at Lulling with heavy baskets and, even more satisfying, a store of news and gossip to keep them happy until the next week.

Ever since Charles and Dimity had gone to live at Lulling, Ella and her old friend met on a Wednesday at The Fuchsia Bush to enjoy a cup of coffee after their marketing. Sometimes they encountered each other at the Women's Institute stall, for Dimity had a standing order for a dozen brown eggs, and Ella always made a bee-line there to buy

any particular item that took her fancy before the stall was
sold out.

On this particular Wednesday Ella was at The Fuchsia
Bush first and managed to find a corner table near the doors
to the kitchen.

It was not her favourite spot. She much preferred to be
near the window where one could see the life of Lulling
passing by. However, on a Wednesday the place was
crowded, and she was lucky to get a table at all, as well she
knew.

She had just unearthed her cigarette-making equipment
when Dimity appeared, much encumbered by a large basket and an armful of single summer chrysanthemums.

'What a crush!' she said, depositing her burdens on the
floor. 'I couldn't resist these chrysanths. Such a delicate
pink.'

'Very pretty,' agreed Ella, putting away the battered
tobacco tin, 'but I don't like to see them as early as this.
Makes me think of autumn, and that comes soon enough
these days.'

'Have you ordered?'

'Well, no. No one's been along yet. The service gets
worse in this dump. I reckon we'd do better at The Fleece.'

'Oh, Ella,' cried Dimity, rather agitated, 'I really don't
think Charles would like me to be seen frequenting The
Fleece.'

'Why on earth not? It's a perfectly respectable hotel, and
in any case we should only order coffee, shouldn't we?'

'Yes, I know all about that, but I'm old-fashioned enough
to *mind* about women going to pubs alone.'

'You wouldn't be,' pointed out her friend, 'I'd be there.'

Dimity tut-tutted with exasperation.

'You know what I mean. Without a man to escort her.'

'Probably be strong drink then,' commented Ella. 'Ah! Here's Mrs Peters.'

The owner of The Fuchsia Bush, looking somewhat harassed, came to the table.

'I'm so sorry to keep you waiting. We've trouble in the kitchen, and we're short-handed.'

'I'm sorry to hear that,' said Dimity. 'Someone ill?'

'Just coffee, please, and some of your shortbread,' said Ella.

'No shortbread I'm sorry to say. Mrs Jefferson isn't here to make it.'

'Is she the one who is ill?'

'She fell down a flight of steps at a neighbour's house, and has broken a leg and two ribs.'

'The poor dear,' cried Dimity, genuinely distressed.

'Well, she would go and take some tea into this next door friend who was in bed with a new baby, and she couldn't see where she was going because of the tray, and down she tumbled.'

Mrs Peters spoke as though this was only what could be expected if one were so foolhardy as to minister to neighbours. There was definitely a note of censure in her remarks.

'So we're run off our feet, and I shall have to advertise for another cook while she's laid up. Meanwhile, we're struggling as best we can. Will digestive suit you?'

Taking this to mean that digestive biscuits were being offered instead of the usual delectable home-made shortbread, the ladies assented, and Mrs Peters bustled back to the kitchen.

'A broken leg,' mused Dimity.

'And two ribs,' added Ella. 'Not funny. A long job, I should think.'

'Weeks,' agreed Dimity. 'I must let Charles know. He will want to visit her.'

Ella took out a cigarette paper and began to fill it with tobacco. She rolled it thoughtfully, licked the edge and stuck it together. Dimity watched resignedly.

Ella lit up and then gave vent to her favourite phrase.

'Tell you what, Dim. What price that Nelly Piggott in the kitchen here? She's bored to tears I hear, and a first-rate cook. Shall I have a word with Mrs Peters now?'

Dimity smiled across the cloud of blue smoke.

'Why not?' she said.

That same evening, as soon as The Fuchsia Bush closed, weary Mrs Peters climbed into her little car and turned its nose towards Thrush Green.

She had spent the day trying to deputise for the absent Mrs Jefferson, and at the same time attempting to galvanise her lethargic staff to greater efforts.

Really, thought Mrs Peters, it was much simpler to do the job oneself rather than urge such lumps as Rosa and Gloria to give a hand. Mrs Jefferson had been one of the old school, punctual, hard-working and taking a pride in all her kitchen creations.

The two women had much in common and had grown to admire and respect each other. Both were widows, and both had been obliged to work to bring up their children single-handed. They were equally energetic, willing to put in many hours of work, and both deplored the slackness of the younger generation.

Mrs Peters drove up the steep hill to Thrush Green, mourning the temporary loss of her old colleague. She did not know Nelly Piggott, as far as she could recall, but it was worth seeing her from what Miss Bembridge and Mrs

Henstock had said, although she was not particularly hopeful.

She drew up outside Albert's cottage, much to the interest of the clients in The Two Pheasants who gazed unashamedly as she waited on the doorstep next door.

The step, she noticed, was freshly whitened, and the windows gleamed. It boded well, though Mrs Peters.

The door opened and Nelly stood before her looking a little puzzled. As soon as she saw her Mrs Peters realized that this was the fat lady who at one time had attended the Misses Lovelock as a char, and whom she had seen passing The Fuchsia Bush. She remembered now that she *cleaned*, but did she *cook*? She only had the two ladies' word for it.

'I'm from The Fuchsia Bush,' began its owner. 'I wondered if you could help me. Miss Bembridge mentioned you to me this morning.'

'Come in,' said Nelly.

The kitchen shone as cleanly as the doorstep, noticed Mrs Peters with pleasure. She took the chair offered her, and put her gloves and handbag on the checked tablecloth. A bunch of pinks, in an old-fashioned earthenware honey pot, scented the air. Mrs Peters had not seen such a honey pot since she was a child, and felt a warm glow of nostalgia for such a homely vessel.

Albert was out at his church duties with his young assistant, and Nelly had obviously been knitting a jumper so vast it could only have been for herself. A delicious smell of cooking mingled with the scent from the pinks.

'You said something about help,' said Nelly, tidying away the knitting.

Mrs Peters told the sad tale of Mrs Jefferson, and Nelly listened attentively. Her spirits rose with the unfolding of the story, but she tried to hide her excitement. It all sounded too good to be true.

'Well, I've never done cooking for *numbers*, if you follow me,' she said, 'and I always believe in having the very best ingredients. No substitutes or made-up stuff, I mean.'

'We only use the best at The Fuchsia Bush,' her prospective employer told her, with a touch of hauteur. 'I have my reputation to consider.'

'Oh, I only mentioned it,' replied Nelly hastily, 'because I occasionally cooked a meal for them Lovelocks, and the food wasn't what I've been used to at all.'

Mrs Peters unbent at once. The Misses Lovelocks' cuisine was a by-word in Lulling. Her heart warmed towards Nelly.

'I'm sure you would soon get the hang of coping with numbers,' she assured her, 'and of course I should be there to help you. It's mainly small cakes and biscuits, and at midday we offer a cold buffet or one hot dish, something simple like curried lamb and rice, or cottage pie. And there's always soup. We keep a very good stock pot.'

At the thought of a very good stock pot Nelly was quite won over. It would be lovely to play in a really properly equipped kitchen, instead of this poky little place of Albert's. And she would be free of him for best part of the day, and what's more earning some money of her own.

'What wages were you offering?' she asked.

Mrs Peters mentioned a sum which seemed extremely large and generous.

'Well, if you think I can do it,' said Nelly diffidently, 'I'm willing to try my hand with you.'

Something sizzled in the oven, and Nelly excused herself as she bent to open the oven door. A gust of delicious cooking odours blew into the room, reminding Mrs Peters how famished she was.

Nelly bore a magnificent pie to the end of the table where a wooden mat was waiting. The crust was golden brown and neatly indented round the edge. Four beautiful leaves splayed across the top, glossy with egg-yolk gilding. From the centre where the pie-funnel stood, came a little plume of fragrant steam. It was a vision of beauty. It was quite enough to convince that connoisseur of pies, Mrs Peters, that here was a mistress of her craft.

'Steak and kidney,' said Nelly. 'I like a bit of puff for that. Lighter than shortcrust, I always think, and my husband suffers with his stomach, so I have to be careful what I put in front of him. Personally, I enjoy making a nice raised pork pie, but it's too rich for him these days.'

'A raised pork pie,' echoed Mrs Peters, quite faint now with hunger. 'Perhaps you would like to make a really large one for the cold table when you come?'

'Nothing I'd enjoy more,' Nelly assured her. 'And when would you like me to start, ma'am?'

Now that she was engaged, Nelly started as she meant to go on, with due respect. Who knows? She might be taken on permanently if she proved satisfactory.

'You couldn't manage tomorrow, I suppose?' ventured Mrs Peters, her eyes still on the masterpiece before her.

'I'd just love to,' said Nelly sincerely, and stood up as her visitor rose.

'I'm so grateful,' said Mrs Peters. 'Tomorrow then at nine, or eight-thirty if you can manage it.'

'Eight-thirty, ma'am,' promised Nelly.

And with a last look of longing at Nelly's pie, Mrs Peters went to her car, her stomach rumbling protestingly at being denied its rights.

Within a few days the news of Nelly's new job had flashed round Thrush Green.

Nelly had told no one but Albert, who seemed to be little interested. When asked outright by the landlord of The Two Pheasants he admitted grudgingly that the news was correct.

'Give her something to do,' added Albert, 'and the money'll come in useful. Suits me to have a bit of time to meself.'

Certainly Albert's usual dour demeanour remained un-changed by Nelly's good fortune. The truth was that as long as his food was provided, and Nelly kept a civil tongue in her head, he was quite content to let things drift on as they had done since her return.

Dotty Harmer and Connie heard about it when they went to tea with Winnie Bailey one hot afternoon.

Connie took her aunt for a drive after her rest, and they

trundled through nearby villages and enjoyed the leafy beauty of the country lanes. Honeysuckle scented the air, and a few late dog roses starred the hedges. The blackberry flowers, pale pinky-mauve, were prolific, and promised a bumper crop later on.

Dotty's spirits were high. She was enjoying her outing and looking forward to tea at Winnie's.

She rattled on in her usual inconsequent vein, and Connie, immersed in her own thoughts, hardly heard her, until she realized that her aunt was busily discussing the old people's homes being erected at Thrush Green.

'But, you see,' rambled Dotty, 'I don't think I should care to be on one floor. One really *should* go upstairs to bed, don't you agree? It's not only the *rightness* of mounting steps to one's bedroom, but the fact that *anyone* could look in as they passed on foot. Friends of my dear father's retired to a bungalow, and she had the most dreadful shock when she realized that the baker was looking in as she was standing in her stays. Very upsetting. She took to dressing in the bathroom, I remember, at least up to her petticoat, and as that was always Vedonis and lock-knit, it was *perfectly* respectable.'

'You're surely not considering applying for one of the houses?' queried Connie, slightly bewildered. A sudden through struck her. 'You haven't already applied for one?' Dotty was quite capable of doing such a thing, Connie was well aware.

'Oh, no, no, no!' tutted Dotty. 'I shouldn't dream of it. As I was saying, I like to go *upstairs* to sleep, and in any case I have no intention of leaving my own dear house.'

'Thank heaven for that!' said Connie. She turned the car in the direction of Thrush Green. They were in comfortable time for Winnie's tea party.

'I can't think why you thought I wanted to live in one of Edward Young's little places,' went on Dotty. 'Do you think I ought to apply? Are you finding me too much of a problem, Connie dear? I should hate to *exploit* you. Perhaps I do? Oh, dear, I should have realized I am very demanding. And of course the cottage is rather small. Only three bedrooms, and perhaps you find it *cramped* with us both in it? As you know, it will be yours one day, and if you feel like taking it over *now* instead of *later*, I should readily agree to any arrangements you might like to make –'

Dotty's voice had risen in her agitation, and she sounded slightly tearful. Connie drew in at a convenient field gate and switched off the engine. It was unthinkable to let poor old Dotty work herself into such a state. If she were not careful she would be arriving at Winnie's red-eyed and sniffing.

She turned to face the old lady and smiled at her.

'You've got it all wrong, Aunt Dot. The last thing I want is to turn you out of your home. You know that. You are *no bother at all* to me. Just the opposite. I love you dearly, and enjoy living with you. And I hope we'll have many years of life together. Now, is that better?'

Dotty took a long breath, and found a beautifully folded handkerchief in her pocket. She dabbed her eyes and returned it.

'That's all right then. As long as you are happy, dear, I am too. Did you notice the rather nice scent on my handkerchief? Winnie Bailey gave it to me last Christmas, and I thought it would be a gesture to use it today. And have you noticed, dear, in books and plays, that the heroine never seems to have a handkerchief *at all*, and is obliged to borrow one from the hero? I mean, who on earth ever goes out *without* a handkerchief? It's quite unthinkable. Although I

once knew two sisters who *shared* one. At parties you heard
them say to each other: "Have you got The Handkerchief?"
So insanitary, we always thought. They were odd girls.'

Not the only ones, was Connie's private comment as
they mounted the hill to Thrush Green. Dear old Dotty, she
needed more attention daily, thought Connie indulgently,
and she would make sure that she had it.

Winnie Bailey apologised for it being what she called 'a hen
party' in her drawing room. Ella Bembridge and Dimity
Henstock were there and Phyllida Hurst from Tullivers
next door.

'You wouldn't have kept Frank away,' said the latter, 'if
he had been at home. The poor dear's at a publishers'
conference in Leamington.'

'And Charles,' added Dimity, as the only other married
woman present, 'is at a diocesan conference. Do you think
men like conferences, or do they just enjoy getting away on
their own now and again?'

'I've never liked to enquire,' replied Phyllida. 'Have you
heard about Nelly Piggott?'

An animated discussion followed, and the general feeling
was that such employment might be the making of Albert's
rather shaky marriage.

'Perhaps,' ventured Dimity, 'Doris Hodge would be
happier with a nice little job.'

'The worst of it is,' said Ella, 'that nice little jobs are jolly hard to come by. I met that objectionable Frances Thurgood this week, and she was telling me that Janet is getting quite desperate searching for some employment.'

'Can she do anything?' asked Connie.

'Nothing as useful as Nelly Piggott, but she's got strings of art qualifications for what they're worth. What about Doris? Any hope as a barmaid again?'

'I gather not,' said Winnie. 'I agree that they are thrown too much together, and Percy is a difficult man, you know. His first wife thoroughly spoilt him, and Doris doesn't. It's as simple as that.'

Later that day, when all the ladies had departed and Winnie and Jenny were clearing up in the kitchen, the subject was raised again.

'How are things going at the Hodges'?' asked Winnie, cake tin in hand.

'Haven't you heard?' replied Jenny. 'He had a letter this week, so Mrs Jenner told me, to say Doris is not coming back.'

'Oh Jenny!' sighed Winnie. 'I am sorry.'

'Not as sorry as I am,' said Jenny grimly. 'I only hope he doesn't try his tricks here again.'

And Winnie was relieved to see that her brave Jenny was prepared to repulse any invaders of her territory.

14 Thundery Conditions

THE SUMMER weeks slipped by. The honeysuckle flowers had fallen and clusters of garnet berries took their place. Hard little knobs of green replaced the bramble blossom, and the wild late summer flowers, knapweed, agrimony and scabious, enlivened the verges.

Everything was beginning to look shabby. The grass was turning brown. A few leaves were already floating down from the trees. The combine harvesters were at work in the fields, and the lucky people with greenhouses were enjoying a bumper crop of tomatoes.

In the vicarage garden at Lulling Charles Henstock and Caleb were busy.

Caleb was pushing the lawn mower at a leisurely pace, and the smell of freshly cut grass floated pleasantly about the place. Charles was engaged in trimming the edges of the flower beds with his long-handled shears, given to him by Dimity on his last birthday. They were, he noted with infinite satisfaction, a great advance on the old pair of hand shears with which he used to tackle this job. What was even more pleasing was the fact that he didn't get the knees of his trousers stained crawling on the grass.

The air was warm and sultry, and there was no sunshine. Hordes of minute insects, called thunder flies by Lulling folk, filled the garden, tickling Caleb and Charles as they worked. Every now and again the sound of a slap and a

vexed exclamation disturbed the peace, as the two men tried
to displace their ubiquitous adversaries.

Despite these interruptions, Charles's flow of thought
continued. He was in a philosophic mood, brought about,
no doubt, by the rhythmic nature of his present labours and
the soporific atmosphere of a warm August afternoon. He
had put aside, as best he could, his earlier worries. Mrs
Thurgood's absence from church could not be helped, sad
though it was. It was true that several families had trans-
ferred their presence to other establishments, but on the
other hand Charles had welcomed several newcomers.

The person who had rifled the poor box, or rather the box
asking for help with the fabric of St John's church, had not
been found. The police had strongly suspected a young man
who lived in one of the riverside cottages by the Pleshey,
but he was able to prove that he had been practising his
bowling at the nets on the local sports' ground when the
felony occurred, and the police were obliged to look fruit-
lessly elsewhere. Charles had long ago put the matter
behind him. A stronger box had been put in its place, and
the alms were collected nightly by the rector himself. One
could do no more.

On the whole, as the months passed, he began to feel
more at ease, although he was still deeply conscious of his
own shortcomings when he compared himself with
Anthony Bull. But there it was. Anthony was Anthony,
charming, a trifle flamboyant, able to talk and laugh easily
with all and sundry, an inspiring orator and as handsome as
a matinée idol.

He could not hope, nor did he wish, to compete. He
could only pray that his parishioners would recognise his
own sincerity, his loving care of them and his desire to serve
them well. He wanted to be accepted as himself, and not

constantly compared to his predecessor. Only time, Charles sighed to himself, scratching his tormented neck, could put that right, he feared. Patience was all.

He straightened up, and saw Dimity approaching with the tea tray. He hurried to help her.

'I thought it would be nice to have it out here,' said Dimity.

'Perfect, my dear. Although there are no end of those horrible little thunder flies.'

'They're worse in the house,' Dimity told him, lifting the milk jug. 'Quite static in there, like veils of treacle.'

' "Veils of treacle," ' echoed Charles. 'Can you have veils –?'

'You know what I mean,' said Dimity. 'One has to *push* through them. Out here they do at least move about a bit. Call Caleb, would you? I'm sure he's as parched as we are.'

And still pondering on his wife's extraordinary description, Charles went across the newly-striped lawn to fetch Caleb to the feast.

Some half a mile away, in the kitchen of The Fuchsia Bush, Nelly Piggott found the thunder flies as irritating as the rest of Lulling.

She had just spread coffee-flavoured water icing carefully over a large square of spongecake, and was now placing halved walnuts at equal distances on the sticky surface. Her intention was to cut the whole into twenty squares, each suitable for a delectable portion to be eaten with coffee or tea by the lucky customers.

The thunder flies seemed bent on committing suicide upon Nelly's masterpiece. She moved it from the kitchen table into the larder, but there seemed to be no escape from the maddening little midges.

'Nothing for it but to pick 'em off with a knife point,' said Nelly to Mrs Peters when she came into the kitchen. 'I'd best open that extra tin of home-made biscuits, ma'am, for this afternoon.'

'Yes, that would be best,' agreed her employer, looking doubtfully at Nelly's icing. 'With any luck these wretched midges should clear away as soon as a storm comes, and I think that's on the way already.'

She vanished again into the shop and Nelly was left to her own devices.

She had not been so happy in years, thought Nelly, putting out biscuits. Albert, although no ray of sunshine, was comparatively good tempered, and certainly did not upbraid her about her absence with the oil man, which she fully expected from him. Perhaps he was mellowing with age? Perhaps he felt, as she did since her time in hospital, that peace at any price was the best guideline? No one could call Albert's cottage a love nest, but at least it was a port in a storm.

The main thing was that she was really blissfully happy whilst at work, and she was in The Fuchsia Bush's kitchen promptly at eight-thirty each morning and content to stay there for as long as Mrs Peters needed her. The café closed when afternoon teas were over, and the arrangement had been that Nelly could leave as soon as the cakes and sandwiches were ready, and the kettles on the stove, sometime before four o'clock. Two part-time kitchen helpers came from one o'clock until five-thirty, so that there was no need for Nelly to remain, but more often than not it was nearer five when she departed.

It seemed to suit Albert too. One of Nelly's perks in the new job was a certain amount of spare food which Mrs Peters allowed her to take home. Very often Nelly had no need to cook a meal for Albert on her return, and for this she was grateful, for a long stint in the kitchen, much as she enjoyed it, and the walk up the steep hill to crown the day, did seem to take its toll of Nelly's strength, and made her realize that she had still not fully recovered from the operation.

Her one fear was that as soon as Mrs Jefferson reappeared then her job would come to an end. So far, Mrs Jefferson's injuries had taken their time in mending. 'It's an ill wind that blows nobody any good,' Nelly had quoted silently to herself, when she heard how slowly her predecessor was recovering. The broken ribs had led later to bronchitis, and this in its turn to a troublesome and painful cough. It was obvious that the patient could not expect to return to her duties, and lifting heavy objects and other arduous kitchen duties were going to be beyond her for some time.

Mrs Peters considered herself extremely fortunate in having Nelly in the kitchen, and never ceased to be grateful to Ella and Dimity for suggesting her.

There was no doubt about it, Nelly was superior in every way to Mrs Jefferson, but Mrs Peters had no intention of depriving her old friend of the job and would welcome her back just as soon as she was fit.

If only, thought The Fuchsia Bush's owner, she could employ them both. But would the business stand it? And would the two ladies work together in harmony?

Well, time enough to worry when her former cook returned, she told herself. Something would turn up, no doubt. It generally did.

Kit Armitage returned from his visit to Wales looking remarkably refreshed.

Mrs Jenner was delighted to welcome him back, but

within half an hour of his home-coming she had poured out the story of her sister-in-law Doris's perfidy.

'But surely she'll come back?' said Kit. 'Isn't it just a little tiff?'

'To my mind, she's finished with Perce. I can't make up my mind if he wants her back or not. He misses his comforts, that I do know, and asked me if I'd take him in. He's fond of my cooking.'

'And are you going to have him here?' asked Kit, feeling some alarm.

'Dear me, no! I'm in my seventies, and I'm not taking on a silly chap like Percy, brother or no brother. He's old enough and ugly enough to look after his own affairs, as our mother used to say, God rest her. I've never worried Perce with my troubles, and apart from offering him a meal if he blows in at the right time, I'm not making a rod for my back.'

Kit heartily approved of this downright approach to the problem, and said so.

'So you see,' went on his landlady, 'this will make no difference to your arrangements. I only hope you'll be able to stay for a long time to come. You've been the Perfect Lodger, if I may say so.'

'You're very kind,' replied Kit, 'and you make me so comfortable I could easily be persuaded to stay for ever. But I really must find myself a house. Prices go up every month, and I'm determined to put my shoulder to the wheel now, and get settled.'

'Well, don't hurry on my account,' said Mrs Jenner.

There was the sound of someone wiping feet on the door scraper at the back door.

'I'd better go. Probably Perce with some vegetables. He's just in time for a cup of coffee. It's my belief he keeps one eye on the clock.'

And downstairs she went to greet the grass widower.

Kit's first port of call was to see Connie and Dotty.

He found the two ladies shelling peas in the garden, with Flossie at their feet eagerly snatching up any stray pea and munching it with enjoyment.

'That's an odd taste for a dog, isn't it?' he asked, when he had greeted the ladies and was settled in a decidedly rickety deckchair.

'That's nothing,' Dotty told him. 'We had a sweet little cat once who enjoyed peppermints. Not the really strong ones that Papa had for his indigestion, but the mild sort. Sometimes I made her peppermint creams, for a treat. Quite simple, you know, just icing sugar and a few drops of peppermint essence. No doubt you made them yourself as a child.'

Kit confessed that he had never tried his hand at peppermint creams.

'But I did make Everton toffee once,' he said, 'and ruined the saucepan. It went black before my very eyes.'

'Tell us about Wales,' said Connie. His appearance had given her so much delight that she had felt herself blushing, much to her horror. It was really absurd at her age, she scolded herself, to behave like someone of sixteen, and she could only hope that he put her rosiness down to the sun. With any luck, he had not noticed, but men, usually obtuse, were often disconcertingly sharp, just when one would rather they were not.

Kit launched into an animated account of his holiday, and fished from his pocket a folder of photographs.

The colander of peas was set aside, under the seat in the shade, as the two ladies studied them in turn.

'This is the River Dovey,' he explained, 'and this is one of the tributaries where we did most of our fishing. Here's the Olivers' house. Here's the church. And this is Diana.'

Was it just Connie's imagination, or did his voice sound particularly loving as he handed over the last photograph? The subject was certainly stunningly attractive. Connie noted ruefully the excellent figure, the smooth dark hair and the enchanting smile.

'She looks lovely,' commented Connie.

'She is,' agreed Kit, tucking the photographs back in the folder.

'And when are you off next?' enquired Connie.

'I'm not,' he assured her. 'I'm now applying myself whole-heartedly to finding a house. There are two in this week's paper which sound hopeful, and I believe the agent has another two possibilities. And Justin has heard of a place south of Lulling, so that gives me plenty to be going on with.'

He hesitated for a moment.

'If it's not too much to ask, would you like to help me? Both of you, of course. I'd be glad of a second opinion.'

'I should love to,' said Connie.

'Well, I won't promise,' said Dotty. 'I'm making our bread now, you know, and it all takes time. And the early plums need bottling. But, thank you for the invitation. If my duties allow, I should be delighted.'

'Then that's settled,' said Kit, throwing himself back in the chair. A terrible rending sound followed, and Kit gradually subsided through the worn canvas amidst cries of distress from the ladies.

'Are you hurt? That wretched chair! It should have been thrown away years ago,' cried Connie, bending over her laughing visitor who was struggling to rise from the débris.

'No harm done, but look at your peas,' said Kit, standing upright.

The colander was on its side. At least half the peas had gone, and the back view of Flossie, with her tail between her legs, was vanishing through the hedge.

'We asked for that,' commented Connie.

'Excellent roughage for her,' said Dotty indulgently. 'Dear little Floss! So intelligent!'

Kit was folding up the tattered chair.

'You know, the frame's perfectly sound,' he said, studying it. 'I'll get some more canvas and mend it for you.'

They began to protest.

'No, I'd like to. I may not be a dab hand at peppermint creams,' he told Dotty, 'but I can mend deck chairs as well as the next.'

'In that case,' said Connie, 'I'll bring out the other three for your attention. They are all at that stage, believe me.'

The prolonged absence of Percy Hodge's wife made itself felt in places farther afield than Mrs Jenner's.

The example of one stone thrown into a pool creating ripples far around it, is nowhere more to the point than in a small community.

Winnie Bailey, and more particularly, Jenny, were both on guard against any unwelcome intrusions by a would-be suitor.

The regulars at The Two Pheasants discussed the affair avidly, and Albert, as a once-deserted husband, had plenty to say.

'She'll come back all right,' he told his listeners. 'Mine did, didn't she? I just bided my time. Acted dignified. Never run after her. She come back, and now she knows when she's well off.'

'You went down to see her in hospital,' put in the landlord. 'As I remember, you was shamed into it.'

Albert feigned deafness. That was the worst of village life, he mused. No one ever forgot any little mistakes you made. You could slip up perhaps twenty years ago, and some know-all would remind you of it.

He button-holed a woe-begone Percy one day and enlarged on the theme of wife-management.

'You mark my words, she'll come to her senses in time! Just don't give way, Percy my boy. Once she sees you can manage all right without her, she'll come running back. Women is awkward creatures. Like to think they can manage without us. But they can't, of course.'

'I don't know as I wholly *want* her back,' said Percy. 'She's led me a proper dance, and spends money like water. I never had that trouble with my dear Gertie. And her cooking was streets ahead. Marriage is a lottery, Albert, and that's a fact.'

'Don't I know it!' commiserated Albert. 'I've had my share of trouble, and that's why I'm giving you my advice.

You let things ride for a bit. You may feel different if she comes back all humble-pie. On the other hand, if you finds you don't want her you could set about a divorce one day.'

Percy started as if stung by a wasp.

'Divorce? But that costs money!'

'Ah!' agreed Albert morosely. 'But anything worth-while does, don't it?'

They turned over this sad fact in unhappy silence.

'What about half a pint?' said the sorrowing widower at last.

And together they entered The Two Pheasants.

Even as far away as Lulling, Percy Hodge's troubles were causing ripples. Charles Henstock, who had been relieved to find that Nelly had returned to the marital home and had understood that Doris's absence was simply a visit to her sister, was now dismayed to find that pressure was being exerted, yet again, for his ministrations.

'I'm really most reluctant to interfere in any little upset between husband and wife,' he told Ella when she brought up the matter. 'Ten chances to one it will all blow over, and I shall simply appear as a meddler.'

'Well, I can't see it would do any harm,' said Ella forth-rightly, 'if you told Percy to fetch her back. And another thing, you could let him know he's a fool to keep throwing Gertie in Doris's face. What second wife is going to stand for that? I ask you!'

'It would only add fuel to the fire,' exclaimed Dimity, rushing to her husband's support. 'You must see that it can only put Charles in a most difficult position. If Percy comes to him for advice, that's quite a different proposition, but I'm sure it's a case of "Least said, soonest mended" here.'

'Well, I don't know,' protested Ella. 'If you've joined

them together in holy matrimony I should have thought a bit of adhesive is needed if they come unstuck. Still, no doubt the bishop gives you guidance on this sort of thing.'

Charles laughed.

'He will if it ever gets to that stage, I'm sure. But at the moment I think we'll simply hope for the best.'

'The best being Doris's return, I suppose? I'll tell you what. Poor Jenny will be jolly relieved if she does deign to come back.'

As it happened, poor Jenny was destined to confront Percy within a day or two of this conversation.

She had walked across to the post box at the corner of Thrush Green, and then decided to take a short walk along the Nidden road.

The recent thunderstorm had cleared the air, and there was a freshness in the breeze that held a hint of early autumn. There were dahlias out in the gardens, great shaggy ones like floor mops, spiky ones of every hue from pale lemon to dark crimson, and dozens of the gay little pompom variety which Jenny loved best.

She was admiring them in a cottage garden when she became conscious of Percy emerging from a field gate.

It was too late to flee. Jenny stood her ground, as Percy approached.

'Nice day, Percy,' she said civilly.

'Would be if things was a bit different,' was his melancholy reply.

Jenny scented danger and took evasive action.

'Well, we'd all like some things different, I daresay,' she began briskly. 'Can't stop, Percy. I've got my ironing to do before tea.'

She turned and set off at a smart pace towards her home.

To her dismay she found Percy at her elbow, pouring forth a stream of self-pity.

The well-worn phrases of 'never-understood-me', 'I-was-too-hasty-in-marrying-again' and 'I-always-tried-to-please-her' flowed like water off a duck's back as Jenny hastened along.

But when Percy was rash enough to puff explosively, for their pace was punishing: 'It was always you I wanted, as you well knows, Jenny,' she stopped, so suddenly that Percy nearly tripped over her.

Jenny faced him furiously.

'Stop that, Percy Hodge!' she cried. 'You're a married man and I won't hear no more. Any more of this nonsense and I'll set the police on you, and that's flat.'

Percy's mouth dropped open. The movement seemed to rouse Jenny to still greater heights of fury.

'And take that to be going on with!' she added, giving a resounding slap to her suitor's cheek. It was delivered with such wholesale venom that Percy stumbled into the verge, and while he was recovering his balance, Jenny marched away in triumph.

15   Under Doctor's Orders

THE NEW school year was a few weeks old when little Miss Fogerty was taken ill.

For the last two or three months she had diligently done her exercises, and tried to keep to Doctor Lovell's arduous diet.

'I really think that my *muscles* have toned up very well,' she told Dorothy Watson. 'It's just that I seem to get so *tired* these days, and I have lost so much weight that my skirts are slipping down.'

'You know what I think,' responded her friend. 'You are half-starved, my dear, and it's time John Lovell noticed it.'

'But I see him regularly every six weeks,' protested Agnes, 'and he is delighted with my arthritis. He says my blood is very much purer than it was, and I'm making excellent progress.'

'Towards the grave, at this rate,' commented Dorothy tartly. 'I really think you should go and see him. You're right down to skin and bone, Agnes, and far too pale.'

'Well, I'm due to see him again in a fortnight's time. We'll see what he thinks then.'

But it was in the same week, a golden one of mellow September sunshine, that little Miss Fogerty gave a small cry, rather like a kitten's, and slid to the floor from the breakfast table.

Dorothy Watson was much alarmed. She knelt beside her

unconscious friend and tried to remember all the right things to do to resuscitate the fainting.

She had a fleeting memory of a railway poster seen in childhood of how to cope with those electrocuted. It showed a railwayman, complete with splendid moustaches, lying comatose, whilst another in gold braid – presumably the station master – was loosening the patient's collar as shown in Figure One.

Agnes's collar did not need loosening, and Dorothy was just about to put a cushion under her head when Miss Fogerty opened her eyes and said quite lucidly:

'It must be time for school.'

'That can wait,' replied Miss Watson. 'You lie there, my dear, while I fetch a rug.'

'Thank you,' agreed Agnes, with such docility that Dorothy's alarm grew.

She hurried upstairs for a travelling rug and took the opportunity of looking from the bedroom window across to John Lovell's surgery. It was with relief that she saw his

car was already there, but Miss Pick's, his secretary's, was not.

Miss Pick, although an excellent secretary, was over-anxious to spare her employer, so she frequently kept patients from talking to him on the telephone. It did not endear her to those in emergencies such as the one now confronting Dorothy.

Agnes appeared to be dozing when she returned. She tucked the rug round her, closed the door carefully, and made her way to the telephone in the hall. She did not want Agnes to hear the conversation.

John Lovell answered himself.

'I'll bob over now,' he said, 'before surgery. I'll leave a note for Miss Pick, but no doubt I'll be back before she arrives. Just keep her warm and lying down.'

He was heartily reassuring after examining the patient, and accompanied her upstairs to her bedroom.

'Bed for the rest of the day,' he told her, 'and I'll be over this evening.'

Dorothy followed him downstairs. She was fond of this conscientious doctor, and grateful for his prompt arrival, but this was not going to deter her from speaking her mind.

'I can't help thinking, you know, that this results from that diet you prescribed. She seems to have been taken off all really nourishing food. She's lost far more than a woman of her size can stand, and her job is *most* demanding. I put this collapse down to weakness and anaemia.'

John Lovell smiled indulgently.

'Well, we'll see later. She seems to have been making pretty good progress so far under my treatment.'

Miss Watson curbed any further comment. It could wait until Agnes was seen again this evening.

She mounted the stairs again to see that her old friend had

all that was needed for the next hour or so. The school bell was now ringing, and Agnes would be anxious.

Miss Watson explained what had happened to the only other member of staff at Thrush Green School.

She was a fresh-faced young woman in her probationary year, and listened to her headmistress with some concern.

She was genuinely fond of little Miss Fogerty and sad to hear of her sudden illness, but she felt even more anxious about her own ability to cope with the infants' class in her absence.

'I shall take your class and mine together,' Miss Watson told her, 'until I can get the office to send me a supply. I know that Mrs Billing is free at the moment, and perhaps we can persuade Mrs Trent, who is due here for the half-day tomorrow, to stay on.'

She went with her young assistant to see her settled in at the new classroom across the playground where Agnes usually held sway.

The children seemed awed by the news of Miss Fogerty's indisposition, but considerably elated at having a new teacher.

They began to converge upon her desk, full of news about their own illnesses, but Miss Watson soon put a stop to that.

'You must stay in your desks until Miss Potter tells you to come out,' she commanded. 'I shall want to hear what good children you have been at the end of the day.'

'I was sick last night,' announced a smug six-year-old in the front row. 'All over the clean counterpane. My mum said a swear word.'

Miss Watson leant towards Miss Potter.

'Keep them busy, dear,' she whispered. 'That's the secret.'

She departed towards her own quarters, checked that her double class was obediently reading in semi-silence, and went to the school telephone in her own tiny office.

She rang Isobel Shoosmith, her good next door neighbour, and told her what had happened to her old college friend.

'To be frank, I'm not surprised,' said Isobel. 'She's been looking pretty groggy for weeks. At least this will make her rest. Don't worry. I'll go and see her now, and I can stay with her until you get over at playtime. Betty Bell's here, and Harold is about too, so don't worry if you are held up.'

Much relieved, Dorothy Watson put down the receiver, and went to resume her duties.

True to his word, Doctor Lovell came again before evening surgery and spent a quarter of an hour with his patient. At Agnes's request, Dorothy waited below until he had finished.

'Well, how is she?' she asked anxiously, when he appeared in the sitting room.

'Nothing that a rest and good food won't cure,' he told her. 'She's very run down, and needs fattening up. I think perhap's she's been more than usually conscientious about her diet.'

'Agnes is always conscientious,' said Dorothy. She could have added a great deal more, but was wise enough to refrain.

'And I want her to take some iron tablets. Here's the prescription. And of course, no going to work for a week at least.'

'What about the diet? Should she try and keep to it?'

'Well, no. I'd see she has plenty of milk, and a good light diet – eggs, fish, that sort of thing. I'll keep in touch.'

Miss Watson, with commendable restraint, made no comment on this complete reversal of Agnes's treatment, and saw him to the door with sincere thanks for his help.

'As I thought,' she said aloud, as she straightened the sitting room curtains, 'half-starved and anaemic! Poor little Agnes!'

The warm September sunshine continued, and Agnes was soon able to sit out in the garden and enjoy her much-needed rest.

It was during this fine week that Charles Henstock found himself the bewildered owner of a dog.

It all began with the arrival of the milkman bearing a pint of gold top Jersey milk and an urgent message from Tom Hardy of the water-keeper's cottage.

'He's ill abed, sir,' said the milkman, 'and says could you come? He said something about hospital tomorrow, but I couldn't hear it all, him speaking so low and that river fair rushing by. I said I'd tell you. He don't write all that well, and of course there's no telephone.'

'Don't worry,' said the rector. 'I've a short service to take in half an hour and I'll go down there immediately after.'

The milkman departed, and Charles told Dimity about it.

'Probably wants a lift to the hospital tomorrow,' said Dimity. 'Are you free?'

'I'm sure I can manage it,' answered the rector. 'I shall be glad to help old Tom in any way.'

He was at the cottage by eleven o'clock. It meant leaving the car a little distance away, and walking across the spongy turf to Tom's door.

This time he did not bother to knock, but entered by the back door, and began to mount the stairs.

'You there, Tom? I'm coming up.'

A grey muzzle pushed its way through the banister railings. Polly made no noise, but her plumed tail wagged in greeting.

'In here, sir,' called Tom.

He was propped up on pillows and looked unusually sallow.

'And what have you been up to?' enquired Charles, drawing a chair to the bedside and sitting down. The Welsh collie put her head on his knee, and he stroked her silky neck automatically as he studied the dog's master.

'Doctor wants me to have some tests in hospital. Something in my stomach, he says. Probably have to have it out, I shouldn't wonder.'

'And you want a lift? I'm quite free to take you.'

'No, no. That's all arranged for me. It's Polly.'

'Polly?'

The dog looked up with her one bright eye and one opaque, and wagged her tail on hearing her name.

'My neighbour, Mrs Johnson, she's been seeing to me, and she was going to have Poll, but her bitch had six pups yesterday, and she'd go for Poll and anyone else she thought'd upset the pups, so the only person I could think of was you, rector. Polly's always taken to you, and she's a good obedient animal. I dare not leave her here, she'd fret so, even if she was fed regular, and I don't hold with kennels. She'd pine away there, that I do know.'

Charles saw, with great pity, that tears were rolling down poor Tom's furrowed cheeks. He was obviously very weak and the anxiety about the dog was more than he could bear.

Charles patted Tom's hand.

'Of course I'll have her,' he said heartily, 'and for as long as you like. Dimity loves dogs as much as I do, and we'll take the greatest care of her. I take it as an honour to have been asked.'

Tom gave a great sigh of relief.

'Well, I don't mind now what they do to me. As long as old Polly's in safe hands, I'm content. You know, sir, you truly are a man of God.'

'I should like to think I was,' said the rector humbly. 'Now, Tom, I'm going to get us both a cup of tea. I can find my way round your kitchen. I know everything's clearly labelled. Then you can tell me what I should know about Polly's diet and her routine before I take her off.'

'You stay here, Poll,' said Tom. He was calmer now. The tears still glistened on his face, and he made no attempt to dry them.

Charles went downstairs and waited for the kettle to boil. He admired again the simple, purely functional, furnishings. The tea pot stood by the kettle. The canisters on the mantelpiece were clearly labelled. A few plates, a mug or two and a cup and saucer were lodged on the rack over the sink. The drawer of the scrubbed kitchen table held a few knives, forks and spoons. Life could not be simpler, thought Charles, and found the place deeply tranquil.

The milk was still on the step, and Charles poured it into the two mugs straight from the bottle.

'Sugar?' he called up the stairs.

'Not for me,' came the reply.

He mounted carefully, a mug in each hand.

They sipped in silence. Outside the River Pleshey splashed and gurgled. A blackbird chattered, and in the distance could be heard a pheasant's sharp croak.

'My, that does you a power of good,' said Tom, putting his mug carefully on the stool by the bed. 'And now I'll tell you what Poll likes. Best of all she likes company, and that's why I couldn't leave her alone, for all Mrs Johnson promised to feed her. She eats anything you've got, scraps and that, and there's a sack of biscuits and some tins in the cupboard downstairs. I'd be obliged if you'd take 'em, sir. I'd feel better if you did.'

'I'll do that willingly,' said Charles. 'What about exercise?'

'She don't need much these days, like me,' replied Tom. 'If she can potter about after you in the garden, she won't hurt. And you'd best take her lead. It's hanging on the kitchen door.'

He fondled the dog's ears.

'I do hope she won't be a bother. If I tell her you're her master for a bit she'll understand.'

'I'll go and get the lead and take the mugs down,' said Charles, deeming it best to leave the two old friends together for a few minutes. 'Anything else I can get you?'

'No, thank you all the same, sir. Mrs Johnson will be down in an hour, and she's coming with me to the hospital tomorrow.'

'I'll come and see you as soon as they'll let me,' promised Charles, setting off with the mugs.

He rinsed them at the sink, and replaced them on the rack. There was no sign of food anywhere for Tom, and he presumed that Mrs Johnson would be bringing him a light meal.

He found the dog food and the lead and took the latter upstairs.

Tom fastened it to Polly's collar.

'Now you do as I told you,' he said earnestly. 'You're Mr Henstock's dog till I come back.'

Much to Charles's relief Tom seemed quite calm, and Polly came with him without any fuss.

'Good luck, Tom. I'll ring the hospital tomorrow and tell you how Polly's settled in.'

'She'll be safe enough with you. I know that, and bless you I do, sir, with all my heart.'

Polly led the way downstairs, across the grass and waited by the car door while Charles opened it.

Without any demur, she jumped in and lay down on the back seat.

Charles drove off gently. What would Dimity say, he wondered, when she saw their new visitor?

He need not have worried. Dimity was overjoyed to have the quiet old creature, and the cat, after a preliminary hiss, decided to ignore the interloper.

Charles was astonished and greatly touched by Polly's docility and ready obedience. As Tom had said, she liked company, and the only time she seemed at all disturbed was when a door opened. Then she looked up eagerly, as if expecting her old master, and when she found that he had not come back, she sighed, and drooped her head once more in resignation.

It almost broke Charles's heart.

The fine spell came to an end with a week of high winds and rain.

Work was at a standstill on Edward Young's new project. The children at the village school could not get rid of their high spirits in the playground, and Miss Watson was greatly relieved to have a supply teacher allotted to her by a sympathetic education office. Mrs Trent, who came occasionally each week, to help with what Miss Watson in her young days called "backward children", now came full time while Miss Fogerty was recovering.

'They were always called "less able children" in my

time,' she told Miss Watson. 'What is the latest term?'

'I've an idea it's "disadvantaged",' replied Dorothy, somewhat impatiently, 'but don't ask me why. I only know the present-day inspectors talk about "remedial classes" when I used to know them as "backward classes'. It's all very silly, to my mind.'

Mrs Trent agreed, and asked if Miss Fogerty would soon be back.

'I very much hope so, but I'm insisting on her getting really fit again. It will take her some time to get over the doctor's treatment.'

It was Isobel Shoosmith who put forward a plan with which Dorothy readily agreed.

'Let me take Agnes to the sea for a few days. I've talked it over with Harold who entirely agrees.'

'To Barton-on-Sea?' enquired Dorothy. Barton was her idea of Paradise.

'Well, no. Harold suggested the east coast. So bracing, you know. But I pointed out that it is so wickedly cold at times, and what Agnes needed was lots of *warm* sea air. Winnie Bailey and Jenny went to a very nice quiet hotel at Torquay, and it sounds ideal.'

Agnes, as was to be expected, was unhappy about postponing her return to school, but was soon over-powered by the determination of Isobel and Dorothy, backed by Doctor Lovell's blessing.

'Very well,' she said at last, looking at the driving rain lashing across Thrush Green. 'If you all think a holiday will do me good.'

'Of course it will,' they chorused. 'And the weather will be quite different in Torquay!'

A particularly vicious squall had removed Justin Venables'

hat in Lulling High Street, and sent it bowling along the pavement outside the Georgian front of the Lovelocks' fine house.

Justin dodged between lowered umbrellas and wellingtons to try and retrieve it. It seemed as if the gods were intent on teasing him, for as fast as he pursued it the faster it went, ricocheting off wet lime trees and railings, being run over by the odd pram, and generally behaving as if it had a life of its own, and a very mischievous one at that.

Luckily, the fishmonger fielded it for him, and Justin, breathless with the chase, thanked him sincerely.

'Not that it's going to be much improved after that,' observed Justin, turning the wet object in his hands. 'I can see I shall have to fork out for another one.'

He retraced his steps, facing the gale again, and heard a peremptory rapping at the Misses Lovelocks' window. Miss Ada was beckoning him in, and Justin knew better than to ignore this command.

'We saw you in trouble,' said Ada at the front door. 'Now you must come in and get dry. What brought you out in such a storm?'

'Business,' replied Justin, handing over his wet coat and hat. 'But it can wait a minute.'

Violet and Bertha now appeared.

'Let us get you some coffee,' said Bertha.

Justin refused politely. He knew the Lovelocks' coffee of old. It took at least half an hour to prepare and was atrociously weak after that.

He was ushered into the chilly drawing room, and the four old friends settled down for a gossip.

'I'm sure I'm keeping you from your affairs,' protested Justin.

'Not at all. Luncheon is cold today,' said Ada.

'Corned beef and a hard-boiled egg,' added Bertha.

'And some very good lettuce,' finished Violet.

'It sounds delicious,' lied Justin bravely.

'And do you ever patronise The Fuchsia Bush? It's so handy, and I hear the new cook is a great asset,' asked Ada.

Amazingly, Justin had not heard about Nelly Piggott's new post, and the ladies were happy to enlighten him.

'We found her a little *extravagant* when she cooked once or twice for us,' commented Bertha. 'Inclined to put *butter* in the mashed potato, and once went so far as to beat in *an egg* as well! Of course, we soon put a stop to that!'

'Naturally,' said Justin solemnly.

'But I must say she has got an excellent reputation with Mrs Peters. Of course, with a *business* one can afford to be rather more lavish than in a private establishment.'

Bertha then told him about Isobel and Agnes's proposed holiday, Ella Bembridge's nasty cold, Percy Hodge's truanting wife and Kit Armitage's fruitless house-hunting.

'Something will turn up, I'm sure,' said Justin. 'I wish he would get married again. I must admit that I had hopes of his recent meeting with Diana Oliver, but there you are. One can never plan for others.'

To his surprise Miss Violet had turned very pink, and her sisters were exchanging meaning glances.

'Well, I must get on,' he said rising. 'The rain seems to have eased a little. It was so kind of you to take pity on me.'

The three ladies helped him on with his coat, and lent him an umbrella. The battered hat was rammed into his pocket.

'That, I fear, is done for,' he said ruefully.

'When it is dry, Justin, do please put it aside for our next Jumble Sale,' begged Ada.

'I won't forget,' promised Justin, and went off with plenty of thoughts in his bare head.

16 House-Hunting

ELLA BEMBRIDGE's cold persisted. She was as slack as Dotty Harmer in looking after herself, and Dimity was much alarmed.

'I'm sound as a bell,' Ella said, her gruff voice belying the statement. 'Just a bit thick in the clear. Nothing to worry about.'

'Well, I hope you are not going out in this rough weather. You know I can do any shopping that's needed.'

'There's just one thing,' said Ella, blowing her nose with the sound of the last trump. 'I promised to take my weaving and canework over to John's gallery for the exhibition. It's all ready in a couple of boxes. Do you think Charles would mind taking it over?'

'Of course not. Let me have it now.'

'Too much for you, Dim. Tell you what, ask Charles if he'd pick it up next time he's by. The stuff's supposed to be over there next week, but I don't suppose it matters if it's a day or so late. That young John Fairbrother, who's taken over, is such a worry-pants he always wants everything far too early to my mind.'

Dimity secretly had every sympathy with the nervous young gallery-owner who had to deal with a number of dilatory artists and craftsmen like Ella.

'Don't worry. We'll take it willingly. I always enjoy browsing round his things. I might even find a few Christmas presents.'

'Good grief, Dim! Don't start thinking of that yet. We're hardly into autumn.'

'It tends to sneak up,' Dimity pointed out, as she made her farewells.

The rain had ceased when Charles and Dimity set out in the car to collect Ella's handiwork.

Lulling High Street was busy, and Dimity waved to a dozen or more friends. By The Fuchsia Bush she noticed Janet Thurgood, an unattractive figure in a long bedraggled skirt and a number of shabby garments overlapping each other on her upper half. She wore a rather grubby scarf tied round her hair, and a pair of broken-down sandals on her bare feet. Altogether she looked the Complete Artist. Dimity did not wave to her, but snorted her disgust.

'Sorry?' queried Charles.

'Just saw that dreadful Thurgood girl. She could do with a bath.'

'I'm rather sorry for her,' said Charles, stopping suddenly to allow a dignified Labrador to cross the road. 'With that *mother*, I mean, and no job to do, or so I hear. Life must be rather wretched for her.'

'Well, they both make life wretched enough for other people,' replied Dimity trenchantly, 'and so they must expect a taste of their own medicine now and again.'

Charles said nothing, and Dimity knew that he was sad to hear her make such a remark. What a difficult thing it was to live with a saint! In many ways, life with Ella had been much simpler.

The boxes were packed into the back seat and off they went. The gallery was some five or six miles south of Lulling in a converted barn. A small cottage adjoining it was the home of John Fairbrother, a clever but timid young man, who worked extremely hard at running the gallery.

He was busy setting out pottery on some low shelves when they arrived, and was delighted to have Ella's work.

'I was beginning to wonder if I should ring her to remind her about it. It's so easy to put off a job, and I'm afraid several of the contributors had quite forgotten about the exhibition.'

He waved towards the pottery.

'Isn't this delightful? Three young men have just set up together and I think we shall get plenty of customers for their work.'

Dimity privately was doubtful. It was thick and of a dreary porridge colour. One of the tankards must have been uncomfortably heavy to lift when empty. When full of beer or cider it must have needed the strength of ten to lift it from the table, thought Dimity.

Charles had drifted to the wall and was surveying some pretty miniatures of wild flowers. He suddenly turned to the owner.

'Do you know Janet Thurgood?' he asked.

The effect of this question was remarkable. A look of awe transfixed the young man's face.

'You mean the abstract artist?'

'Well, yes. I suppose she is best known for that sort of work. Does she ever exhibit here?'

'No, I'm afraid not. And I should never dare to ask her. She would ask far more than my clients could afford. She is very well thought of in artistic circles.'

'You don't want any help in arranging the exhibition, I suppose, or manning it while it's in progress? I happen to know she is free at the moment. I just wondered if you would like me to speak to her.'

The young man turned quite pale at the thought.

'I certainly do want someone, and there's a notice on the door advertising for temporary help, but I doubt if such an eminent artist as Janet Thurgood would even consider such a post. The pay is very small for one thing.'

'Would you like me to approach her? I've a feeling she would love to help, if you are willing.'

'I'd be more than grateful. In fact, I'd be downright honoured,' admitted young Mr Fairbrother, and there the matter was left.

Dimity managed to escape from the pottery, but salved her conscience by buying some tiny straw figures which would look attractive on the Christmas tree when the time came.

'Are you really going to bother with that wretched girl?' she asked as they drove home to get Polly's tea-time biscuits and Tabitha's saucer of milk.

'I am,' said Charles firmly. 'You call her a wretched girl, Dimity, and I fear, from the glimpse I had of her this afternoon, that is exactly what she is. Simply wretched!'

It so happened, that while Charles and Dimity had been engaged in the gallery, Kit Armitage and Connie had been less than a mile away looking at one of the houses on Kit's list.

It had been built in the thirties, so that the garden was mature if rather small. It had three bedrooms looking out to the rolling countryside, and faced south.

Connie liked it. Her only private sorrow was that it was some way from Thrush Green, and it meant that she would see less of Kit. She admitted to herself how fond she was of him, and the pangs of jealousy she felt when considering the distant Diana Oliver were so completely foreign to her nature that she was obliged to face the fact that she was fast falling in love with the man. It was all delightful, but rather disconcerting, she found, for a sensible woman in her forties.

'Not much ground,' was Kit's comment. 'What do you think?'

'Do you need a lot? The garden's very pretty, and private too. I should have thought it would be big enough to keep you busy.'

'But not big enough for animals,' objected Kit.

This was a new idea altogether, and Connie felt puzzled.

'I didn't know you proposed to keep any animals,' she replied.

'Oh, just a few hens and things,' he said vaguely, and went to investigate a small greenhouse built at the side of the house.

They toured the rooms again. It seemed an ideal house for a bachelor, to Connie's mind, compact, light and easy to run. One of the bedrooms was small, but Connie was old-fashioned enough to think that every house should have a boxroom, and this would make a splendid place for all those things like trunks, odd chairs, fire screens, boxes of spare curtains and such like which need a space to jostle in.

This would leave a large bedroom for Kit and an equally large one for his spare room. However, it was apparent that he had taken a dislike to the place, for some reason best known to himself, so Connie kept her thoughts to herself.

'Well, shall we push off? Let's have tea at The Fuchsia Bush. You aren't in a desperate hurry to get back?'

'No. I'd love that. Aunt Dotty's not expecting me till six, and Albert is milking Dulcie, so she'll have company too. The Fuchsia Bush has some splendid scones these days, thanks to our Nelly. I'm glad she came back to Thrush Green.'

'Sensible woman,' commented Kit. 'Can't beat Thrush Green. This place is too far from it for my liking.'

His spirits seemed to have recovered, and they drove back to Lulling gossiping cheerfully. Tea was as delicious as ever under Mrs Peters' indulgent eye, and the two returned to Dotty's in great heart.

'No luck?' queried Dotty.

'Too far away,' said Kit.

'Well, you both look all the better for your outing,' said Dotty, 'and I've had a most interesting talk with Albert. Do you know his mother gave him a fried mouse to eat when he had whooping cough as a child? And he used to clean his teeth with sage leaves.'

'No wonder they've dropped out,' was Kit's comment.

Tom Hardy made good progress in Lulling Cottage Hospital, and was always eager to hear about Polly when Charles visited him.

'I've got another favour to ask of you, sir,' he said one afternoon. 'It seems I can go out from here if there's someone to look after me.'

Charles began to rack his brain for some willing neighbour who was free to oblige. The sad thing was that it seemed that everyone was out at work. Where had all those nice single aunts gone? They had been the mainstay of family crises in the rector's own childhood.

'Well, I can't go home, that's flat,' continued the patient. 'But they can fix me up at a convalescent home down Cheltenham way till I'm up and about again. The thing is, of course, old Poll.'

'You needn't worry on her account,' the rector assured him. 'We both love her, and she is the best-behaved dog I've ever come across. We'll keep her with us until you are well enough to have her.'

The old man gave a gusty sigh of relief.

'That's a weight off my mind. I tell 'em here I'll be doing for myself again in a week or two's time.'

But as the good rector returned home, he began to wonder if old Tom would ever be able to look after himself again.

And then the thought of Edward's old people's homes came to him, and he decided to see what could be done about one for his old friend, if the need arose. The biggest snag, of course, would be Tom himself. He loved his simple quiet home, with only the joyous sound of the river splashing alongside for company. How would he feel about neighbours living so close to him, and the sound of traffic nearby? There was no doubt about it, one's home meant so much. He recalled talking to Isobel Shoosmith when she had been house-hunting, and more recently he recalled Kit Armitage's comments.

They had all agreed that each house had an aura about it, and one which was quickly recognized.

'Some really welcomed you,' Isobel had said. 'You felt that the people who had lived there before had loved the place and been happy there. I felt it at once in our present home.'

'I felt it too at Lulling Vicarage,' agreed the rector, 'although I believe there have been some pretty rum incumbents over the centuries.'

'I definitely loathed one cottage I looked at beyond Nidden,' chimed in Kit. 'Couldn't think why. Roses round the door, south facing, sheltered by a little hill, it seemed perfect, but there was something sinister about it. I'm the last chap to claim to be psychic, but I wasn't a bit surprised to hear from Mrs Jenner that a couple lived there at the turn of the century who neglected their six children so appallingly that two of them died. It was a pitiful tale. The squalor alone was enough to curdle you, let alone the cruelty. There's a lot that goes on in the country that is hidden by pretty thatch and leaded windows.'

'I'm afraid you are right,' agreed the rector.

In the evening of the day they visited the gallery Charles rang Mrs Thurgood's number. He had not been in touch with that formidable woman since the disastrous meeting in the church which had led to her departure from his congregation.

A lesser man might have shirked the job, and been content to write a note to Miss Thurgood herself. But Charles had never lacked courage in a tight place, and he was confident that it would be better to explain matters over the telephone to Janet and to be prepared to answer any questions.

Luckily, it was she who answered the call. On hearing who it was on the other end of the wire her voice became somewhat cool, but Charles was not deterred.

He explained about their visit, the advertisement on the door, and the real need of the young gallery-owner to have help.

She listened attentively and sounded thoughtful when she spoke.

'I should like to help him. Should I write, do you think?'

She sounded more friendly after hearing the news, and Charles was relieved.

'I must stress that John was most reluctant to worry you. He has a great regard for your work, and thought you might be too busy with your own painting to bother with other people's efforts. He is refreshingly modest, I may say, and did remark about it being an honour if you felt you could help at the exhibition.'

'Really? How very kind!' exclaimed Janet, sounding quite enthusiastic. 'I think I will ring him now and find out more about it.'

'An excellent idea,' agreed Charles. 'And I hope you don't think me impertinent for mentioning your name to him.'

'Far from it. It was excessively kind of you. Especially in the – er – circumstances.'

'Not at all.'

'Well, a thousand thanks, anyway. I'm really rather at a loose end, and it will be lovely to have something useful to do. I'll let you know what happens.'

'Thank you,' said Charles. 'I should be interested.'

He rang off, and bent to stroke Polly.

'And how is the wretched girl,' asked Dimity, with a smile.

'Not quite so wretched,' Charles told her.

The days of early autumn were warm and cloudless. The tractors were busy in the fields turning over the golden stubble in long chocolate-coloured furrows.

The sun was still pleasantly warm. The plums and apples were ripening, and prudent housewives were busy storing the last of the runner beans and late peas in readiness for the winter.

Agnes Fogerty, greatly rejuvenated by her few days at Torquay, was now back in the classroom, and Mrs Trent reverted to her half-day's remedial work with backward, or possibly less-able, children.

Edward Young was now at the interesting stage of deciding on the best colours for interior and exterior decoration of his masterpiece. There was still plenty to be done for, as is usual during building operations, it seemed that one operator was always waiting for another to do something before the former could begin. The plasterer waited for the plumber. The plumber waited for the electrician. The electrician waited for the electricity board to supply the correct poles and wires, and so the merry-go-round went on.

'Some time,' cried Edward to Harold Shoosmith, 'I suppose it will get done. In the meantime, I'm trying to visualize what yellow walls would look like in the kitchens.'

'Depends on your mood,' observed Harold. 'They might make you feel sunny or bilious. I suppose the homes have all been allotted by now?'

'I wouldn't know, but I think it's likely. The council copes with that, and I don't envy it the job. I've heard they could be filled five times over.'

'You'll be getting on with the next few then, I take it?'

'Oh well,' said Edward cheerfully, 'these will change hands quite quickly, what with the "natural wastage" as it's so prettily expressed.'

'Deaths, do you mean?'

'That's right. Let's face it, Harold, most of them are on their last legs when they get one of these. However, it's jolly good luck for those on the waiting list, isn't it?'

He smiled brightly at his friend and mounted a ladder nimbly to inspect some guttering.

'It's strange, isn't it,' said Harold to Isobel later, 'how differently people look at life? Or death, for that matter.'

That afternoon Dimity was sitting in her drawing room mending her own and Charles's underclothes.

It was a job which she did not enjoy, and one which she had put off for so long that the pile beside her on the sofa was now formidable.

Polly lay beside her on the floor, thumping her fringed tail whenever Dimity spoke to her. Dimity often wondered what thoughts lay behind those odd eyes and the satiny head. Did she think of Tom? Did she secretly pine for him? Or was she as contented as she seemed to be, staying at the vicarage?

Dimity was a great animal lover, and secretly thought the idea, held by some people, that animals' spirits did not survive death, was desperately wrong. If goodness were anything to go by, there were a dozen or more cats and dogs known to her who had far more noble qualities than their owners. She dare not tell Charles of her beliefs, although she suspected that he felt as she did.

She put down the petticoat she was mending and gazed about her. Everything came to its end at a different age. Look at that lampshade, for instance, made by dear Ella for her last birthday, and already unravelling at the seams. And yet the chest it stood on had been her grandmother's, and had been made between 1780 and 1800 according to an expert in such matters. That surely would survive for another hundred years or so.

Or take Polly. She stroked the smooth head, and the dog thumped her tail with pleasure. Her end must come within the next two or three years. The roses on the table would be over in two or three days. It was an interesting thought.

At that moment, the telephone rang and Dimity put aside the petticoat.

A girl's voice spoke.

'Is your husband at hand, Mrs Henstock? It's Janet here.'

'Janet?' queried Dimity. She found it difficult to recognize voices on the telephone, and she knew three Janets.

'Janet Thurgood,' said the girl.

'No, I'm afraid he's visiting,' said Dimity, trying to disguise the coldness in her tone. 'Can I take a message for him? He will be back for tea.'

'It's just that I have started work at the gallery, and simply love it. John Fairbrother is such a dear, and I haven't been so happy for months. And it's all thanks to your kind husband. Please tell him.'

Dimity thawed at once. Praise of Charles was the surest way to her heart.

'He'll be delighted to hear it,' she said warmly. 'And so am I.'

17   Future Plans

IT WAS by means of the competent bush telegraph of Thrush Green and Lulling that Nelly Piggott first heard of the probable return of Mrs Jefferson to her kitchen duties at The Fuchsia Bush.

Albert had heard the news in The Two Pheasants. His informant was his young assistant Cooke, and he had heard it from Betty Bell who had heard it from the postman, Willie Bond, who was her cousin. Regretfully, no one seemed to know who had told Willie.

How much the tale had been embellished or confirmed in its roundabout journey, Nelly could not say, but she did know that quite often a rumour ran about several weeks before the fact emerged. She was very upset, but did her best to disguise it.

'I'd have thought Mrs Peters would have said something if that's true,' she told Albert. 'Always been straight with me. I bet this is some barmy idea one of your friends next door has thought up when he was half-seas-over.'

'Well, you wait and see,' replied Albert, nettled at the response to his bit of news.

She did not have to wait long. Mrs Peters met her in the kitchen of The Fuchsia Bush a few days later. It was the first thing in the morning, and they were alone.

The owner came to the point at once. She had been giving a good deal of thought to this tricky problem, but was determined to try to keep Nelly if she could. The sales of home-made cakes, at which Nelly excelled, had risen sharply since her arrival in the kitchen.

'If you would be willing to take sole charge of the cake side,' said Mrs Peters, 'I'm sure Mrs Jefferson will be able to cope with the rest. She will be coming in at ten o'clock for a little while, just to see how things go. That would help over the lunch time, and once that was cleared away she would go home. The new kitchen maids seem capable girls.'

Nelly agreed to all these plans with fervour. It meant that she would have the kitchen to herself for the first hour or so of the day, and this she relished. It also seemed that she could fit the afternoon hours to please herself.

'Take two afternoons off,' said her employer. 'We may be able to work out something half-time for you and for Mrs Jefferson, but we'll have to see how things go for the time being.'

When Nelly told Albert about these temporary arrangements he was somewhat smug.

'What'd I tell you? Now the old girl's back, same as we was told. Two afternoons off a week's not bad going either. You thinking of taking another little job?'

'No, I'm not,' responded Nelly flatly. 'I might spend one evening at Bingo. Must have a bit of fun now and again, and Mrs Jenner mentioned it to me the other day. She goes regular. Sees a bit of life there, she says.'

Which made it plain that Nelly was beginning to find her usual form.

'Well, I only hopes you keep the housekeeping money separate from your own bit,' replied Albert, damping down any unnecessary revival of spirits.

It was about this time that Charles Henstock heard that Tom Hardy was back at home and asking to see him. He was quite fit enough to manage to cope with Polly, was the message, and would take it kindly if the reverend could bring her home one day.

Dimity said farewell to her charge with real regret. She patted the docile old lady as she sat meekly on the back seat of the car.

'Take these too, dear,' said Dimity handing over a basket. 'They will save Tom bothering with catering for a day or two.'

Charles drove circumspectly towards the river. The willow trees were pale gold in the autumn sunshine. Soon they would be stripped bare by the first winds of winter. Already there were drifts of crisp leaves beneath the beech and horse chestnut trees, and chrysanthemums and dahlias outnumbered the roses in Lulling's front gardens.

There was already a chill in the air at dawn and dusk. Dimity had lit the fire in the drawing room on several recent evenings. Far too soon the curtains would be drawn at tea time, and the long dark nights would be upon them.

Not that Charles was wholly sad at the prospect. There was something remarkably satisfying about the domestic side of winter. He enjoyed splitting the logs that Tom had supplied earlier in the year, before his illness had struck him down. He liked piling them in the hearth, ready for the evening's comfort. He relished the long hours of reading or listening to his beloved Mozart on their ancient record player.

Secretly too, he was relieved to see the garden at rest for a few months. He knew quite well that such a vast expanse would benefit from the attention of a full-time gardener, if not two, but Charles's salary would not rise to it. He was lucky to have Caleb's help and advice, but it was evident that the garden was not kept in the pristine state it had been during Anthony Bull's incumbency.

In the winter, with the curtains safely drawn across, the garden was hidden from Charles's eyes, and his self-reproach was lessened.

But although he relished the snugness of his new house and rejoiced to see Dimity so happy in it, the winter brought hardship outside. Despite the blessings of a welfare state, which Charles was the first to acknowledge, there were still families among his parishioners who were short of the basic needs of shelter, food and fuel. There were animals too who suffered, and this grieved the good rector sorely.

The wild birds who flocked around his bird table, the stray cat who came nightly from a neighbouring barn, were given his bounty and his blessing. But there were one or two dogs, chained to kennels, and a few poor farms where the sheep and cattle never seemed adequately fed and housed which touched Charles's tender heart. He spoke his mind to the owners of these unhappy creatures, for when his duty was clear Charles shirked nothing. Sometimes matters improved, sometimes not, and for all his flock, both human and animal, Charles knew that winter could be a cruel season.

As he approached Tom's cottage, basking in the thin sunshine, Polly began to show signs of excitement. She stood up on the seat, her nose pressed to the side window, and began to make curious little growling sounds which were new to Charles.

'Nearly home, Poll,' he told her. 'Soon see your master. Soon see old Tom, Poll.'

He drew into the grass verge, and fastened Polly's lead. The dog was now quivering with excitement and leapt from the car with more energy than Charles had ever seen.

She tugged so strongly that the rector was almost pulled off his feet. She began to bark, high frantic yelps of rapture, and at that moment the door opened and Tom stood there his arms wide in welcome.

Charles let go of the lead, and Polly raced across the gap between them, still yelping hysterically.

'Poll! Poll!' called Tom.

The old dog leapt upon him, almost knocking him down. Tom stooped to caress her, and she licked his face with her large pink tongue, making ecstatic little cries, and dancing on her back legs. Charles was much moved by this reunion.

'Well, Tom old boy, she knows who is her true master, doesn't she?'

'Ah! I knew she wouldn't forget. How's she behaved? Any trouble?'

'None at all,' Charles assured him, 'and we're both sorry to lose her.'

He paused on the threshold. The cottage was as spruce as ever, and Tom seemed quite strong, if somewhat thinner.

'I forgot the basket,' confessed Charles. 'You go in out of the wind, while I fetch it.'

By the time he returned, the old man was sitting in his wooden armchair with his feet propped up on a stool. Polly lay across his lap, almost covering him, with her head resting on his shoulder.

'You'll have to stay there for the rest of the day,' said Charles. 'It's quite apparent she's not going to let you get away again.'

'And I'm not going, sir, that's a fact. I'm managing well, and my good neighbour keeps things up together for me, and does a bit of shopping. I'll be all right now.'

Charles wondered if he should broach the subject of one of the new homes on Thrush Green, but felt that the matter

could wait. He turned his attention to unpacking the basket instead.

Dimity had sent a home-made cake, some eggs and rashers and some kedgeree in a screw-top jar. There was also a packet of dog biscuits and the bone which Charles recognised as the residue from yesterday's leg of lamb.

'It seems you've both been provided for,' he said, setting out the provender. 'Now what can I do for you while I'm here? Do you want coal brought in, or anything fetched?'

'No indeed, sir. But if you like to put on the kettle, I'd be pleased to make you a cup of tea when I can get out from under this great silly of a dog.'

And the rector gladly obeyed.

The equinoctial gales came with unusual force, and the leaves came tumbling down. Housewives began looking out extra blankets and warmer underclothes, and those who had forgotten to order coal and logs during the summer, made hasty arrangements for quick deliveries.

'I don't like to see it getting parky so early,' observed Mr Jones of The Two Pheasants. 'Makes you think of frosts, and my hanging baskets are still ablaze with colour. I don't relish bringing them in so soon.'

Next door at the school house Miss Watson and her assistant also deplored the sudden cold weather.

'We shall have to get the stove going if the weather stays like this,' said Dorothy. 'I must mention it to Betty.'

'But what about the office? You know they really frown upon the stoves being lit too early.'

'The office can lump it,' said Dorothy tartly. 'Good heavens, it's October this week, and I'm not having the children suffering. Nor you, Agnes, for that matter. You must be kept warm. We don't want you laid up again.'

'Oh, I shall be all right. My arthritis is really so much better since I've been doing my exercises.'

'Since you've been eating properly,' her friend corrected her. 'Which reminds me. I must leave those beef bones to simmer for stock before we go across to school. This weather makes one think of soup.'

Some half mile away, at Dotty Harmer's, Connie too was dealing with stock and was busy dicing vegetables to put in with a chicken carcase in Dotty's largest saucepan.

Kit had asked her to go with him to see yet another house, this time quite close at Nidden. He had arranged to pick her up at half past two. Dotty had declined the invitation, and said she preferred to take a nap but would see them at tea time.

As Connie chopped carrots and onions her spirits were high. She cherished this friendship with Kit, and knew it was something more than that on her part. As for Kit, who could say? He was cheerful, kindly, attentive and perceptive. She suspected, and hoped, that he too felt as she did.

Farther than that she would not go in her thoughts, as things were at present.

One thing bothered her considerably. Why were the houses that he went to see so much too large for a bachelor? And why did he consider that so much garden was essential? Even if he proposed to marry again – and here Connie resolutely put aside the memory of the delectable Diana – there would be no children presumably. And he was not an avid gardener, nor a man who would consider keeping animals. Connie did not like to broach the subject, but it did perplex her.

Squalls of rain were veiling Lulling Woods when Kit arrived, and Dotty, snuggled under the eiderdown, was glad that she was not facing the elements.

'Something smells good,' commented Kit.

'Only stock,' Connie told him. 'I often think it smells better than a whole dinner cooking.'

'Mrs Jenner cooks a great saucepan of odds and ends for her chickens,' Kit remarked. 'The most delicious scent floats up to my flat. Makes me quite hungry. She mixes in some sort of stuff called "Karswood". I tell her she ought to dish it up for us, it must be good enough.'

He held her mackintosh while she put it on, and they set out to the car through the blustery weather.

Mr Jones's hanging baskets were swinging in the wind outside the pub. A window was banging at Albert Piggott's, and the playground of Thrush Green school was awash with puddles.

'What a beast of a day! I was hoping to show you this latest house in brilliant sunshine.'

'Is it a large house?'

'Four bedrooms. Two bathrooms, and just over an acre of ground. The paddock next to it is up for sale too.'

Connie could keep silence no longer.

'Do you really need anything so big?'

There was silence for a few moments, and Connie wondered if he were offended. His face was serious.

'No,' he said. 'I don't need anything as big. Not for myself.'

A most unwelcome vision of Diana Oliver floated momentarily before Connie's inward eye, blotting out the flicking windscreen wipers and the view beyond.

The road widened here, and a fine beech tree towered on the left hand side. Russet leaves eddied beneath it in the whirling rain.

Kit drew up beneath it and turned to face Connie.

'I should have said all this long before. I wanted you to see the houses because I hoped – I dared to hope, let's say – that I might persuade you to live there with me. And Dotty too, of course.'

'Oh Kit!' said Connie, with a most unromantic hiccup. 'But what about Diana?'

'What Diana?' replied Kit, too much taken aback to bother about correct grammar.

'Diana Oliver,' said Connie, now hiccuping with unbecoming regularity.

'Good God!' cried Kit. 'She doesn't come into it! Anyway, she got married a month ago. I forgot to tell you.'

'I'm glad to hear it,' said Connie. She took a deep breath in order to quell the hiccups.

'Well, my dear, I am trying to ask you if you would think of marrying me. You must have known. I've been trying to say it for weeks!'

Connie looked at him, scarlet in the face from holding her breath. She let it go with a crescendo of hiccups.

'Think of it?' echoed Connie. 'I've thought of nothing else ever since we met.'

A hiccup interrupted her.

'Is that hopelessly unmaidenly? And don't worry about these damned hiccups. I always get them when I'm suddenly happy.'

Kit put his arms around her.

'There's nothing I like more than a hopelessly unmaidenly woman. And what you need is a lump of sugar. I shall carry some in my pocket for the rest of my days.'

Mrs Cooke, pedalling against the wind on her bicycle, was intensely interested in the sight of Mrs Jenner's respectable lodger locked in a close embrace with Dotty Harmer's niece.

'Fine goings-on,' she muttered to herself, as she struggled past the car. 'And both old enough to know better.'

She felt obliged to express her displeasure at the scene when she met Betty Bell on her way to her duties at the school. It was hardly surprising that the famous bush telegraph was humming before many hours had passed.

Bemused, the two elderly lovers drove to the house and followed its owner from one room to the next with unseeing eyes. They nodded vaguely at the conservatory ('very large'), the larder ('north-facing – always cool'), the four bedrooms ('all doubles, if the bed isn't too big') and the monkey-puzzle tree in the garden ('such a feature of the place').

The seller was surprised at their lack of interest, and even more surprised to see them holding hands.

'I take it you are married,' she said at last.

'Not yet,' replied Kit, with such a doting look at his

companion, who occasionally emitted a hiccup, that their guide was quite scandalised.

They promised to let her know their decision in a day or two. She showed them to the front door with alacrity, and watched them battle through the rain to their car.

'Well!' she exclaimed as she shut the door. 'They talk about the young ones' behaviour! But what about that?'

Before they reached home, Connie bade Kit stop the car. Reason was beginning to return and almost succeeding in routing the bliss in which she was engulfed.

'We must talk before we go back to Aunt Dotty. You see, it's really out of the question for me to leave her.'

'I know that. That's why I've wanted plenty of ground for the animals, and a big enough place for her to have a room or two of her own.'

'Yes, I see it all now, and love you even more because of it. But still, it would never do, Kit.'

'Why on earth not?'

'I can't ask her to leave her own house. It would be like prising a snail's shell from its back. She's lived there for years now. She couldn't bear to be uprooted.'

Kit gazed at his affianced's troubled face. At least the return of reason, however damping, had stopped the hiccups. He thought she looked prettier than ever.

'Well, don't worry about that now. Let's ask her before you upset yourself. She may jump at the chance to move. You never know.'

'I don't think she will. You see, she's so old and quite groggy. I simply must stay with her. I'd marry you tomorrow, but do you really want to have us *both* on your hands?'

'Try me and see,' said Kit.

★

Betty Bell, vigorously scouring the school wash basins, turned over Mrs Cooke's disclosure with much pleasure.

It certainly would be nice for Miss Connie to be married, and that Mr Armitage seemed a good sort of fellow. Bit long in the tooth, perhaps, and set in his ways, but *very clean*, and had been quite handsome years ago, so she'd heard. And come to think of it, he had plenty of money, and that was always half the battle in marriage. Mrs Jenner had said that he always paid in advance, and gave her extra for doing his smalls, though she'd never expected it. Yes, one way or another, Miss Connie should be all right.

She paused from her scouring to fish up some extraneous matter from the plug hole. It felt like bubble gum, and when she held it to the light she saw that that was exactly what it was. Children! A good thing Miss Connie was past having any, decided Betty, depositing the revolting pellet in her bucket.

At that moment, another thought struck her. What about Dotty? Surely Miss Connie wouldn't abandon her?

Perhaps they would all move to one of these places Mr Armitage had been viewing. But would Dotty go?

Just then Miss Watson appeared, and broached the subject of the stove. What did Betty think?

'You're right, miss. I'll put a match to it first thing tomorrow. This place is getting proper clammy.'

Miss Watson agreed.

Betty wrung out her cloth and spread it to dry on the edge of the sink.

'I've just heard a piece of good news,' said Betty. 'Seems as Romance has come to Miss Harmer and Mr Armitage.'

'Miss *Dotty* Harmer?' queried Dorothy, in stupefaction.

'No, no, no! *Young* Miss Harmer!'

'Well, how very nice! I'm delighted to hear of it. Who told you?'

'Mrs Cooke.'

Dorothy Watson's face dropped. Mrs Cooke had been a thorn in her side, both as mother of many of her pupils and one-time temporary – and most unsatisfactory – school cleaner.

'Oh indeed!' she said frostily. 'I should advise you, Betty, not to repeat the news to *anyone*. We both know how unreliable that lady can be. I shall keep the news to myself – much as I hope that it is true – until I have it confirmed.'

Betty Bell, bursting to confide in all and sundry, nevertheless saw the wisdom of Miss Watson's remarks, and sighed.

'I reckon you're right, miss. But isn't it *romantic* if it's true?'

And Dorothy Watson conceded graciously that it certainly was.

18 Charles Is Melancholy

WHEN KIT and Connie returned they found Dotty cutting bread and butter. The loaf was of her own making, slightly burnt on top, craggy, and remarkably resistant to the knife.

The slices, when Dotty had managed to hack them from their source, were of the doorstep variety. Kit wondered if he should ever be able to work his way through one.

'You must be starved,' said Dotty, busy with the butter. 'I thought we'd have some of my bramble jelly with this. Full of all the vitamins you need to face the winter.'

Connie made the tea, and it was not until they were settled by the fire that she felt she could tell Dotty their news. But Dotty got in first.

'I had the most peculiar dream,' said Dotty, trying to spread runny jelly. 'I thought I was swimming with dear Papa, and he somehow got out of his depth and was about to drown. And do you know, I was *hesitating*, about rescuing him!'

Very Freudian, was Kit's private thought. From all he remembered of Dotty's formidable parent, drowning seemed a relatively painless demise for one so sadistic.

'I can't remember now if I did or not,' went on Dotty, sucking a sticky finger, 'but the odd thing was the water was warm. How extraordinary things are. And how was the house?'

'Not very suitable,' said Kit, putting down his slice of

bread and determined not to pick it up again. 'As a matter of fact, we've wonderful news for you.'

'You've found a better place?'

'No, not that. But Connie has been persuaded to marry me.'

If the happy pair had been expecting any excitement from Dotty at this stupendous news, they were disappointed. Dotty replied in a very matter-of-fact tone of voice.

'Well, I'm so glad to hear it. You've both looked so sheep's-eyed for weeks, I wondered when it would happen. I'm never wrong over these things. I've seen it hundreds of times, you know, with Dulcie and Flossie, not to mention the poultry, though with all those feathers one doesn't get quite the same clarity of facial expression, if you follow me.'

'But you're pleased, Aunt Dotty?' said Connie, with some anxiety. It was not exactly flattering that she had looked like a love-sick female goat, dog, or hen, for some time, but knowing her aunt's little ways she could ignore any such pin pricks.

'Well, of course I'm pleased,' cried Dotty. 'And when's the marriage?'

'We haven't got that far,' said Kit. 'Being engaged is quite enough for today. Could I have some more tea? I find that all this excitement makes me terribly thirsty.'

'Very natural,' said Dotty approvingly.

'It's something to do with the hormones, I believe. I must look it up in my veterinary encyclopedia.'

Dotty poured his tea, and under cover of her preoccupation with the tea pot, Kit smuggled the revolting remains of his bread to the attentive Flossie, who took it, and with commendable intelligence, hid it under the sofa.

Local reaction to the news was predictable and congratulatory. Harold Shoosmith, who had also made a late marriage, was particularly delighted.

'I wonder you didn't tell us, Betty,' he said to her when she was trundling the vacuum cleaner along the hall. 'Miss Harmer rang herself to tell us, but I wouldn't mind betting you knew about it long ago.'

Betty Bell looked smug.

'To tell the truth I heard a couple of days ago, but as it was from that Mrs Cooke, I never said nothing to nobody. I'm not a one for idle gossip, as you know.'

Harold, if asked, would have said quite the opposite. Most of their local intelligence came from Betty. However, it was plain that she was enjoying the fruits of unaccustomed prudence on this occasion, and Harold was quick to commend her for her virtue.

'I wonder if Miss Connie will have a white wedding? Look lovely, wouldn't she? I mean, even if you are past your best there's something dignified about a long white frock.'

Most of the ladies at Thrush Green were also interested in Connie's wedding attire, but the general vote seemed to go to a suit or a frock and jacket.

'Much more sensible,' said Jenny to Winnie Bailey. 'Be able to wear it afterwards. After all, when can you get the wear out of a wedding dress? Most of 'em end up cut down for a christening robe, and I shouldn't think Miss Connie would need to do that.'

Winnie managed to evade comment, but was amused to find that Connie's age was a cause for discussion among her friends.

'Won't be bothered with the patter of tiny feet, anyway,' was Ella Bembridge's comment.

Phyllida Hurst confessed herself rather sad at the thought of no children.

'Although there was that woman in the Old Testament who had a child when she was about eighty. But of course, they reckoned their ages differently. In cubits or something,' she added vaguely.

Isobel Shoosmith, happily married for the second time, gave whole-hearted support to the proposed union and declared that age had nothing to do with the case, while at Lulling Charles and Dimity rejoiced, and Justin Venables in his office wrote a most beautiful epistle in his best copperplate, and sent Muriel out specially to catch the next post.

The three Misses Lovelock heard the news by telephone from Dotty herself. Miss Ada had answered the telephone in the hall, and Bertha and Violet hovered nearby anxious to be told the message.

'Good gracious!' said Ada. 'Well of course, I am delighted. So will my sisters be. We shall write at once. How nice of you to ring, Dotty. Do give Connie our love and congratulations.'

She replaced the receiver carefully.

'How is Dotty?' asked Bertha.

'Like a cat with two tails. Connie's engaged. You can guess who to.'

Violet was white, and seemed unable to speak.

'Kit?' queried Bertha.

'Yes, Kit Armitage. She's a lucky girl. I'm sure they will be admirably suited.'

'I think I will see if I have closed my bedroom window,' said Violet faintly, making for the stairs.

Bertha and Ada exchanged looks. Bertha began to follow Violet, but Ada shook her head violently.

Violet mounted alone.

Once in the sanctuary of her bedroom, she sank down upon the stool before the dressing table, and gazed at her reflection with unseeing eyes.

So that was that! It was only to be expected, of course, but it made the blow no less painful. She had always known that she could never hope to become Kit's wife, but she had enjoyed such pleasure in these last few months of dallying with the idea of love.

When she had caught a glimpse of Kit striding up the High Street, or he had waved to her from his car, her heart had quickened as if she were still a young girl. His many kindnesses had warmed her. She recalled the little compliments, the appreciation of her plum tart, his gratitude on being told about Mrs Bassett's house, and she felt both loved and loving. Now all the daydreams must end.

For they were only daydreams, she knew full well. It was not so much that she had lost Kit, for in her heart she knew she had never been able to call him her own. It was the inescapable fact that this was the end of all hope of love, and that she must resign herself to being one of the three old

Lovelock sisters until the day she died.

She became conscious of her reflection in the mirror. Her hair was still thick and wavy, but wholly silver in colour. Her neck was scrawny, her mouth had little lines radiating from it, and two tears shone on her papery cheeks. The hand she lifted to wipe them away, was bent and bony, old and claw-like. There she was, an ancient crone becoming more fragile and forgetful every year. This was the sad truth which she must face. Those last youthful flutterings were now stilled for ever, and had vanished with the once-golden hair, the round pink cheeks and the smiling red mouth.

She rose from the seat and went to look out of the window. The life of Lulling flowed by unheedingly. The dustman was humping a dustbin from The Fuchsia Bush. The greengrocer across the road was holding out a cauliflower for young Mrs Hurst's inspection. The black and white dog, who had so enjoyed the snow earlier in the year, was now sniffing along the railings by his house, and in the distance the church clock struck ten from St Mary's tower.

'Well,' said Violet, stuffing her damp handkerchief into her pocket, 'that's all behind me! Now to work!'

She made for the door, but stopped abruptly by a fine mahogany chest of drawers. On it stood a faded snapshot in a silver frame.

It showed half a dozen young people in the tennis clothes of the late twenties. Among them, taller and handsomer than any, smiled Kit.

Violet swallowed hard. She put the photograph into the top drawer and went resolutely downstairs to face her sisters.

'I think,' she said, to forestall any comments, 'that I have a cold coming.'

'You must take things gently then, my dear,' said Bertha kindly.

'Why not lie down for an hour or two?' suggested Ada. 'We can bring you up some soup at lunch time. It's no bother, Violet dear.'

'You don't want to start a cold so early. Time enough for that after Christmas. Would an aspirin help?' asked Bertha solicitously.

'The thing that would help most,' said Violet steadily, 'is to carry on as usual. It's my day to make the pudding, I believe. Would you both like trifle?'

'Delicious, Violet,' said Ada.

'Nothing better,' agreed Bertha.

Sisters, although often maddening, can be of great comfort at times, thought Violet, on her way to the kitchen.

The blustery weather continued, and it became much colder.

'Very unseasonable weather,' commented one of the customers in The Two Pheasants.

'Means a hard winter,' prophesied Percy Hodge morosely. His wife was still absent from home, and any hope of her returning grew dimmer as the weeks passed. Percy was much cast down.

'Well, that's healthier than weather that's too muggy,' Albert told him. 'Doctor Lovell told me once he'd sooner see some good sharp frosts than a mild winter. Unhealthy, see? Frost kills the germs. He told me that when I went about my last operation. Did I tell you, Perce?'

'Time and time again,' growled Percy, putting his beer mug on the counter. 'I know more about your inside than me own, and that's a fact.'

'All right, all right!' cried Albert. 'You wants to keep a

check on your temper. I don't wonder your Doris left home.'

There was a sudden silence. Percy stood up slowly and menacingly. Albert realized that he had gone too far.

'Sorry, Perce, sorry! Forget it.'

'I don't know as I want to,' said Percy dangerously.

Mr Jones bustled round from the other side of the bar.

'Now, now, gentlemen! We don't want no silly talk in here. You sit down again, Percy, and have the other half. It's on the house.'

'Oh, it is, is it?' said Albert nastily.

'And I hope you'll have a half pint too,' said Mr Jones, with hasty diplomacy. 'Come on, boys! Sit down again.'

The two men obeyed with some reluctance. The beer was put before them, and they acknowledged the gift with nods.

The mugs were half empty before Percy spoke, after wiping his frothy mouth with the back of his hand.

'She ain't ever coming back, you know,' he said at last to Albert. 'All that advice you give me about being dignified and that, and then she'd come back! Well, it don't work, Albert. I wrote to her a week ago, and I had a letter this morning. She's got a job at Marks and Sparks. Likes it too, and her sister's putting her up. I reckon I made a fool of meself there, Albert.'

The beer was beginning to make him maudlin.

Albert did his best to be a comforter.

'I reckon you're better off without her, Perce. She don't know when she's well off. A good chap like you – she must be off her rocker to throw you over. Forget her, is my advice.'

'It's all right for you,' grumbled the abandoned husband. 'You've got your Nelly back safe and sound.'

'Well, to tell the truth, that ain't all beer and skittles by a long chalk. She's taken up Bingo twice a week, and I gets cold supper them nights. And what she's spending I dursen't think.'

Percy nodded sadly.

'Women is nothing but trouble,' he sighed. 'Well, Albert, best get back to work, I suppose.'

He linked his arm in Albert's, and the two set off rather unsteadily to the door.

Mr Jones watched their departure with infinite relief.

On one of the cold windy evenings, Charles Henstock made his way from the vicarage to St John's church.

He had arranged to meet the organist there to decide on the music for a recital to raise money for the Church Fabric Fund. Raising money had never come easily to the good rector, and now that he had four churches under his care he found the upkeep of them a formidable problem.

The loss of the fund's box had been a setback, although Charles realized, since he had made a point of emptying the new one daily, that contributions were very small indeed.

He did not blame people. He knew only too keenly how short of money so many families were these days. He too denied himself in many things, and was glad to do so, embarrassed at times by the multitude of expensive gimmicks he found in the homes of some of his parishioners.

He was beginning to realize too that Anthony Bull and his wealthy and generous wife gave readily to St John's, something which he could not do in his more humble circumstances.

The rector pondered on these things as he sat in his accustomed place in the chancel, awaiting the arrival of Bill Mitchell.

The church was cavernous and dark. Only the chancel

light was on. It was also bone-chillingly cold, and Charles wished that he had put on a thicker coat.

It had been a sad day. The post had brought a letter from a friend of his schooldays to tell him of the death from leukemia of their only son. Charles had been the boy's godfather.

The sense of shock had remained with him throughout the day. The death of one's parents' generation one could accept, albeit with sadness.

When the time of life came, as it had to Charles, that his own contemporaries were common in the obituary columns, it was always a severe shock. But when, as today, one heard of the young, the children, the rising generation going untimely to the grave, it was enough to break one's heart.

He had gone about his duties all day with a shattering sense of loss. He normally enjoyed robust health. Today he suddenly realized how fragile and empty he felt, as vulnerable as a wounded bird, or a broken sapling. How rapidly, it seemed, one could change from a strong being to an invalid. It was a sharp lesson on the frailty of life.

The weather had done nothing to raise his spirits. Mist had risen from the river and engulfed the little town. People moved like ghosts, emerging from greyness to vanish again within yards. No wonder the Americans called this the fall of the year, ruminated Charles, sitting in his chilly church. It was not just the falling of the leaves, it was the decline of abounding life everywhere, the quiet slide from summer's joy towards winter's death.

He stirred himself and peered at his wrist watch. What could have happened to the organist? Bill Mitchell was always so punctual, and now he was ten minutes overdue.

He traversed the long aisle, and opened the south door.

Dead leaves had gathered in the porch, and rustled as he walked through them. He made his way to the wrought iron gate. The bulk of his own vicarage loomed dimly through the mist.

Nearer at hand, beyond the graves, were six ancient almshouses. The lights shone mutedly in the mist. Waiting by the gate, his hand on the clammy metal, Charles saw one of the doors open. The clinking of bottles made him aware of the milk bottles being put out on the stone doorstep, ready for the morning.

The radio was on quite loudly, and a violin sobbed across the gloom. It had a haunting sound, 'a dying fall', which affected Charles with unaccustomed melancholy. He was glad when the door slammed, and he heard it no more.

The trees dripped dismally. There were puddles in the path. Really, thought Charles, all the approaches to the church needed fresh gravel. There was so much to do, and at times he felt that it was all beyond him. He mourned his loss of physical strength, his lost youth and vigour, his lost companions. Perhaps the succession of pinpricks, the criticisms, the petty comparisons with Anthony's ministrations, the departure of people like Mrs Thurgood from his flock, had contributed to his present low spirits. But the overwhelming feeling was this poignant one of loss.

Even dear old Polly had now gone, he remembered with a pang. And his old rectory was no more. He had been happy there, and had grieved far more keenly than his wife and friends over the charred remains. There were still precious objects which he missed. His old crucifix was one, a Bible given to him at his confirmation, a letter-opener he had made as a child, and innumerable dearly-loved books which could never be replaced.

Charles sighed. He was about to retrace his steps when a

car skidded to a halt in the road, a door slammed, and Bill
Mitchell ran towards him.

'I'm so *very* sorry,' he cried. 'Some poor chap had crashed
his lorry and blocked the road. It was full of bottles of
tomato ketchup, so the place looked like a battle field,
besides bristling with glass.'

'No one hurt, I hope?'

'Only Constable Darwin who slipped up in the mess and
sat down. But he's quite all right. Directed us all round the
houses, which is why I'm so late.'

They entered by the south door, which the rector locked
behind him. In the light of the chancel Bill Mitchell looked
at the rector.

'Are you all right? You look as though you might have a
chill.'

'No, no,' protested Charles, touched by this solicitude. 'I
find this weather a little depressing, but that's all.'

'Good! Well, let's get down to the music. That will cheer
us up. Music always does.'

'You are quite right, Bill,' agreed Charles, rubbing his
cold hands briskly. 'Music always does!'

19 Marriage Plans

THE ENGAGEMENT of Kit and Connie afforded general satisfaction to their friends in Lulling and Thrush Green, but after the congratulations came two questions.

The first was: 'Where would they live?' The second was: 'Would Dotty live with them?'

Connie had been the first to pose them, and it was she who insisted that she would broach the subject with Dotty when they were alone.

'It's the best way,' she told Kit. 'If she's willing to move and come with us to a new place, then that settles it. But, if she won't, and I think that's more likely, we shall just have to think again.'

Kit agreed, and Connie awaited a suitable opportunity. It did not arise until two or three days after the engagement.

The two women were sitting by the fire, Dotty engrossed in brushing Flossie, and Connie trying to do the crossword. Kit was calling at half past three, and Connie decided that this was the moment to grasp the nettle.

'Where would I live?' queried Dotty, pausing momentarily from her work. 'The point is where are you deciding to live?'

'As you know, Aunt Dotty, Kit hasn't found anything yet. We must know if you would be willing to make a new home with us. One thing's certain. I shan't leave you, and Kit knows it, and approves.'

'That dratted dog!' exclaimed Dotty, as Flossie made her escape and went to ground under the sofa.

'Well, dear,' continued Dotty, putting down the brush. 'I've been giving a lot of thought to this matter ever since Kit appeared on the scene, and it was as plain as a pike staff to me that he had his eye on you.'

'You make me sound like a bargain!' protested Connie.

'And so you are. Now, I can't think why you keep fussing about looking at houses when you know this one is yours. I know it's not all that commodious, but you could always build on. Edward Young could probably run you up a nice little annexe. He's quite intelligent, and those homes of his are really very pleasant for people who don't want to go upstairs to bed.'

'But its *your* house, not mine!'

'It's left to you, as you know, and I shall be in Thrush Green churchyard before long,' said Dotty cheerfully. 'And I only hope that Albert Piggott will have gone too by then. Such a muddler at his work. I still think they would have been better advised to let my goats crop the grass there. The mowing is deplorable.'

Connie sat pondering on this development. Dotty was quite right. There was plenty of space round the cottage on which to build. It would solve the problem too of Dotty's future.

The only thing was how would Kit feel about settling at such close quarters with this dear, but slightly mad, relative?

As if reading her thoughts, Dotty rambled on.

'You see, there are *three* bedrooms after all, which would make one apiece. Though, of course, when you are married it would be quite in order, dear, for you to share one room.'

'I had realized that,' said Connie.

'And it would be a very good thing to be on the premises when the builders were working. Some of these fellows can be very dilatory, and I know for a fact that the men who renovated Tullivers, for the Hursts, were not above sitting down and *playing cards!*'

Dotty made it sound like one of the deadly sins.

'I said to them often: "This wouldn't do for my father, you know. You would have got short shrift had he been employing you!" They were quite impertinent, I remember.'

Dotty grew quite pink at the memory.

'Very naughty of them,' agreed Connie, wishing she had been on the scene at the time. 'Well, Aunt Dot, it's a marvellous offer, and I shall tell Kit about it. But could you bear to share your house?'

'It's *your* house! And there's nothing I should enjoy more than having you both under this roof. I could keep an eye on you, and make sure that Kit treated you properly.'

'I don't think he will turn out a wife-beater,' said Connie.

'You never can tell,' replied Dotty. 'Do bend down, dear, and fetch Flossie out. She badly needs kempting.'

'Kempting?' echoed Connie.

'Well, if she's *unkempt*, which she most certainly is, then she should be made the opposite. Now, where did I put that brush?'

Walking into Lulling with Kit that afternoon, Connie told him of Dotty's plans.

'There's a lot to be said for it,' he agreed. 'It settles Aunt Dotty's future, and I honestly think we could have a lovely house there if it were sensibly enlarged. The site is perfect and I shouldn't think there would be any planning difficulties. If you like the idea, I'll have a word with Edward, and see what he thinks about the possibilities.'

'I'm all for it,' said Connie, 'but are you truly happy about these arrangements? I can see some men refusing point blank, and I shouldn't blame them. Aunt Dotty's not everybody's idea of a close companion.'

'My dear girl, I know quite well I shall never get you to leave her, and I respect you for it. Therefore, if I want you – and God knows I do – then I'm more than happy to take on dear old Dotty as well. I think she's being uncommonly generous in making the offer. Let's jolly well enjoy it. We ought to have a lot of fun planning the new building.'

'It's an enormous weight off my mind,' confessed Connie. 'Let's have a cup of tea at The Fuchsia Bush to celebrate.'

Kit's landlady, Mrs Jenner, was delighted on her lodger's account to know of the forthcoming marriage, but told him frankly that she hardly dared to hope that she would ever get such a paragon again in her upstairs flat.

'Nonsense!' Kit said. 'You wait and see. There'll be a queue from here to Nidden when the word goes round that there's a flat here to let. You'll be able to pick and choose, and state any rent you like.'

'I'm not sure I shall let at all,' said Mrs Jenner. 'Percy

keeps badgering me to have him here for good. I've said to him, time and time again: "Look here, Perce! I don't want you, so stop asking!" But, you know, he won't take a hint.'

Some hint, thought Kit privately! It sounded a straightforward ultimatum from sister to brother to him. He hoped that Mrs Jenner would not weaken. It was time she had life a little easier, and Percy could look after himself quite well, if he would get over his self-pity.

'I tell him,' went on his landlady, 'that I want the place to myself now and again. Percy would expect a cooked dinner prompt at twelve o'clock, meat and two veg and a proper pudding. Well, I'm not starting. A boiled egg and a slice of toast does me, and I've had my fill of cooking over the years. Besides, I'm enjoying getting out of an evening now. I like my choral nights, and Bingo.'

'Have you won anything?' asked Kit.

'Well, I once won eighty pence, but you'll never believe this! Nelly Piggott won fifty pounds last week. Think of it! But don't breathe a word, will you?'

'Of course not. But surely there were dozens of people present who know all about it?'

'Maybe, but Nelly doesn't want Albert to hear of it. She's putting by as much as she can in case he ever throws her out again.'

This was news to Kit, who had always understood that it was Nelly who deserted Albert, not the other way about.

'She's a good sort,' went on Mrs Jenner, 'and a real hard worker. They say The Fuchsia Bush is coining money since she started cooking there. I've got quite fond of her over the last few months, and I reckon she's had a hard time.'

'Well, you can count on me,' Kit assured her. 'I shan't say anything about her winnings. But I hope their marriage won't break up again.'

'Well, marriage is a proper lottery, isn't it? And when's yours to be?'

'Soon after Christmas. There's quite a bit to be arranged. I must sort out some of my furniture still in store for one thing.'

'And it will take some time to get the plans passed for the new wing on Miss Harmer's place, won't it?' said Mrs Jenner conversationally.

As neither Kit himself nor Connie had breathed a word of their hopes to anyone, he realized that this was just another prize example of rural communication at work.

'That's quite right,' he agreed resignedly.

As Dimity had remarked to Ella on an earlier occasion, Christmas seemed to have sneaked up on Lulling and Thrush Green, and no doubt on the rest of the British Isles as well.

At Thrush Green School Miss Fogerty had set her children to making Christmas cards and calendars already. Miss Potter's slightly older children were promoted to bookmarks with tassels, knitted string dish cloths and covers for the *Radio Times* and *T.V. Times*, in crash embroidered with lazy daisy stitch.

Miss Watson's class, as befitted the most experienced and talented members of the school, were engaged on such heady projects as tea-cosies, handerkchief sachets, decorated boxes and tea pot stands.

As well as all this handicraft activity, Christmas carols were being practised and plans were afoot for a Christmas party. Anything more ambitious had been vetoed this year after much earnest discussion in the school house.

'I really don't think I can face another nativity play,' confessed Miss Watson. 'I know the mothers are marvellous in getting the costumes done and helping with the make-up, but there's always some crisis or other. Do you remember when the three wise men all wore dreadful robes which clashed terribly? And then John Todd's mother was so difficult about providing a beard for Joseph? And really the floorboards are far too splintery for all that kneeling, and I do detest taking my rug over for the front of the manger. In any case, I don't think Axminster looks reverent enough.'

'A nativity play certainly makes a lot of work,' agreed Agnes. 'And the one pantomime we tried years ago was a little amateurish, I felt.'

'To be honest,' said Dorothy, 'I suppose we are getting past all the effort. But after all, if things had been as we wanted we should be retired by now. I really don't think we need to feel too guilty, at our age, for making Christmas simpler.'

'In any case,' pointed out Agnes, 'we are having the carol service in the church this year, instead of at the school. It should be a very impressive afternoon, and I'm sure the parents will appreciate it.'

'Mrs Todd won't. She's staunch Plymouth Brethren, and is refusing to let John set foot in St Andrew's.'

'Sometimes one wonders if church unity will ever be realized,' said Agnes, shaking her head.

'Well, I've a scheme which I think ought to be realized,' said Dorothy, changing the subject. 'As soon as term ends, I propose that we spend Christmas at Barton and have a thorough rest.'

'What a wonderful idea! But can we afford it?'

'We're going to,' said Dorothy firmly. 'You are not really fit yet, and my leg is still a nuisance. I think it would do us both a world of good to have a week by the sea, and to let other people wait on us. What's more, we might even hear of a little house for sale while we're down there.'

'But what about the parties we usually go to? And the Christmas Day service at St Andrew's?'

'They'll have to do without our presence for once. No, Agnes, my mind's made up. No bothering with Christmas catering, no standing about at cocktail parties drinking stuff you don't want while your headache gets worse, no last-minute presents to deliver. We're going to have a very quiet, lazy week indulging ourselves. And surely, Agnes, at our age, we deserve it?'

'Indeed we do,' agreed little Miss Fogerty.

Across the green, Christmas preparations were also going on. Jenny was surveying a splendidly rich fruit cake, and deciding on its future icing. Ella Bembridge was sorting out scarves and ties of her own weaving for the unfortunate recipients of her bounty. Joan and Edward Young were trying to fix a convenient date to have a mammoth Christmas shopping spree, and in every house where there were children notes were being sent up the chimney to Santa Claus, most of them asking for presents of such magnitude and expense that parents' hearts quailed.

At Lulling the pace was even faster. The shops were beginning their pre-Christmas fever, and the council men were threading the lime trees with coloured lights.

The Fuchsia Bush had a mouth-watering display of Christmas cakes, boxes of home-made sweets and short-bread, most of them made by Nelly Piggott and her helpers. Mrs Peters was looking forward to a bumper Christmas this year, and congratulated herself on being able to keep Nelly in her employ as well as Mrs Jefferson.

Next door, the three Lovelock sisters were already going

through the little gifts which had been put aside throughout the year. Some had been bought at local bazaars or coffee mornings. Some had been given to them and were unwanted. This useful store was now being allotted to various friends, many of whom would recognize the gift, when the time came, as something they had given to one of the sisters on an earlier occasion. It was all part of the fun. One particular vase, of hideous shape and unsteady on its base, had been bandied about the Lovelock circle for more years than could be recalled, and was looked upon as a peripatetic old friend. People had been known to say with pride: 'I've got the vase this year!'

It was early in December that Charles and Dimity had unexpected visitors.

The morning was clear and cold, the grass glittering with hoar frost. At Dimity's bird table greenfinches, tits and chaffinches squabbled for the nuts and fat, and on this sharp morning even the rooks from the trees in the churchyard had flown down for Dimity's largesse.

Charles was in the greenhouse picking dead leaves from his geranium cuttings, and doing a little watering. He found the brilliant morning a comfort to his spirits, for he had been unable to throw off entirely the unusual melancholy which seemed to envelop him.

He had said nothing about it to Dimity. The feeling was nebulous, and Charles chided himself for harbouring these unwanted spells of sadness. They would pass. He did not intend to burden anyone, and certainly not his dear wife, with such vague twinges of discomfort.

Working among his plants, ministering to their needs in peaceful warmth, the good rector felt calmed and useful. He set about repotting some penstemon cuttings, enjoying the feeling of the moist compost in his hands, and the sight of tiny white roots thrusting bravely into the world.

He was so engrossed in his job, cares forgotten for a while, that he was surprised to find that his wrist watch said eleven o'clock. Dimity would be brewing coffee, and he dusted his hands, and went off to the house.

The frost still furred the grass, and there was ice on the bird bath. But the sun was beginning to shed warmth, and the sky was a brilliant blue.

Hurrying to the front door, Charles was surprised to see a large shining car there, and recognized it as Anthony Bull's.

He and his wife had just arrived and Dimity was taking their coats. Her face was alight with joy.

'Isn't this marvellous?' she said. 'I was just going to send a search party for you.'

The Bulls were equally pleased at this reunion.

'We are on our way to Cirencester,' Anthony said, 'to deliver Christmas presents to an aged uncle of mine, and we couldn't resist dropping in. Have we interrupted anything vital?'

'Nothing!' Charles assured him.

The two women went out to the kitchen to superintend the coffee making.

'It all looks splendid,' said Anthony, gazing across the garden to his former church. 'And how are things going?'

'I love the place,' said Charles, 'and so does Dimity. And I have had the greatest kindness from so many people.'

'From *all*, from what I hear.'

'I'm afraid not *all*, Anthony. You know, you were a difficult man to follow. I lack so many fine qualities which you possess, and which, I think, my congregation misses.'

'Rubbish!' exclaimed Anthony. 'You must not belittle yourself, Charles. You have got a wonderful reputation in the parish – in all four parishes – and the Bishop has told me several times how highly he thinks of you.'

Charles looked at his friend in amazement.

'We see quite a bit of him. He stays with us if he has a meeting in London. He's pretty shrewd, and has his ear to the ground. He's told me about a score of happenings here which have warmed his heart. And mine too, for that matter. There's no doubt about it, Charles, you are a far more conscientious parish priest than ever I was.'

'I don't believe it,' protested Charles.

'It wasn't all plain sailing for me, you know. Every clergyman has to face criticism from some quarter. I may have given satisfaction to those who enjoy a good sermon and a well-decorated church. I hope I did. But I faced quite a bit if suspicion from others. I think they resented the fact that my wife is a wealthy woman. The less generous of them were inclined to sneer at "too much display", as I heard one call it. I often thought about the camel and the eye of the needle, Charles, and I came to the conclusion that you simply can't please all the people all the time. So one just gets on with the job, as best one can, and that's it.'

Charles felt much comforted by this sound reasoning.

'But I can't believe that you ever met such slights. I've only heard good of you, Anthony.'

'You only hear from those who are articulate. There are plenty in Lulling who say little to one's face, but who make their feelings known to their friends. Take heart, Charles! What does it matter in the end? We are both doing our humble best. Let the Almighty judge our endeavours.'

Charles smiled at his old friend.

'You've done me a power of good. And you're quite right. Ah! I hear the coffee arriving.'

And he bustled across to open the door.

THE WEDDING of Kit and Connie was arranged for the first week in January, and the banns were read at St Andrew's church.

It was to be a quiet affair. Apart from her aunt Dotty, Connie had few relatives, and Kit was similarly placed. Some old friends from Thrush Green and Lulling were invited, and the service was to be at eleven o'clock. Joan and Edward Young insisted on the wedding breakfast being held in their house.

'It will be a buffet affair,' Joan said. 'Kit and Connie are off to Heathrow before two, but it will give us time for wishing them well.'

The honeymoon was to be spent in Madeira, and they were not returning until the end of January. The fact that they had this opportunity to spend over three weeks in the sunshine was due mainly to Winnie Bailey's insistence.

As soon as she had heard the wedding plans she called to see Connie whilst Dotty was aloft having her afternoon nap.

'Let her come to stay with me, Connie. Jenny and I would love it, and we have plenty of room. It would never do to leave her here, even if she had someone living in. You know full well she would be out in the garden, and coping with the animals, whatever the weather. And she really would revert to her catering ways – an apple in her hand as she wandered about, and nothing cooked.'

'I know exactly what you mean,' said Connie. 'I was going to ask Mrs Jenner if she could have Kit's old room while we're away. I know she would care for her, but it hardly seemed fair to expect her to take responsibility for dear old Dotty. She is rather a handful.'

Winnie thought that this was the understatement of the year, but not the moment to say so.

'I know Mrs Jenner goes out on some evenings,' said Winnie, 'and really Dotty shouldn't be alone in the house. If she were with us there would be two of us to care for her, and also she wouldn't be tempted to potter out to see to things as I know she would if she were here, or even at Mrs Jenner's. Do think it over, Connie, and say "Yes".'

And so it had been arranged. Albert Piggott had jumped at the chance of looking after the animals, night and morning, and of taking complete charge of the goat Dulcie on whom he doted. Betty Bell would continue her ministrations twice a week. All the post would be delivered to Winnie Bailey's address, and far more important than any of these plans was the enthusiastic agreement of Dotty herself.

Kit and Connie approached Edward Young with their ideas for the enlargement of Dotty's cottage, and the three of them spent many hours discussing possibilities.

It was only a few days before Christmas when they agreed Edward's final design which he promised to submit to the local planning committee.

'And I don't think there should be any difficulty,' he assured them. 'You've got a marvellous site there, and whatever is built is not going to affect anyone nearby. Everything's there already in the way of drainage, electricity and so on, and there's easy access for the builders so that they will have no excuse for uprooting hedges and

chopping down trees when no one's looking. Leave it all
with me, my children, and go and enjoy yourselves.'

'We intend to,' said Kit. 'But none of it would have been
possible without friends in Thrush Green.'

Matters at the Piggott household continued to run with
unaccustomed harmony. Nelly, still happy in her job at The
Fuchsia Bush, was made still happier when she discovered
that she had lost almost a stone in weight and felt all the
better for it.

It was not lack of food. She usually had a substantial lunch
provided by The Fuchsia Bush, but there was no doubt that
the semi-run downhill to Lulling, and the arduous plod
back after work, were giving the lady much-needed exercise.

Better still, from Nelly's point of view, was the healthy
state of her Post Office savings' account. It now stood at one
hundred and seventy five pounds, boosted most satisfactorily by the fifty-pound Bingo winnings.

All in all, Nelly found life at Thrush Green much pleas-
anter than she had expected on her nervous return from the
perfidious Charlie. Of him, she had heard nothing. She
assumed that his entanglement with his new love still
engrossed him. They were both welcome, Nelly told herself. She had had quite enough of love. Good health, a nice
job and money behind her really provided a much more
satisfactory state of mind, and she said as much to her new
friend, Mrs Jenner, as they puffed uphill one evening from a
Bingo session.

'You're quite right, Nelly,' said Mrs Jenner. 'I know
Albert's behaving himself very well at the moment, and
looking forward to spending time with Dulcie, so he's in
good spirits, but you watch your step, my dear! Put as
much in your account as you can. There's nothing like a bit

of money behind you. That way you can be independent, and I don't care what all the book-writers say about love and marriage. To my mind, you can't trust men.'

And with this sentiment Nelly heartily agreed.

The visit of Anthony Bull had done much to comfort Charles. To be told that he was considered by his Bishop to be a conscientious parish priest made Charles feel humble as well as proud.

He treasured too, Anthony's own kindly comments, and only hoped that they were not exaggerated. It was amazing to Charles to learn that there had ever been any adverse criticism of his predecessor, although he realized now that, as Anthony had pointed out, no man in the public eye could expect to be free of censure in some form or other. Those few exchanges with Anthony had put matters into perspective for Charles, and he felt greatly heartened.

Dimity was much relieved to see this improvement in his spirits. She had grieved to see him cast down during the past few weeks, and guessed the cause. Primarily, she blamed Mrs Thurgood. Charles had taken her wounding remarks much to heart, Dimity considered, and she could never forgive her for making her dear husband so unhappy.

Charles, of course, would have none of it, brushing aside Dimity's queries, and insisting that he was in perfect health and spirits. Now it really seemed that the doldrums were over, and Dimity rejoiced.

A week or two before Christmas she left him immediately after lunch to spend the afternoon at an old people's Christmas party in Lulling.

It was bitterly cold, with a cruel northerly wind sweeping the High Street, as she made her way to the hall at the other end of the town.

The shops were gaily decked for Christmas, and a fine Christmas tree was being put in place in the little square by the Butter Market. Dimity, ignoring the wind, thought it all looked remarkably gay.

Across the road she saw old Tom Hardy with a large parcel under his arm. Polly was on a lead, trotting quite briskly, and although Dimity waved to him, he did not see her, and continued steadily up the street towards Lulling church. He was certainly walking well, thought Dimity, and it was good to see the two old friends united again.

It was some minutes later that Charles went to the back door. There stood Tom and Polly.

'Come in! Come in, out of this dreadful wind,' cried the rector, ushering them in. 'It's good to see you both.'

Polly's tail wagged in greeting, and she moved towards the study where she guessed correctly that the rector had a fire.

Tom carried the parcel with him and settled in an arm chair.

'I've brought you and Mrs Henstock a little Christmas present,' he said, pushing the parcel across the rector's desk. 'It's not much, but I made it myself.'

'May I undo it?'

'Of course, sir. Tell me if you think it'll do.'

Charles unwrapped it carefully. The old man had done it up beautifully, and the parcel was stoutly secured with string. It took some time to get the present free, but at last it was revealed.

Tom had made a fine sturdy birds' nesting box with a cleverly thatched roof.

'It's superb!' the rector told him. 'A marvellous piece of work! Dimity will be delighted.'

'Well, I know she's one for the birds, and I thought it

would give you both pleasure. It's just a little return for all your kindness to me and Polly.'

The dog, hearing her name, thumped her tail on the hearth rug.

'I wish my wife were here to thank you too,' said Charles. 'She will be sorry to have missed you. I can assure you, Tom, you couldn't have given us anything more welcome. Now, let me get you a drink.'

'No, no, I won't if you don't mind, sir. I've another call to make, and then I'll get back before it's dark.'

He stood up briskly, and Charles was pleased to see how much stronger he seemed.

'Then I won't keep you, but thank you again for a perfect present. Come out this way, Tom, it's quicker for you.'

He led the way to the front door, shook hands with the old man and patted Polly.

He watched the two setting off down the drive. They had reached the gate when a car turned in.

To Charles's dismay, he recognized it as the one belonging to Mrs Thurgood.

'Will you come into my study? I'm afraid the drawing room fire isn't alight yet. Dimity is out this afternoon.'

'No doubt about her good works,' said Mrs Thurgood, graciously accepting a seat.

Her eye alighted on Tom's nesting box.

'What an attractive object!' Charles found Mrs Thurgood's smile almost as disconcerting as her withering tongue, but at least it seemed that she was in a pleasant mood.

'Tom Hardy made it,' said he. 'It's an early Christmas present. I'm looking forward to showing it to my wife.'

'Yes, I've heard about your kindness to that old fellow,' replied Mrs Thurgood. 'One of your *many* kindnesses, let me add, which is why I have called.'

Charles was nonplussed. This complete change of attitude was puzzling enough, but he could not recall any particular favour he had given Mrs Thurgood. Their paths had not crossed since their last stormy meeting.

'I wanted you to know that Janet is going to be married shortly, and you were the person who introduced her to her future husband, John Fairbrother.'

'I'm delighted to know,' said Charles. 'He seemed a very pleasant young man, and much admired your daughter's work, I remember.'

'Yes, he really does recognize her remarkable artistic ability, I'm happy to say. Of course, he has very little money, and is rather shy in manner, but he is *very well-connected*. The Shropshire Fairbrothers, you know.'

'Indeed,' said Charles. The phrase, 'very well-connected' was one which the good rector heard often from the lips of his more socially-conscious parishioners. He had once overheard: 'I know that he is seriously addicted to drugs, and has spent several months in prison, but he is *very well-connected*.' It seemed to excuse all.

'We should so much like the wedding here at St John's,' went on Mrs Thurgood, coming to the point, 'probably just before Easter. Such a pretty time of year with all the daffodils out. And, of course, I do so hope that you will agree to take the service. Having introduced them, you know, so very fitting.'

Mrs Thurgood gave the rector another unnerving smile. He rallied his strength.

'I shall be delighted to officiate,' he assured her. 'It will be a pleasure as well as a duty. With so much in common, they should be a very happy pair.'

Mrs Thurgood gave a little sigh of relief. It was plain to the rector that this confrontation had needed courage, and his tender heart was touched.

Mrs Thurgood rose to go.

'I am so glad that you will take the service. I was afraid that perhaps you might dislike the idea. My daughter and I have sometimes felt that we were a little – how shall I put it?'

'Don't attempt to put it,' said Charles impulsively. 'Let bygones be bygones. There are no hard feelings on my side, I promise you, and I very much appreciate your coming here today.'

He opened the study door and accompanied his visitor down the hall.

'Ah! Just one moment,' she said, rummaging in her large crocodile-skin handbag. 'Open it when you are alone,' she ordered him, thrusting an envelope into his hand.

'Thank you,' said Charles, somewhat bemused, but imagining that this was a Christmas card which she was very sensibly delivering by hand to save postage.

'Well, this is the season of giving and goodwill, isn't it?' said Mrs Thurgood, climbing into her car. 'Very glad that we are friends again.'

She waved, and drove off.

Charles returned to his fireside and opened the envelope. It did indeed contain a handsome card depicting the nativity. But within that was a folded cheque.

It was made out to St John's Church Fabric Fund, and had more noughts on it than Charles had ever seen on a cheque before.

He had to sit down suddenly to recover from the shock.

By the time Christmas arrived most of the inhabitants of Lulling and Thrush Green were quite exhausted with all the many preparations, and were looking forward to having a rest as soon as possible.

The weather had turned mild and tranquil, as is so often the case at this time, making a mockery of the Christmas card scenes of stage coaches in deep snow, children constructing snowmen and winter landscapes complete with skaters.

In Lulling gardens a few tattered roses still clung to unpruned bushes, and one or two early crocuses and snowdrops were thrusting through the damp soil. The more morose inhabitants, such as Albert Piggott, reminded each other of the old saying that a green Christmas meant a full churchyard.

But on the whole, people rejoiced in the mild spell, and among them was Charles Henstock. He had been able to go about his visiting, and to attend the plethora of pre-Christmas festivities, unencumbered by slippery roads and snow drifts.

On the morning of the great day he awoke early as usual. Dimity was still deep in sleep, and the rector thought of the duties before him with real pleasure.

It would be a busy day. He was to go to Thrush Green

first, to take Holy Communion at eight o'clock in the church he loved so well. At eleven he would officiate at Morning Service at St John's, and at three-thirty he was due at his most distant church at Lulling Woods for Evensong.

Today, he knew, those churches would be full and he would have the joy of seeing almost all his flock.

He looked forward keenly to his Christmas Day. It was still dark, but by the illuminated dial of the bedside clock he saw that he must rise if he wished to be in good time.

He smiled in the darkness. How lucky he was to have work that he relished! How lucky to have escaped from the gloomy valley he had been transversing, and to have entered the sunny uplands again!

He edged gently out of bed, hoping not to disturb his wife, but she stirred as he moved.

'Happy Christmas!' she murmured, her eyes still closed.

'It will be,' said the rector, with conviction.

ABOUT THE AUTHOR

Miss Read is actually Mrs. Dora Saint, whose novels draw on her own memories of living and teaching in a small English village. She first began writing after the Second World War, mainly light essays about school and country matters, for several journals. Her first book, *Village School,* was published in England by Michael Joseph and then in the United States by Houghton Mifflin Company in 1955. She has since delighted millions of readers with both the Fairacre series and her equally well loved series about the Cotswold village of Thrush Green. Miss Read and her husband, a retired schoolmaster, have one daughter and enjoy a quiet life near Newbury, Berkshire.

Available in paperback: The Fairacre series

Village School   "An affectionate, humorous, and gently charming chronicle."
— *New York Times*

The first novel in the Fairacre series, *Village School* introduces us to that cheerful schoolmistress Miss Read and her lovable group of children, who are just as likely to lose themselves as their mittens.   **ISBN 0-618-12702-X, $12.00**

Village Centenary   "Miss Read reminds us of what is really important."
— *USA Today*

Village Centenary chronicles the year Miss Read's school celebrates its one hundredth anniversary with the help — and, in some cases, hindrance — of many of our favorite Fairacre friends.   **ISBN 0-618-12703-8, $12.00**

Summer at Fairacre   "A world of innocent integrity in almost perfect prose consisting of wit, humor and wisdom in equal measure."
— *Cleveland Plain Dealer*

Summer at Fairacre charmingly recounts one hot — but very welcome — summer, when Miss Read tends to the problems and possibilities that unfold in the lives of her downland village friends against the background of Albertine roses, skylarks, and bees.   **ISBN 0-618-12704-6, $12.00**

Mrs. Pringle of Fairacre   "Miss Read's novels are sheer delight."
— *Chicago Tribune*

Through the eyes of Miss Read and other longtime Fairacre friends, we trace Mrs. Pringle's life from childhood through her stormy standing as the redoubtable (but beloved) cleaner of the Fairacre School.   **ISBN 0-618-15588-0, $12.00**

Changes at Fairacre   "Fairacre offers a restful change from the frenetic pace of the contemporary world." — *Publishers Weekly*

While Fairacre's new commuter lifestyle causes a sharp decline in enrollment at Miss Read's school, Miss Read focuses her attention on the ill health of her old friend Dolly Clare.   **ISBN 0-618-15457-4, $12.00**

Farewell to Fairacre   "Humor guides her pen but charity steadies it . . . Delightful." — *Times Literary Supplement*

The beloved village schoolmistress, Miss Read, is suddenly taken ill and must consider leaving her longtime post at the school. But through the changing seasons in this gentle, humorous drama, the problems of Miss Read and her fellow residents of Fairacre are gradually resolved.   **ISBN 0-618-15456-6, $12.00**

Available in paperback: The Thrush Green series

Thrush Green "Every once in a while ... a book comes along which defies description except by a burble of adjectives such as *enchanting, lovely, gentle, pointed* and *charming*." —*Minneapolis Sunday Tribune*

Thrush Green introduces the inhabitants of the lovely village during the course of events on one pivotal day, May Day, which has always been important to the village, as it brings love, laughter, and the annual village fair.

ISBN 0-618-22759-8, $12.00

Return to Thrush Green "Welcome to Thrush Green, the happy world to which Miss Read introduced us so many years ago." —*Publishers Weekly*

It's spring again, and the change of the seasons means change in the village. The Young family's routine is disrupted by the sudden arrival of Joan's father, and Molly and Ben Curdle consider settling down. **ISBN 0-618-21914-5, $12.00**

Gossip from Thrush Green "A charming little world in which to live ... One learns a good deal about human nature, integrity, and about truth."
— *Christian Herald*

The pristine setting of Thrush Green conceals a flurry of activity. Rumor has it that Mr. Venables is considering retirement just as Miss Watson, the village's teacher, is about to make an important decision. **ISBN 0-618-21913-7, $12.00**

Affairs at Thrush Green "Miss Read's book gently sweeps you right into the heart of the English village she has created." — *Sun-Sentinel* (Fort Lauderdale)

This volume in the Thrush Green series continues the fortunes of the Thrush Green families. The kindly vicar, Charles Henstock, carefully navigates the rivalry between the Fuchsia Bush café and the Two Pheasants.

ISBN 0-618-23857-3, $12.00

At Home in Thrush Green "Here you'll find delicious wit, quirky characters, the colorful intrigues of daily life ... Delightful." — Jan Karon

Charles Henstock loves his new post in the village of Lulling, yet wistfully remembers the rectory of Thrush Green that burned to the ground. Retirement homes will be built on the ruins of Henstock's former dwelling, but who will move in? **ISBN 0-618-23858-1, $12.00**

Friends at Thrush Green "A soothing oasis of tidy living for the frazzled reader weary of an untidy world." — *Kirkus Reviews*

Miss Watson and Miss Fogerty retire to Barton on Sea after many years teaching the children of Thrush Green. They return for visits frequently, however, and meddle in the many goings-on of the village. **ISBN 0-618-23888-3, $12.00**